T0129236

Old Coot

Old Coot

MAY ONE EVIL, CARE FOR THE OTHER.

SHAWN A. JENKINS

OLD COOT
MAY ONE EVIL, CARE FOR THE OTHER.

iUniverse books may be ordered through booksellers or by contacting:

iUniverse
1663 Liberty Drive
Bloomington, IN 47403
www.iuniverse.com
1-800-Authors (1-800-288-4677)

ISBN: 978-1-5320-1000-2 (sc)
ISBN: 978-1-5320-1001-9 (e)

Print information available on the last page.

iUniverse rev. date: 10/20/2016

For he was an odd man. A man with little or no purpose to speak of. He was a being with the sole resolve of simply existing.

There came only a brief period in the man's life when he would discover the absolute and finite meaning of the word "disruption." A moment in his famed history in which time, at least for him, would slow to a miserable crawl.

His story, though at times both vile and wretched, was one worth telling, or re-telling, to those who may not be aware of one of God's most forgotten creations…and the obscure, little town upon which the unusual man tread.

Why should the world care about such a man? Such a reprobate?

It is the final season…

CHAPTER 1

"Come and get me, motherfucker!" Millard cried out as the howling winds pushed his gaunt frame from one end of the living room to the other as though he were as light as a feather.

The tall, old man hobbled down the basement stairs and grabbed his aged Winchester rifle from off its hanger; the same weapon that was always gleaming with a clear and glowing shine on its leather padded sides as if it were brand spanking new.

He then reached over to the tool table that was to his adjacent right, anxiously opened the small drawer up under it and took out the rifle's shells, four in all, and as dusty as unearthed fossils. He was more than confident that they would end up achieving the appreciated results that he craved.

With wet, arthritic hands, he eagerly filled the chamber with one shell after another. It wasn't often that Millard got the opportunity to use such a particular weapon, so despite the current meteorological conditions, he was as overjoyed as a child on Christmas morn just to be living in the moment.

"I got ya now!" He hollered with a growling grunt in the back of his throat as he raced back upstairs and into the noisy living area.

The moment Millard felt that the coast was clear, he crouched down beside the front window that overlooked the muddy driveway and barn outside. He held his trustworthy gun to his sweaty face; the steel felt warm and smooth against his bearded skin as he trembled with eager zeal, waiting for his prey to emerge once more from out of the darkness.

Drips and sputters of rain drained down from the roof and into the steel bucket that sat behind Millard in the middle of the floor. The roof leaked incessantly whenever it rained, causing the entire living room and all the furniture to soak up with musty smelling water. It was a pain for Millard to have to clean up afterwards, but it always left him with something to do for the next day or so.

"Sweet Mary keep callin' me, keep on callin' me home."

Before Millard could even finish the next stanza of his eloquent song, the sound of glass shattering into pieces next to his couch blasted from out of nowhere. The commotion should have set the old man on edge, but instead it only caused his rusty blood to circulate even faster as he turned his attention back to the window in front of him.

"C'mon, sweet Mary," he hummed to himself, "c'mon home and gimme some."

Millard observed his drenched yard outside that was rapidly turning into a muddy trash heap, complete with his woodpile and brick stove floating out into the nearby road.

"Sit your ass down, girl! Can't ya see I almost got 'em?" Millard yelled at his 17 year old, shady brown pit-bull.

Millard shoved aside the mangy animal as not to alert his unwanted foe outside. He knew how agitated she would get every time a storm rolled through, but now wasn't the time for comfort and consolation, for the task at hand, Millard needed every ounce of concentration and cunning he could assemble before heading out into the blustery weather.

"Here I come, ya son of bitch!" The old man wailed as he rose to his feet and bolted out into the blackness of his yard like a charging soldier.

The strong wind-storm that had Sullinger, Mississippi in its torturous claw wildly whipped Millard from side to side as if he were a spinning top. Not even the weatherman could have predicted that the storm would be as horrendous as it turned out to be, but the last thing Millard ever did was listen to other people, on any subject.

Once Millard was able to regain his bearings, he trudged through the heavy and thick mud on his way towards the old barn house.

He couldn't see his intruder thanks to all the blinding rain, but if there was one thing that Millard valued was his uncanny sense of direction. Without a map the man could swim across an ocean and find Australia with little or no trouble at all.

Just a few feet more and he was nearly there. The barn wavered and toppled back and forth like a palm tree, but as far as Millard was concerned it could have all blown away to kingdom come, just one less thing to worry about.

"Son of a bitch," he squealed out in agony as something heavy and hard from out of the thrust of the powerful wind knocked him face first into the muddy ground from behind.

Ignoring his aching back, Millard lifted his head to see what looked like a naked person stagger into the barn house, looking as though it were limping. With nothing but burning fury inside, he got to his feet and reached for his rifle.

Millard raced for the barn while trying not to slip and fall. The moment he was able to reach the threshold, he closed the door behind him and tried to recover both his saturated eyesight and wobbly brain.

He was a filthy mess, but that was about as discouraging as it came when it involved Millard's own well-being.

With the rickety old barn threatening to shatter to pieces at any unexpected moment, Millard ever so carefully traipsed about in the hay with his rifle cocked and ready in his wet hands, just waiting for someone or something to make a blundering move.

He began to play the tune that he was singing back in the house in his head all over again, it was the one thing that seemed to grant him some measure of terrestrial potency, like a theme song to egg on the hero in their moment of danger.

All of the sudden, from behind him, a rustling commotion began to stir from a hay patch. With age, Millard's hearing was obviously fading, but he knew when there was more than one perpetrator in his midst as the rustling noise sprang from one end of the barn to the other, almost simultaneously.

Millard made sure not to make any sudden moves, and the fact that his back was unprotected made it even more thrilling in a demented sort of manner, just more reason to shoot off his rifle.

He continued to stalk around until a tall, thin, blackened silhouette rose up directly in front of him, just a few feet from where he was standing. His reflexes should have been more precise, but for some reason Millard's wet fingers couldn't seem to latch on to the trigger at that painstaking second.

The old man's fumbling fingers gave the dark character enough time to jump up into the loft above with the agility of a startled cat.

Without thinking, Millard raised his gun, and just as he was about to pull the trigger he was immediately tackled from behind and taken down into the hay before being punched mercilessly in the face.

A series of punches to the face were about as damming and harmful as being slapped by a woman to Millard. His old, grizzled face was numb due to years of fighting and wrangling with all the wrong people in life; the ones that didn't know when to leave an old man in peace.

Millard kicked the intruder in the midsection before getting up and searching for his fallen weapon.

"Fuck you, old man!" An angry male voice shouted as he tackled Millard down to the ground again.

Within the blackness of night Millard could see the person that was attacking him, as well as the sharp shears and nails that were once hooked onto the walls of the barn flying to and fro. Even the blowing hay at that point was becoming a hindrance that both men could have done without.

Distracted by the wind's intensity, the man slightly pulled back, which in turn gave Millard the opportunity to claw into his face, nearly tearing out his eyeballs before tossing him to the side.

Millard then tried to stand up, but the wind was to be the ruler that evening as its gusty force shoved him right back down.

The invader crawled over to where a large, rusty butcher knife was lying within the hay before making his way back over to Millard to inflict his final blow. The old man quickly grabbed a hold of the intruder's right arm and fought with all his might to secure the weapon.

He should have been in an utterly hysterical state of mind, but all the brawling in the wet hay only caused Millard to reminisce on the days when he was a boy, rolling about in his grandfather's yard with the farm animals.

Millard continued to fight while still lying on his back, trying his best to keep his invader from impaling him in the eye with his own butcher knife. Only mere inches stood in between the old man's right eye and the tip of the sharp blade.

Then, from out of seemingly nowhere, a bail of heavy, wet hay came crashing down right next to the two men, which in turn caused the invader to become distracted.

Much like the light at the end of a dark tunnel, Millard seized his opportunity. He punched the man in the face and got up. He was determined not to be knocked back down again by the forceful wind as he reached over for his rifle. It was entirely too dark to see where the gun was located, but old Millard seemed to be able to sniff it out like a purebred bloodhound.

The intruder got to his feet and stood strong before Millard who had his rifle pointed straight at him. The man stared dead silent at the weapon while hay and rain whipped across his face.

Millard, with a sneering grin across his face, only looked back at the man who at last, he had at his mercy. Blood dripped from his mouth and chin, the only thing to do was lick it to the side and pull the trigger.

Millard watched with a tickled tummy as the man flew backwards into the hay. He looked on as the assailant twitched and quivered like a fish out of water.

"Now, I gotcha', motherfucker," he gleefully screamed. "Now, I gotcha!" Where the hell is your friend at, huh?"

Just for good and pleasurable measure, Millard kicked the man in the head, nearly decapitating him in the process.

"I got your fuckin' friend, now, I'm comin' for your ass next!" Millard warned as he ran over and began to climb the ladder that led up to the loft above.

The very instant he reached the top, the old man felt a very cold, wet hand grab him by the face and push him right back down to the ground below where the back of his head ended up hitting the blunt end of a power saw.

"I gotcha', motherfucker…tell your mama, I got your ass." Millard slowly slurred as he steadily drifted off into unconsciousness.

Just as he was about to slip away into another land, Millard's lazy eyes drooled upwards to the loft to see a lean, black figure perched upon one of the loft's ledges like a gargoyle, just staring back down at him.

He didn't have the power to even curse at it one final time. That would have been the ultimate finish to his evening.

CHAPTER 2

Like an old car engine turning over after a whole year of inactivity, Millard began to awaken from his embattled slumber. Both the shocking sunlight and drips of water from the roof seemed to only anger the old man to the point where he wanted to swing at mid-air as though it were too much for him bear.

He could taste the sourness in his mouth like a filthy sponge. His entire head throbbed as if someone had kicked him over and over again. His eyesight was hazy and unstable, had he not known any better he would have thought that he was awaking from a drunken stupor.

His ears could catch a glimpse of what sounded like footsteps from a distance. Someone was in his yard, but with the way he was feeling at that moment, mounting an attack was the furthest thing from his mind.

Suddenly, his dog began to bark. Millard could hear her paws racing towards his direction. He was alive, he pondered to himself. Yet another reason to curse.

"Millard, is you in here?" A heavy voice called out.

Millard recognized the man's voice, but trying to respond with such a parched mouth was nearly impossible.

From the barn's threshold appeared a hefty, dark skinned

man who appeared as though he were in his mid-sixties. He was wearing a brown police officers uniform that had the sleeves rolled up. Millard could see the man's heavy, black goulashes clomp into the barn.

"Millard, Millard, is you alright?" The man feverishly asked as he raced over and knelt down to retrieve the old man.

Gradually, Millard opened his eyes all the way to see the man gawk strangely down upon him before raising himself up, only to fall back down; he was too woozy to maintain a stable balance.

"Hold on, just settle down and—

The man suddenly paused his words for a few seconds before standing back up and looking over to see a dead body lying in the hay next to the tool table.

Millard turned around to watch the man study the corpse that he had laid waste to the night before. He could feel the oncoming questions stab at him like a hundred knives.

"What the hell is that, Millard?" The man grunted in a determined tone.

"It's a dead fucker, Leon, that's what it is!" Millard snapped back as he stood to his feet and leaned up against one of the loft's wooden poles.

Millard watched as Leon stepped over and investigated the rotting corpse. The young man's once dark brown face had become a dark pale blue. Mosquitoes swarmed and buzzed around the deceased man; his left eyeball had rolled upwards while the other remained in place, staring lifelessly up at the rafters above. His wide open neck was still a fresh, blood soaked wound that the insects considered a holiday feast.

Unlike Leon, Millard had absolutely nothing to mourn over, he was dead and gone, and that was gratifying enough for him.

Leon wiped his sweaty face with his right hand, turned to Millard and exhaled, "What the hell happened this time?"

"This faggot and his buddy were tryin' to break into my damn house last night, but when they heard 'ole Shirley barkin', they had the nerve to run in here and hide."

"So ya' shot 'em?" Leon gasped.

"You damn right I shot 'em!" Millard adamantly replied.

"What about the other fella?"

"That bitch hit me from behind and then ran up into the damn loft. When I tried to climb up there he pushed me back down again, that's when I hit that damn saw over there."

With a dismayed face, Leon scanned Millard up and down and said, "Well, I reckon he's probably long gone by now. Good God, man, look at your face. I guess he and his friend did that to you?" He pointed.

"Only the dead one," Millard coughed. "Once I was able to grab a hold of my gun, that's when I blew his black ass from here to hell!" He devilishly sniggered.

Leon shamefully shook his head from side to side before saying, "Man, ya can't keep killin' folks every time someone walks onto your land!"

"If the sum bitches would stop tryin' to break into my house in the first place then I wouldn't have to shoot nobody!"

Leon causally snickered and said, "You know good and well why folks keep runnin' onto your land, Millard. Let me take you down to the clinic to get that head of yours fixed up."

"Boy, I ain't goin' to no clinic. I got Band-Aids in the bathroom." Millard relented.

Leon looked back down at the dead man on the ground before sighing, "I don't know how I'm supposed to cover this one up, Millard. Ya shot a man in the damn neck!"

Millard only nonchalantly giggled, "You're the sheriff, you'll think of somethin'".

"Well, I probably could get away with sayin' that the storm killed 'em. Maybe somethin' sharp flew through the boy's neck." Leon contemplated while scratching his own neck.

"Stop whinin', boy. Just bag 'em and get 'em the hell outta here before he stinks up the place!" Millard rattled on as he stumbled out of the barn and into his destroyed yard, holding his sore ribs along the way.

Following in behind Millard, Leon ranted, "I'll stop whinin' when you stop shootin' folks!"

Ignoring the sheriff's obstinate rebuttal, Millard's surly eyes vigilantly surveyed his ungodly looking surroundings; even he was in awe at the total devastation that was left behind.

"Yep," the sheriff moaned, "the good Lord sure put a whoppin' on us last night. It almost became a tornado. I'm surprised that the old barn in still standin'."

Millard didn't respond, he just carried on to his old shack where he stepped through the already opened front door and immediately went straight for a small bureau that sat next to the couch. He whipped open the drawer from within and snatched out a half full pack of chewing tobacco.

"Man, when are you gonna get that old roof fixed? Look at all this water in here."

"When they start fixin' roofs for free," Millard yawned as he turned around and offered a snip of chaw to Leon before chugging a handful into his own mouth.

The sheriff just turned his nose up in disgust at the tobacco. Millard was well aware that Leon didn't chew, but that surely didn't stop him from offering every time he bothered to stop by.

"Man," Leon breathed, waving his left hand in front of his sweaty face, "this here whole town was wrecked last night, and you know it's too hot to be tryin' to fix up houses and stuff like that." He commented before strolling into the kitchen and grabbing himself a can of Coors from out of the refrigerator.

With a hearty chuckle, Millard dropped himself down onto his wet couch and said, "Boy, I sure hope that other sorry fucker comes back again, I got somethin' for 'em this time!"

"What is you talkin' about now?" Leon questioned, strolling back into the living room.

"I'm talkin' about the motherfucker that got away last night; I'll be waitin' for his ass when he comes back 'round here again."

"And just how do you know that he'll be back again, especially after you killed his partner?"

"All nigga's think alike, dead slow. This dumb bastard is probably still around here somewhere, and when I catch 'em, then you can add another dead ass to the lineup."

Leon chuckled before saying, "I don't know how you can stand to live in this old place. No air conditioning in the summer, no heat in the winter, it smells of dog piss and tobacco. You're a better man than me."

With one hand scratching his itchy testicles and the other massaging his aching neck, Millard slumped deeper into the damp couch, and with a blasé expression on his face he responded, "Shit, when you get as old as me, one odor smells just like the other. Hot and cold feels the same. As long as you got a roof over your nappy head, you ain't got nothin' to be worryin' about."

Leon took one last gulp of his beer before letting out a strong belch and saying, "Well, let me get outta here and see what else God fucked up for us. Oh, by the way, Cornelia still wants to have supper with you sometime. Just you, me and her, whenever you get a chance to, that is."

Millard carelessly waved his right hand in the air as to say that he wasn't interested in the kind invitation that had been tossed his way for the past umpteen times.

Leon sucked in his bloated gut and started for the door. "I'm gonna pack this fella up and get 'em out of your yard. And next time, do me a favor, if ya got an intruder, just call me, please." The sheriff pleaded.

"Boy, the day I call the law to come and help me is the day I finally decide to go back to church…never." The old man grunted.

Leon tightened his frustrated lips and stepped out the front door, leaving Millard alone to sulk in his moldy, old couch.

Right above Millard was the spot where yet another hole in the roof had formed thanks to the heavy rain.

Feeling thicker than a ton, Millard sat up and watched as Shirley came blundering into the house with her head hung low.

"And what the hell is supposed to be wrong with you, gal?" He mumbled before spitting out a huge, brown wad of chaw right onto the floor.

Millard patted the shabby animal on top of her head while his red eyes gazed around at his withered shack in dismay.

The brooding appearance on his face would have suggested that he was sorry that the old place had survived the storm at all. The more his eyes scanned the four bare walls, couch, and his 1979 RCA television that sat in front of him, the more he just wanted to get up and go.

He sluggishly lifted his sore body from off the couch

and began for the bathroom. In the half cracked mirror he examined the knot on the back of his head. His frail, 63 year old grizzled face looked as though it wanted to slide right off into the mildew stained sink below; there was such a wretched, almost sad appearance glowing upon him.

The bruises on his face were a sight most customary, a split lip here, a broken nose there, all in a day's happening for the old one. Just as long as there was enough energy left for some quality revenge, the world could have used his iron frame for a punching bag.

He opened the medicine cabinet door and took out a bottle of rubbing alcohol. Once he realized that the plastic bottle was completely empty he tossed it to the floor and lumbered back into the living room where he could hear the sheriff's cruiser pull out of the yard.

"C'mon here, girl, let's see what we can see out here." Millard groaned as both he and Shirley ventured outside into the wasteland that was his front yard.

With only his pair of worn out, muddy blue jeans and his old work boots on, Millard looked to his left, and then to his right. It never struck him when he first came inside from the barn earlier, but stepping out onto the porch with a more focused mind made all the startling difference in the world.

There was hay strewn all over the messy yard, along with seven dead chickens that were lying next to his old, blue pickup truck, as well as the once ten foot high stack of bricks that was now a three foot high stack crumbled into pieces.

Out of all the damage and mayhem that the storm had left behind, the one thing that seemed to bare down most upon the man was the fact that both his shack and barn were still standing, tall and proud. Both structures clearly suffered considerable harm in various areas, but as ancient and decrepit as they were, they were the only things that reminded Millard that he was still on his own property.

Millard and Shirley both came down from off the porch. The dog right away made a mad dash towards the barn while Millard blundered about in the mud and debris with a swollen glare on his face as he scratched at his scruffy, grey hair.

It was an extremely hot and humid Saturday morning, the kind of soaking humidity that made a person feel as though they were swimming in their own skin. And the stench of dead animals only made the air all the more unsafe to breathe in.

Millard carried on towards the dead chickens near his truck, and one by one, he picked up the carcasses before callously tossing them into mud patch beside the barn.

Once he was through covering the fowl with patches of hay and sludge he all of the sudden noticed Shirley whining from within the barn.

"What is it now, gal?" He moaned while lurching towards the entrance to find the dog staring upwards into the loft. "You should be out here helpin' me clean up these shitty chickens."

Millard stood in place and watched his pet ogle the loft with such eager zeal. It didn't take too long for him to figure out why Shirley was so upset at that instant. Not long at all.

"I gotcha, now," Millard wildly screamed while stampeding into the barn and snatching up his rifle from off the ground. From there he climbed the ladder to the loft above, hoping along the way to at least see the look of fear in his intruder's face before sending him first class to another world.

Once he reached the top and saw nothing but stacks of

hay, Millard gazed back down at the dog with a disappointed glare on his face.

"What the hell is wrong with you, gal? There ain't nobody up here!"

But Shirley continued to whine as she placed her left paw on the foot of the ladder, as though she were trying to climb up herself.

"You stop that!" Millard hollered. "You remember what happened the last time you tried to climb up here; I had to listen to that howling all night and day from you for a whole week because you broke your damn leg! Get down from there!"

But the obstinate animal acted as if her master hadn't said a word as she persisted in ascending the wooden ladder.

At his wits end with the dog, Millard stood in front of the ladder and yelled, "I said get your ass down from there before I—

His stern warning was abruptly interrupted by the hay patch behind him moving about. With the energy and alertness of a *20* year old, Millard spun around, cocked his rifle, and pulled the trigger.

The loud noise could possibly be heard from a mile away. But what seemed to confuse Millard was that the buckshot sounded as though it hit something solid.

There was definitely something or someone up under the rustling stash of hay, and the old man wasn't about to let whatever it was get away unscathed.

The hay patch shook and wobbled. Millard stood and watched with bated breath, waiting for enough hay to fall away as to reveal the intruder beneath.

But with every clump of straw that was whisked from side to side, the who or what that was supposedly up under was seemingly nowhere to be found. Ultimately, there was nothing but empty space.

From behind, Shirley started her rampant barking, starling Millard to the point where he nearly dropped his rifle to the ground.

"Get outta here, damn you!" He snapped.

If he wasn't afraid of a mighty windstorm then whatever was allegedly under the stash of hay at one time was about as frightening as a campfire tale.

The old man used the tip of his rifle to scatter away errant strands of hay, hoping to find a rat, possum, or some other form of unwanted rodent.

Completely dumbfounded, Millard took a slight step back while the dog continued to bark like a rabid beast at the bare corner where the hay was moving a moment ago.

"What the fuck is you barkin' at, gal? There ain't nothin' there!" Millard urged.

He had to actually hold the dog back by her neck just to get her to calm down. He was taken aback by her sudden wild reaction; she hadn't behaved in such a manner since she was a pup.

"What is it, dammit? What the hell are you barkin' at?" Millard irately yelled as he struggled with the sixty pound animal as though she were as powerful as a grizzly bear.

Millard looked back at the empty corner while trying not to get bit by his pet's gnashing, foam filled teeth. Finally, too tired to carry on with anymore nonsense, he picked Shirley up and carried both her and himself back down the ladder.

With the dog still barking like a mad lunatic in his arms. Millard stared back up at the loft, and right away conjured up only one solution that could possibly make any kind of plausible sense to him.

"Well I'll be dammed…we got ourselves a spook up in here." He confidently smirked, as though he had solved the mystery.

Millard carried Shirley and his gun quietly and humbly out of the barn and back to the shack to try and calm her down; it would be only the first time she had ever encountered such a phenomenon. She was the only dog in town that ran from mice and covered her head at the sight of a bumblebee, and yet, their new visitor in the barn seemed to at last bring out the true nature in her breed.

She was finally the beast that Millard always wanted her to be…just like him.

CHAPTER 3

It took well over an hour for Millard to bring Shirley back down to earth once again. The moment that arduous mission was complete the old man had yet another mountain to climb.

As sweaty and smelly as he was from the night before, Millard never bothered to shower, he just saw fit to throw on his blue Local Union Workers 40th Division ball cap, a faded blue, short sleeved Ole' Miss t-shirt with the wide open hole in the right underarm, and a pair of brown corduroy pants.

Shirley, with her long tongue hanging from out of her mouth, sat in the open back of her master's beat up truck that on any chilly morning would take nearly ten whole minutes just to start up.

The sheriff was dead on with his description of the town's damage report. Various trailer parks had become wastelands; most houses had their roofs torn completely away, while other homes leaned precariously to the side, just waiting patiently for the perfect stiff wind to finish their descent to the ground.

Dirt roads had morphed into mud packed trails that made it appear as though Sullinger had transformed into some Central American mountain thoroughfare overnight.

Sullinger, Mississippi. Its tentative population, *397*, although that lowly number tended to fluctuate every so often thanks in part to brazen drug dealers moving in for a year and doing their dirty business, then fleeing the moment the sheriff was able to smoke them out like rats in the dark.

Almost an hour later, after touring the demolished outskirts, Millard arrived at the heart of the town, tooling down a half mile strip which was Sullinger's town central.

There was a small market called Barrington's, named after the late Mrs. Charlotte Barrington. Before her passing nine years earlier, she was the town's wealthiest resident, wealthy at *$3,233.42*.

Across the street from the market sat a two chair barbershop, a barbeque pit, a hair salon and gun shop. There were other businesses along the strip, but they were nothing more than long faded memories, along with the abandoned fiberglass plant that sat isolated on the outskirts of the town. The same business that moved its operation out of state and cost the vast majority of the town's residents their beloved jobs.

The barbershop's two front windows, as well as both styling chairs, were all blown out into the messy street. Fallen street lamps and power lines blocked most of the roads people drove along.

And anyone who even entertained the thought of shopping at the market could now do so outside, because every item of food and beverage was scattered up and down the pavement as though a full scale riot had taken place.

Just a few feet outside the strip sat a small diner/truck stop. Nothing extravagant, just a little place folks could stop by and grab a quick meal before and after work. The only damage the diner seemed to sustain was a downed tree limb that missed the establishment by only mere inches, and a TV antenna that was lying in the bushes that before the storm was perched on top of the roof. Beyond, that, the place was virtually untouched.

Millard parked his truck in front of the eatery next to a maroon Chevette. With led feet he climbed out and began for the door while Shirley sat still in the back as she usually would do, waiting patiently for her only friend to return.

Millard stepped inside and immediately took notice of two elderly white men seated in a booth, conversing and smoking cigarettes. Millard knew them and they knew him right back, which was exactly why evil eyes were passed back and forth like ping pong balls.

Without parting his chapped lips, Millard sat himself down in a stool in front of an all-white counter and waited for some kind of attention while the tiny am/fm radio clear down at the other end of the counter played Waylon Jennings' *Amanda* for everyone to hear.

Without the television, which was regularly tuned to the hunting channel, sitting and listening to the sizzling of food on the stove in the kitchen and the coffee pot whistling were alien sounds to those who were accustomed to hearing proper methods on fish gutting and bear trapping.

The old man sat and waited patiently for the waitress who seemed to be busy tending to cooking in the back. If it had been anyone else he would have raised holy hell the minute he bothered to step through the door.

The moment he saw the young woman slap both her spatula and over mitt down on a table and begin her march out into the eating area, Millard right away started to wipe the cold sweat from off his forehead and face. He cleared his throat of the usual saliva buildup.

The attractive, light skinned young lady came out dressed in a dirty white apron and white undershirt underneath.

Upon her head she wore an *Atlanta Hawks* ball cap that hid her long strands of jet back hair. Her greasy blue jeans with the torn hole in the right knee looked as though they were chewed apart by a wild animal.

Millard looked on at her sweaty face, which was emblazoned with a laid back, almost agonizing frown. She stared him down as though he were the most unimpressive being on the planet. The man watched with boiling anticipation as her mug quickly turned red.

The woman snatched out a pen and pad from her back pocket and said with a slight giggle, "Funny seeing you here."

Millard stared at the young lady with his mouth ajar as though he wanted to say something but the words had escaped him.

"What can I get for you, sir?" She wearily sighed, sounding as if she were already fed up with the old man.

"Uh, well…I reckon I'll have the toast and bacon." He hesitantly muttered.

The woman quickly wrote down the order, and without saying another word turned and began for the kitchen.

"I see the TV is off." Millard blurted out.

The young woman stopped in her tracks and let out a brief, excruciating sigh before spinning back around. "The storm knocked the antenna down; you may have noticed it lying near the road outside." She snidely remarked. "Mikey said that he'll have to get the cable company up in Jackson to have it replaced."

"The storm," Millard rolled his eyes. "Speakin' of the storm, how are the boys?"

Millard watched as she tightened her lips, almost biting down in the process before she approached the counter.

"They're alright. It's the first time either of them has ever been through something like that, so they're obviously shaken up…but they're alright." She nonchalantly replied as she began to wipe down the already clean countertop in front of Millard.

"I'm surprised you're here workin' today."

"Bills don't care about storms, and I got plenty of those coming my way, every day." The woman carried on while scanning Millard's bruised face. "Looks like the storm didn't miss you…you've looked better."

"Aww shit, this?" Millard pointed to his swollen left eye. "I just had some…troubles of my own last night. Nuttin' big."

"I guess you couldn't help but to bring those troubles in here along with your muddy shoes, huh?"

Millard cleared his throat before responding, "Yeah, well, my whole yard is a damn mess. I didn't get a chance to clean up much."

With a cunning smirk gracing her face, the young lady said, "I see. Well, I'd better get your order in now."

"I was just wonderin' if—

"Hey, Courtney, darlin', can ya grab another cup 'O Joe here, please?" One of the old men in the booth kindly asked with his cup lifted.

"Comin' right up, Abe," Courtney gladly replied before re-directing her attention back to Millard who appeared shell-shocked at that instant. "You were saying?"

With a mouth full of cotton, Millard quickly rooted around in his frosted brain for something logical to say. "Uh…I'll let you get that boy's coffee first."

Courtney slammed her wet rag down onto the counter in front of Millard before walking around to an adjacent counter while rolling her annoyed eyes along the way.

Millard watched as she carried the steaming pot over to the gentlemen's table and began to strike up a conversation with them.

The old man wasn't a glutton for punishment; he knew when he had had enough. He had no more words left for the young woman to respond to, and he was well aware that she was already at her boiling point with him. Breakfast would have to come later as far as he was concerned.

Millard lifted his smelly body up off of his warm stool and started for the door, all the while trying not to take another coarse glance over at Courtney.

Right before he could reach the door, Courtney announced, "Just in case you care, Virginia will be here tomorrow!"

Millard continued on as though he hadn't heard a mumbling word. In his mind, her final sentence was as insignificant as the people that resided in the small town of Sullinger.

With even more bile welling up inside of him, Millard bolted out the door and hopped into his truck without looking back.

His long, hot day was just beginning.

CHAPTER 4

I f Sullinger was famous for something, among many things, it had to be its tree laden back roads, and Millard was a titan at maneuvering through and in the tight and winding woods that was home to many a wild forest creature; animals that old Millard had no qualms over demolishing just to reach one of his desired destinations.

Once he was clear of the two mile stretch of woodlands, he raced out and onto the muddy main road that eventually led to a disheveled apartment building.

The old man pulled his truck in front of the two floor shanty and parked in behind a downed oak tree. Much like everything else in town, the storm laid waste to the building that *52* people called home for *$120.00* a month.

Small children carelessly played near fallen power lines, while two drunken black men stumbled aimlessly about in the parking lot as though they were completely lost.

Millard got out of his truck and marched straight for what was left of the front door, which was at that point half a door.

"Hey, brotha, can I get a dime off ya?" One of the stumbling drunks slurred as he wobbled towards Millard with an extended right hand.

Without stopping or even giving the man a simple glance, Millard bellowed, "Nigga, get the fuck outta my face before I stomp a mud hole in ya!"

Shoving his way past the rancid smelling individual was only the easy part, once inside, Millard found himself nearly slipping and falling to the saturated floor. The entire downstairs was a soaking wasteland of toys, clothes and beer bottles, all floating about from one end of the floor to the other.

The instant he was able to regain a stable foot hold, Millard headed up the steps while trying to skip and dodge wild playing children who considered all the destruction another excuse to frolic in the nasty water.

There was a foul stink attached to the tenement, and it went far beyond the common beer and weed aromas that permeated the building. Not only was it the stench of moldy water, but also that of human waste. The old man always seemed to feel at home.

At the very end of the grimy hallway sat his desired locale. The noises of women screaming at their children to stop running before they fall and hurt themselves could be heard throughout.

There were the young men, both black and white, who would keep lumbering in and out of their respective apartments clothed in only a pair of dirty boxers on their behinds, and their hair wild and loose before the world.

After stampeding his way through heaps of wreckage, Millard approached a door that had the number *32* printed across the wood in red crayon. He didn't knock on the door; he didn't call out any names. He just twisted the knob before brazenly stepping right in and catching two Hispanic women, one older and the other young, arguing and recklessly tossing clothes in all directions.

Millard slammed the door behind him as hard as he could in the hopes that the racket would put an end to all the incessant quarreling, but instead it just brought Millard face to face with the Spanish speaking older woman and her raging temper.

With a lazy appearance melting all over his face, Millard simply looked over at the younger woman as though the old lady had lost her mind.

"Mama, come away from him and get out!" The young woman shouted as she walked over and pulled her mother away from Millard's presence.

Right off the bat Millard recognized Spanish curse words when he heard them, including the racist ones. The ones that were meant specifically for his race seemed to make him smile a bit.

"Mama, stop saying that and leave!" The younger woman urged while pulling her short mother nearer to the door. "I can take care of myself!"

Any other time Millard would have tossed the old woman out the nearest window and that would have been the end, but on that sticky morning, he had more pertinent matters to attend to.

"Get that stinkin' cunt outta here!" Millard hollered before sitting himself down on the couch.

The two yelled on and on at each other in fluent Spanish until the frustrated daughter was able to fling her mother out the door. Once the door was slammed shut, the infuriated mother could still be heard on the other end, cursing up a storm of obscenities towards both her child the black man that was seated inside the apartment.

The young woman pressed her frail, skinny body up against the door for as long as she could before exhaling and trudging her way over to the couch where Millard was seated.

The young lady stood at an even five- foot three. Her jet black hair supported a tight pony tail that was wrapped in a yellow rubber band. Her paper thin body wore nothing but a yellow tank top shirt and a pair of red polka dot panties.

She sat there next to Millard flustered and out of breath; her one room apartment was a clutter of clothes and notebook paper that enveloped just about every corner of the tiny enclosure.

"I'm sorry about that." The woman sighed with a kind smile attached to her blushing face. "My mama wants me to leave this place and get away from you, but—

"Gal, shut the hell up and come here!" Millard griped as he grabbed the woman by the back of her neck, unzipped his pants and whipped out his penis.

From there he forced her head down and watched as she bobbed up and down on his rod, just as he always did whenever the mood struck him.

His eyes were never closed for the event; it was as though he had to view everything, no matter how incredible it felt.

Millard was well aware of just how much she hated it when it was forced upon her, but he couldn't have cared less. Reckless abandon always seemed to get the old man's juices running, like an animal in heat; and after the night before, Millard felt that he was more than justified in his rambunctious actions.

Fortunately, however, for the young woman's sake, Millard had the staying power of a dead turtle. So when he let loose his load inside her mouth, without warning no less, she breathed a sigh of relief as she came up for air, coughing and chocking.

Millard sat there on the couch, gripping his limp member

in his hands and jerking and jolting as though he were in the midst of a seizure. With one eye opened, he watched the woman get up and take exactly three steps ahead to the kitchen sink where she twisted on the water faucet and began to clean off her mouth and chin.

She then grabbed a paper towel from off the counter before making her way back to Millard, who ended up snatching the towel from her hand. He used the cloth to wipe clean his messy midsection of any excess.

The young lady sat there next to Millard, looking him up and down as if she didn't recognize him all of the sudden.

"What happened to your face?" She questioned in her usual broken English.

"I had to take care of some scabs last night." He grunted. "One's dead, the other's on the loose. I'll get the fucker, though."

"You shot another person?" The lady screamed out in terror.

"You damn right I did!" Millard shamelessly replied. "The motherfucker was tryin' to get into my house! Now I think I got his ghost runnin' around in the barn. As long as he stays away from me, I ain't got no problem with 'em no more."

"Do you know why these guys keep on trying to break into your house? It's been seven years already."

"I know why," Millard smirked, "and I got to kill another one of the stinkin' rats last night, too. What the hell you got around here to eat anyways?"

"I don't have anything, the electricity went out last night and everything in the fridge spoiled." The girl innocently answered.

"You got any eggs?"

"I had to throw everything away, including the eggs."

"Dammit, gal, I'm hungry as a bear."

"I heard that the diner was open today."

"Who the hell cares?" Millard grumbled as he scrounged about on the couch while rubbing his sore back.

"What's wrong with your back, sweetie?" The woman compassionately inquired.

"Don't worry 'bout that."

"Well, did the storm tear your house apart? Because if it did then you can come and live with me." The young lady anxiously panted.

Without looking in her direction, Millard replied in a scornful tone, "I bet you'd like that, wouldn't you? Nope, the storm just got everything on the outside, killed my damn chickens, too."

"Is Shirley okay?" The woman asked with a shot of contempt in her voice.

"Yeah, she was half out of her mind this mornin', barkin' at the barn and all. It had to be that spook 'cause I heard it fuckin' around in the hay. When I pushed everything away, there wasn't nothin' there."

"You know how this old town is. I told you that one day the next person you kill will come back to haunt you."

"Shut the hell up!" Millard suddenly snapped. "What the shit was your mama here for anyways?"

"I tried to tell you, she wants me to move out of here and live with her in Biloxi. She especially wants me away from you, but I can't leave my sweet Tequila behind." The woman warmly smiled as she attempted to wrap her boney arms around Millard's neck.

"Cut all that shit out," Millard growled, slipping his way out of her loving hold. "I'm hungry, I feel like I ain't ate nothin' in days, dammit."

"I'll see what I have left in the cabinets." The girl

somberly spoke as she got up from off the couch and shuffled her way into the kitchen.

"You do that, and I want some bread that ain't molded, too!"

"Alright, Millard," the woman moaned while rummaging through the cupboards. "I sure hope we don't see any more storms anytime soon so we can take that trip down to the Gulf finally."

"Can't leave Shirley behind, you know how she gets when I leave for too long."

"Then why don't you marry Shirley, then?" The woman sarcastically mumbled under her breath."

"What was that? Come again!" Millard struck back as he snatched up a pink short sleeved shirt that was lying next to him and threw it at the woman, hitting her on the backside.

"Stoppit, Millard, I was just playing!"

"Well don't play, motherfucker! And hurry up fixin' that food before I leave this shithole altogether!"

Still worn thin from the events of the night before, Millard laid down on the soft couch and shut his eyes. He allowed his mind to wander on the intruder that got away, the same one that pie-faced him back down onto his power saw.

It was rare for anyone to elude Millard's wrath- filled ferocity, especially after a famed robbery attempt. Nothing in the world vexed him more. No one got the best of Millard... no one.

Suddenly, the blaring of sirens caused Millard to awaken from his half slumber at that instant.

"Who is that for?" The young lady questioned as she stepped over to the window. "It's an ambulance, Millard."

"No shit, dumbass!"

"It looks like they've come for some kid down there."

Millard closed his eyes all over again and attempted to

once more shut the world out. But with his friend's constant, minute by minute updates, he found that gaining a simple measure of peace would be out of the question.

"Millard…where's Shirley?" The young lady suddenly stuttered.

At the snap of a finger, Millard jumped up from off the couch as though it were on fire before racing to the window and shoving his lady aside.

"What the fuck?" Millard frantically hollered as he turned, ran out the door and down the flooded stairs that led outside.

Once Millard reached the parking lot he began to search the muddy ground for any possible paw prints that the dog could have left behind.

Shirley wasn't one for running away, but with her recent raging demeanor, anything could have been a possibility. Not even the little black boy that was being lifted onto a gurney after being electrocuted by one of the downed power lines could derail the old man's blinding hysteria.

The very moment he was able to spot a series of small paw prints in the mud, Millard pushed his way past scores of onlookers, hopped into his truck and started to pull away, nearly dragging his lady by the door handle that she was fighting to hold on to.

"Slow down before you crash!"

"Fuck slowin' down, my damn dog is gone!"

Millard tore down the mud layered road at breakneck speeds; the paw prints ended yards back but the path that the old man was traveling led directly towards his house, therefore, it wasn't hard for him to put two and two together.

There was absolutely no way that his friend was going to stop him from driving so fast and careless down the slippery road. In certain areas there were unpaved ditches the size of craters, and with so much debris strewn about, there was no telling where they could have ended up with just one false twist or turn.

* * *

Ten minutes later, Millard and company arrived at his homestead, in one miraculous piece. Millard stopped on a dime in front of the shack and jumped out to see Shirley perched at the barn's entrance, just staring upwards at the top of the structure with her jaws locked tight.

Exhausted, Millard stepped forward and asked, "Gal, what the hell is you doin' back here? You scared the shit outta me!"

"What is she looking at, Millard?" The young lady questioned as she climbed out of the truck.

While rubbing the dog's head, Millard looked up and replied, "I'm figurin' that spook."

"The ghost is up there, on the roof?"

Millard stared down at the dog and began to wonder to himself just what was taking place. Shirley was never an active animal. Her mother was sick when she gave birth to her and eight other pups. Shirley was half dead when Millard decided to take her in. It was uncharacteristic of him, but there was something about the lowly creature that urged the old man to nurse her back to health. She was shiftless, pathetic in a fight, and an outright nuisance, but Millard kept her around nonetheless, and no one in town ever dared to question why.

For the first time in her life, there was something driving her mad, and Millard could see right through his only friend.

"I don't see anything up there, baby." The young woman carefully observed.

"Well, you know animals can see things people folk can't."

"I can't believe she ran all the way back here just to look at the barn."

Just then, something began to take place, something that could never be explained by word of mouth, only witnessed by human eyes to truly believe and comprehend. Shirley started to whine as she slowly backed away from the barn and towards the house. Her stump tail didn't wag and her eyes never once left the top of the barn house.

It was an utterly amazing and jarring experience to observe, it was as if she were locked in a sort of possessed trance.

Both Millard and his lady stood still and watched in awe as Shirley continued her startling backwards march up the steps of the shack and turn a complete 360 before eventually lying down and under her own forepaws.

Millard looked back up at the roof of the barn to see what he had been seeing since he arrived moments earlier, absolutely nothing.

"Has she ever done that before—

Right before the woman could even finish what she was saying, broken pieces of wood came crashing down from off the roof of the barn and onto the ground, sending both Millard and the woman breathlessly scurrying out of the way.

Millard knelt down, picked up a couple of pieces of the old wood and studied them real hard before gazing back up at the top of the barn with a befuddled glare.

He didn't know what to think, but for him and the small town of Sullinger, odd dogs and falling debris were tame compared to some of the happenings in and around the town over the years.

"Millard, maybe you should come and stay with me for a while, until the ghost goes away." The girl quivered in her own dirty tennis shoes.

"Shit," the old man snorted before tossing the scraps of wood aside, "I ain't goin' nowhere."

"Well, maybe it was some damage from the storm that made all that come down."

Millard just turned and casually grinned at the young lady's naïve take on the situation, as though he had everything under control.

"Maybe you could get Leon to come out and take a look."

Without responding, Millard started to walk back to his house.

"Where are you going?"

"Where the hell does it look like I'm goin'? I told you, my ass is hungry."

"But I wanna go back home!"

Millard stopped before stepping foot on the first porch step, he then turned and said with a salty grimace, "Then I suggest you get to walkin', gal."

With that, the old man took out his house key and unlocked the front door, allowing Shirley to scamper in first before slamming it shut behind himself.

Chapter 5

The harmonizing and often time's raucous singings of the parishioners over at the old church across the field from Millard's property could be heard loud and clear inside his tiny, so called bathroom.

For the first time in over four days Millard was bathing himself in his rusty, steel basin that sat on the floor right next to the tub. It wasn't that the shower wouldn't work; rather, the old man just chose not to pay for the extra water it took to use the thing.

He sat there with his knees to his chest inside his five foot wide tub, stewing over the fact that no matter how many degrees of physical separation there was between him and the church he was still able to hear every song as if the congregation were right there in front of him.

On any other Sunday morning Millard would have been knocked out cold asleep or hung over dead drunk somewhere, but for starters, his own body odor was beginning to overwhelm even him, and, the barn house was still fresh in his head.

If it hadn't been for Shirley behaving so out of character then he would have totally dismissed the whole matter, but anything that got the old, mangy dog so wound up was well worth investigating as far as he was concerned.

On top of all that, even though he would never actually admit it to himself, there was the something out in the barn that unsettled him to no end. Even though Millard, along with other residents of the town, had seen his share of the supernatural through the years, the patch of moving hay was more than enough to alarm the staunchest of disbelievers in the supernatural. He knew that there had to be more behind it all than what his eyes could or could not see.

Once he was through bathing, Millard got up and out of the washbasin and emptied the dirty water into the tub before drying himself off with the same unwashed brown towel that he used every time he felt like taking a bath.

The very moment he was done drying, the old man made his way out of the bathroom, through the living room and outside onto his porch. He then faced the west in all his unbridled nakedness and flagged down both the church and its patrons inside with a mighty middle finger.

From there, he knelt down to pick up a half empty bottle of Coors from off the porch floor and drank up while the bright morning warmness soaked into his skinny, bare body. It was beyond warm, though, it was boiling hot outside, reason enough for Millard to forgo wearing at least a shirt.

Millard stepped back inside the shack with a hearty burp to push him along while a rampaging Shirley buzzed right by her master on her way outside.

Millard curiously looked on as she ran inside the barn, he could hear her wrestle about in the hay, whimpering and whining the entire time.

"Just hold on, gal, I'm a comin'." The old man sighed as he dragged himself to his bedroom and put on a pair of stained white boxers, dingy blue overalls and his pair of work boots.

Millard then shuffled into the kitchen to grab his rifle which was placed next to the refrigerator before stepping outside to the barn as though it was nothing more than a waste of his time.

Nearly tripping over the barn's threshold, Millard cocked his rifle and froze dead in his tracks to take notice of Shirley who was standing on her hind legs while her front paws were reaching for the air, as if she were quietly begging for a treat. The bright sunlight shined down on the animal, causing a soft glow to gleam off her dusty coat.

Millard continued to stand in place. He wasn't afraid, just thrown off his game plan; his one and only friend had suddenly become something else out of nowhere.

"Hey, gal…whatcha doin'" Millard cautiously whispered as he slowly crept forward to the dog.

Gradually, Shirley turned her head to face Millard, the moment her entire face was in sight, Millard could see blood trickling down her face from her eyes. At the drop of a dime, the old man threw down his weapon and ran over to console his ailing friend. He wiped away the dripping blood from her eyes while checking the rest of her body for any other sort of damage.

As Millard continued to wipe and clean, Shirley began to growl, Millard just ignored it while speaking soothing words to try and calm the dog.

All she could do was stare into her master's eyes as if she were entranced by the blackness in them, until, without warning, she snapped at him, almost biting Millard in the face before releasing herself from his grip.

"What the fuck is wrong with you, gal?" Millard hollered as he fell backwards and stared angrily at the animal.

Foam began to drip from Shirley's mouth, foam that wasn't there when Millard first entered the barn. The dog then wildly shook her head from side to side before wagging her tail and galloping out of the barn.

The old man got to his feet, wondering just what he should do next. Chase after his soul mate, or investigate his haunted barn?

He picked up his rifle and started to meander about in the hay, searching for anything that could possibly explain what exactly was going on. The more he stalked the ground the more he could smell what resembled an overflowing sewer, much like his own house.

He rooted around for the source of the foul stink, believing that maybe it was a dead animal, until the smell could be located towards the base of the loft's ladder. Millard looked up and raised his rifle in the air; the barn had never smelled that way before, so then, all of the sudden, there was something that was making itself at home. Millard lived only with his dog and no one else…that was the way he liked it.

Ready and waiting to end another life, Millard stepped onto the first rung of the wooden ladder and began his ascension, only to be met halfway by a bitterly cold breeze that all but wiped the sweat completely off of his face.

Overlooking the disturbance, he continued on. The cold grew more intense, so extreme that it became almost intolerable to where the old man became dizzy enough to fall backwards onto the soft hay laden ground below.

Millard looked up with a pair of foggy eyes at the loft; he could hear the same crunching sounds that he heard the day before stem from the top of the loft, expect now, the ruckus was moving towards him.

He looked up only to hear what sounded like a pair of heavy feet hit the ground directly in front of him before the feet ran out of the barn as if they were being chased. Its thick presence before him was deafening. Dismissing the blurriness in his eyes, Millard got up and began to run towards the barn's door with his rifle pointed directly ahead of him.

"Whoa, man, I just came to visit!" A young, dark skinned man pleaded with his arms up in the air.

"Get the hell outta my way, boy!" Millard screamed as he ran around the young man, nearly knocking him over.

Millard scanned his entire yard, but could only see his usual filthy surroundings stare right back at him.

"Damn, man," the young man said as he carefully stepped behind Millard, "you look like you 'bout to kill someone!"

Millard didn't want to discuss what just took place, he didn't have to, all he had to do was play it off and grin devilishly at the boy.

"So, how long you plan on stayin' out of jail this time, boy?" Millard asked as he turned and made his way towards his shack.

"Aww, man, those crackers ain't gonna put me back in that place no mo'. I got too much to do out here, daddy." The boy gleefully replied, following his father into the house.

Millard sniggered before saying, "That's what ya said thirteen months ago and they still ended up haulin' your black ass away."

"That wasn't my fault." The man urged. "Besides, I got a plan this time for some money. I ain't gotta rob homes no mo'."

"A plan," Millard rolled his eyes. "What kind of plan, nigga?"

"I got a plan to open my own beeper shop." The young man proudly proclaimed. "Everybody needs a beeper."

"Not me," Millard nonchalantly responded while examining his rifle's chamber.

"Maybe not, but there's a whole lotta folks out there that talks a lot, and I'll be the only nigga in town who can give it to 'em."

"Boy, the majority of folks in this here town can't even afford to pay for water. What the hell makes you think they can afford a pager bill every month?"

Millard looked up at his child, awaiting an answer sooner than later. When it took too long for him to reply, the old man eyed his boy from head to toe as though he were disgusted with his attire.

Uneven cornrows, a scraggly, unshaved beard and a pair of blue jeans with a white, sleeveless shirt. Millard knew that the boy could do better, but at nineteen, there was only so much a father could expect from his son. The only piece of clothing that didn't seem too inappropriate were his all white Chuck Taylor's, which were too clean for a recent parolee.

The boy haplessly snickered before at last replying, "I was just thinkin', that's all."

Millard just pathetically shook his head from side to side before reaching into his pocket and slipping out his wallet.

"Hey, daddy, who you gonna shoot at?"

"I need to get to the shop; I gotta get some more shells."

"Can I come?" The boy practically begged.

Millard looked up at his son as though he were staring at a small child before sighing, "I reckon so; you can hold my damn gun."

"You got anotha' dumbass up in your yard again, daddy?"

"You could say that. Did ya happen to see where Shirley ran to when you came into the yard?" Millard asked as he parted the dusty blinds in his front window and peered out.

"I didn't see her at all when I got here. Did she run away?"

"I dunno, but she needs to bring her crazy ass back here."

Millard warned as he and his boy exited the house, got into the truck and pulled out of the yard.

Millard wasn't much for carrying on a conversation, and talking to his own son about anything was the last thing on his mind that bizarre morning.

"Man, I'm 'bout to meet up with this one bitch I've been writin' to since I was locked up in County." The young man announced. "She be sendin' me naked pictures and letters almost every week."

Millard sat silent as his two eyes remained focused upon the road ahead of him. He heard his son's words, he just chose not to respond until something worthwhile came out of his mouth.

"She's up here talkin' 'bout gettin' married and—

"Gettin' what?" Millard suddenly awoke. "Boy, what the hell have you gotten yourself into now?"

"I ain't the one who wants to get married, it's her." The young man hastily explained as though his life depended on it. "She already got five kids from five other dudes. I ain't tryin' to hear all that marriage shit. I got some hoes I'm supposed to be meetin' up with tonight anyways."

"Ain't you learned nothin' all these years?" Millard protested. "You don't wanna keep a woman. Women are like elephants, they're fun to ride on every now and then, but you don't ever wanna own one. You don't need the aggravation."

"Well, I'll just hit it and then quit it."

"Women have only two purposes in this here world, havin' babies and givin' blowjobs, other than that, they ain't shit. But I'll tell ya, that mama of yours sure could suck one mean dick when she was alive. Niggas used to say that she could suck the skin off a dick and still keep on suckin' away!" Millard gaily laughed out loud as if he had told the funniest joke ever.

For moments, there was an eerie quiet that prevailed in

the truck as they tooled down the dirt road. Millard never even bothered to look over at his son who had become obstinately silent all of the sudden.

"Is you still messin' around with that Mexican girl, daddy?" The boy soberly questioned.

Millard let out an exhaustive sigh before replying, "Yeah, that gal still don't know when to leave a nigga alone. I sent her ass home yesterday. Like a dummy she walked all the way back to that rat trap apartment of her's."

The young man chuckled before asking, "You ever see that fine ass Courtney anymore?"

At that moment, Millard almost immediately reverted back to the comatose state that he was in before their conversation arose earlier. Just the mere mention of the woman's name crooked Millard's already stiff neck.

He didn't want to even hear the name Courtney. In Millard's state of mind, he was the only person inside the truck.

* * *

The town's supply store that was located just around the bend from the main strip was more than just a supply mart, it also sold bullets for just about every gun every manufactured, as well as hardware items and straight from the tap, ice cold beer. It was a safe haven for the men of the town.

Millard pulled his pickup truck in front of the one room house-like building that was missing part of its roof in the back. He then snatched his rifle from out of his son's lap and got out.

The second Millard entered the store, with his son hot on his heels, he right away saw two middle-aged white men seated at a table drinking beer and playing cards, and an old white man behind a counter counting money. The very instant the elder man caught sight of Millard's son, he more than quickly stuffed his wad of bills into his cash register and pretended to dust off his glass counter while straitening his thin eyeglasses.

"Well, look who's out of the pokey again, boys, it's 'ole Brett!" The old man announced with an amiable but cautious smile on his wrinkled face. "How long you plannin' on stayin' out this time, young fella?"

With his hands planted in his back pockets, Brett bashfully replied, "I hope forever, Mr. Roberts."

"That's what ya said the last time, and look what happened, son." The heavy set card player said while stroking his grey beard.

"Man, whatever," Brett scornfully mumbled.

Ignoring all of the incessant chatter at his son's expense, Millard approached the counter and slammed his rifle down onto the glass.

"Well, whaddya want, now?" Mr. Roberts asked.

"You know damn good and well what I want, ya sum bitch!"

"Don't come here in startin' no trouble, Millard!" The heavy man spoke up. "Don't ya think this town has had its share of trouble after that storm?"

Slowly and methodically, Millard turned his attention from the old man, and with a stunned face, directed his eyes solely on the fat individual seated at the table.

The burly man immediately stood up from out of his seat and boldly stepped forward to face Millard down.

It was hard to say just when old Millard lost his fear of humankind, or any other kind for that matter. He just stood his ground as he usually did, with his feet planted firmly to the floor beneath him.

Even though both men were of the same height, the

heavy man outweighed Millard by at least two hundred pounds, but not once did one bone in Millard's lanky body budge. And no matter how hot it was both outside and in, not one bead of sweat dared to form upon his forehead.

Both of them looked as if they were two prizefighters just waiting for the opening bell to go off. The store smelled of underarm funk and stale beer as a tape deck that was placed behind the counter played Willie Nelson's "*Blue eyes Cryin' in the Rain.*"

Neither man flinched; Millard's cold, dark eyes were dull and sullen as though the three hundred pound behemoth that stood in front of him was a mere, unfunny joke.

It wasn't the first time the two had ever faced one another, but after so many years of eventual showdowns, something drastic had to give.

"You wanna say it…don't you?" Millard sneered, practically daring the man to even blink. "Well go on then, son, I'm waitin'."

The big man stood steady while Mr. Roberts, Brett and the other gentleman seated at the table all looked on in uneasy anticipation as if another storm were looming on the horizon.

"Brett, my boy," the big man exhaled, "you best take your daddy on home before someone gets disruptive in here."

Millard stood and watched as the man broodingly turned and stumbled back over to the confines of his card table.

"C'mon, daddy, ya know I can't afford to go back to jail again." Brett patiently pleaded as he placed his right hand on Millard's shoulder.

To Millard, it was as if someone had placed a dead bird on his shoulder because the wicked expression he handed his son at that instant would have suggested that the boy had only seconds to remove his hand or else.

Ever so quickly, Brett withdrew his trembling hand and sheepishly turned away from his father's hateful face.

Millard cut his red eyes away from his startled son and turned back to look Mr. Roberts dead in the face. "Give me my fuckin' shells, ya cracker." He bitterly mumbled.

Millard realized that the man would have climbed the tallest mountain in the world just to get him out of his store as soon as possible. To Millard, it was a cute little game that he enjoyed, all because he could enjoy it.

Mr. Roberts knelt down and took out a box of shells, he then handed the box to Millard who in turn snatched it away.

"You know the price." Roberts sternly said with an outstretched hand.

Millard reached into his pants pocket and whipped out a crumpled fifty dollar bill before tossing it into the man's face. With his newly purchased bullets, Millard Lang turned and stormed out the door.

"Daddy, you forgot your change!" Brett said as he came running out of the store behind his father.

"No I didn't, it's on his cracker ass." Millard replied, climbing into his truck. "Now, what was you sayin' about some gal's you were gonna meet up with?"

"Oh yeah, I met these two fine ass bitches up in Jackson, but I gotta go pick 'em up if you'll let me borrow your truck. They're black, too."

"I don't give a shit if they're polka dot." Millard shrugged. "Can they suck a mean one?"

"You know it."

"What time ya bringin' 'em by?"

"Anytime ya want, I reckon."

"Come around eight, and bring the beer, too."

"But I ain't got no money, daddy."

Millard looked over at Brett with a confident glower upon his unshaven face and grinned, "Well, I reckon you best be doin' what you do best then…boy."

CHAPTER 6

It was well after eight-thirty that evening; the bright sun was taking its sweet time setting, leaving in its faltering wake a red and orange glowing luster over an otherwise dismal and demolished town.

The sweltering heat was still apparent, but the somewhat cool breath of nightfall would possibly give a glint of relief to weary sleepers. However, for Millard, sleep was the very last thing he desired that twilight. Pacing back and forth on his porch with an anxious zeal, the man just couldn't shake the unsettling fact that there was something sinister prowling his property.

Millard stepped down from off the porch and began to skulk about the yard in search of Shirley whom he had neither seen nor heard from since earlier in the day. He checked the stinking barn house which was by then cool enough for a person to lay back and enjoy a respite from the deep Mississippi heat.

Shirley wasn't a pet that ran off on a usual basis; the animal was smart enough to recognize the difference between her safe yard and the road.

Millard wasn't in any kind of mood to be searching for a crazy dog all night long, especially when he knew that he was on the verge of "getting some" that evening. Brett was late, Shirley was out of her mind and two figures were slowly making their way across the field behind Millard's house.

Just as he was about to head back inside, Millard heard the grunting of his truck's engine rumble down the road and towards his house. He impatiently waited as Brett pulled into the yard. The very second the young man and his two female companions stepped out of the vehicle, Millard instantly began to tear into him.

"Boy, where the hell have you been?" He snapped.

"I had to pick up the girls, daddy." Brett shuddered.

"I thought you said that they was up in Jackson, not Jupiter!"

"Well, I also had to make a stop at a buddy's crib and pick up some weed, too."

"Did ya get the beer?"

"Yes, sir, and it's still cold, too." Brett proudly grinned.

Millard stood in place on the soaking ground and looked over the two young ladies that Brett brought with him.

One was a dark young lady while the other was caramel skinned. Both women appeared as though they had just finished up with previous clients just hours earlier with their unkempt hair and ragged clothes.

"Check this out, daddy. This right here is Tammy, and her cousin Belinda."

Millard wore a smug and mighty glare, like he was judging both women for a beauty contest. His hungry eyes scaled Belinda, the dark woman, up and down, noticing her black boots that reached her scratched up knees.

"Damn, girl, ain't you hot in those boots?" Millard frowned.

"Not really," Belinda muttered, "you get used to this heat after a while, sir."

"Hey, daddy, Tammy is goin' to college up in Jackson, and—

"Boy, I don't give a damn if she's goin' mountain climbin', get they're asses in the house and let's get down to it!" Millard anxiously barked.

The ladies timidly glanced at each other, appearing as if they had just made the worst mistake of their young lives.

"Hello there, Brotha Lang!" A deep voice called out from the other end of Millard's wooden fence.

Millard spun around to see a short, fat black man and a thin black woman make their way onto his property. He had all but forgotten about the two figures that were trekking across the field, and he planned on forgetting about them even more once he was inside his shack.

"Say there, Brotha Lang, I was wonderin' if I could get a moment of your time, sir."

Millard knew who they were; the man was the pastor at the little church at the other end of the pasture, and the woman was his wife. In the fourteen years that they had attended the church, the couple made the sad mistake of crossing over into Millard's yard only once, ever since that fateful encounter, the husband and wife respected the boundaries that separated them.

"What the fuck do ya'll want?"

"Brotha Lang, you don't have to use that evil language." The pastor said.

"Would you like for me to use somethin' else, boy?"

"Brotha Lang, we just stopped by to let you know that your dog was scratchin' at the church's door just a few hours ago, and—

"You've seen my damn dog?" Millard's head snapped forward. "Then why the hell didn't you say anything before now, nigga?"

The pastor's wife all of the sudden stepped forward and

skittishly replied, "Well, because once I made my way around to see what was happenin', your dog took off. He looked like he had got into a fight or somethin', his eyes were bleedin'."

"It ain't a he, it's a she. Did you see a dick on that old thing?"

"Brotha Lang, I told you that there was no reason for that kind of talk." The pastor struck back with bitterness in his baritone voice.

With a smirk on his face, Millard asked, "Boy, do you remember the last time you was over here? Do you remember almost losin' your life that day?"

"Brotha Lang, for all your hateful behaving, my Lord and Savior Jesus Christ is always on the side of justice. No weapon you have forged against me shall prosper."

"Then you tell Jesus to save your black ass when I go inside and get my damn gun! We'll see if he can save you both from a bullet!"

Tense minutes of hostile staring passed before the pastor's wife began tugging at her husband's sleeve and said, "C'mon, Marvin, I told you we had no business comin' over here to begin with!"

"You better listen to your old woman there, fat man. She ain't as dumb as she looks."

Both the pastor and his wife started to slowly back away and turn to the field behind them, but the pastor was determined to have the last say, no matter what.

"I'll pray for you, Brotha Lang. God loves you, too!"

"He's also gonna love for me to get inside these two hoes before the sun goes down, too!" Millard hollered back. "Now, get the hell outta here!"

"For your information, I ain't no hoe!" Tammy snapped back with her hands placed firmly on her hips.

As though he heard someone tell him the most shocking

news ever, Millard ever slowly turned around and eyeballed the young lady like she had lost her mind.

Dueling words wasn't what he was in the mood for that evening, especially when the words happen to come from someone he believed to be a lesser life form. When his point was spoken, the case was closed.

Giggling like a nervous wreck, Brett whispered into Tammy's ear, "Hey, girl, he didn't mean it like that."

"Then how did he mean it, then?" Tammy asked in a belligerent voice.

"My daddy just has a way of sayin' stuff, that's all."

"What's that smell?" Belinda coughed as she covered her mouth and nose with her left hand.

"It's just the sewers backin' up, right, daddy?"

Millard didn't answer, he just snatched Belinda by the arm and practically dragged her into the house. Once all four individuals were inside, Millard slammed the front door shut before forcing the Belinda down to her knees.

"Damn!" she squealed. "You aint gotta yank me all over the place!"

"Just the shut the hell up and get ready!" Millard sniggered as he hurriedly unzipped his pants. "Get me a beer, boy."

Brett did as ordered and pulled out a tall can of Coors from his brown paper bag. He then reached into his pants pocket and whipped out a small plastic bag full of weed before rolling up the material into numerous thin paper sticks.

Millard grabbed his beer and snapped open the cap, he then reached over and helped himself to a newly wrapped roach, all the while looking down at Belinda serve him as only he truly desired.

The disagreement he had with the pastor and his wife, his dog, and even the odd visitor inside his barn had all but become mere echoes in his hazy brain that evening. He didn't care how he treated either of the women that dared to entertain him; to Millard, it was their duty as females to submit.

The battle weary man was at last at peace.

*   *   *

The nighttime, such as it was, was one of unbridled carnality. Beer, drugs, sex and two gleeful men. Absolutely nothing else on earth could have felt better. Not a single soul on earth could have disrupted the occasion; it was the perfect tie-on to what Millard Lang would have aptly phrased as "his paradise away from heaven."

As the old, naked man got through with his business with Tammy, he got up from off the floor and stumbled over two other naked individuals on his way to the kitchen. He was both high and drunk as sweat drooled down his face, causing his already blurred vision to become even unclear.

As he attempted to turn on the water faucet, his ears caught the buzzing of a commotion above him. With a head that felt as if it could drop right off of his shoulders, Millard looked up at the black ceiling. Like the drunkard that he was, Millard toppled back and forth against the sink while listening to the ruckus above that to him sounded like someone were walking across the roof.

His drooling eyes looked back and forth but just could not seem to focus upon one particular thing at once. He dropped his head and leaned up against the sink before listening to his stomach churn and groan.

Just as soon as he was about to make his way back into the living room, Millard felt tiny spurts of wetness drip down onto his head. He looked back up again and listened intently at the fuss that was taking place above, but in his hazy frame of mind, the noises that he was hearing could have been all in his head. The sprinkles that he was feeling could have possibly been rain. It was all water under the bridge as far as the old man was concerned.

No sooner did he take one step forward, a sound like that of a yelp, shot out. Millard lazily turned back around and scanned the dingy kitchen before wiping his nappy head and resuming his stumble back into the living room.

Behind him was the noisy racket on the roof that continued on and on, making it sound like the roof itself were about to collapse.

Millard Lang shoved the noises out of his mind; he couldn't be bothered that evening. He dared the individual to even entertain the very thought of disrupting his frivolity.

Chapter 7

Millard's head pounded with thunder. He could see flashes of light blink on and off repeatedly, while the familiar whiff of weed breezed into his nostrils. He had been in such a place before, but never had the storm been so loud to where he could feel it in his chest.

The old man realized that he was dreaming, but the more he tried to open his stinging eyes, that was the louder the thunder grew until it eventually got on his last nerve.

With a body that weighed twice its original density, Millard sat his fully naked self up on the filthy smelling couch upon which he was lying and gazed around the living room to find beer bottles, squashed roaches in an ashtray and condoms all over the floor. Nowhere were Brett and his female companions to be found. But one thing was truly with him no matter what, the thunder that seemed to only grow louder the more his mind and ears could fully comprehend what was taking place.

With about all of his energy, Millard picked his crusty body up off of the couch and carried it straight to the front door, the place where the thunder was emanating. The closer he got to the door the more forceful the knocks became. It beat at him so vividly that the buzz he had lingering inside of him from the night before had all but diminished.

With the force of a mighty wind, the man swung open the door and roared, "What the fuck do you want, motherfucker?"

The overbearing sunlight exploded right into the living room and onto Millard's dreary face, causing him to shield his eyes.

"Uh…it's me, dad." A strong voice stuttered from the other end of the door.

From behind his hand Millard could make out two wide shapes standing side by side. It took perhaps a few moments for certain things to register in the old man's watery head, but after a while it slowly began to sift in.

Millard huffed before turning back around and groaning in a worn out tone, "Oh…what the hell is you doin' down here, boy?"

Millard sat down on the couch and watched as the two individuals, both fat, black men, came inside. Getting himself dressed was the last thing on Millard's mind at that moment, his entire body felt like sun-dried mud; just the slightest movements drained him all the more.

He looked up at the two men. One of the fellows wore a white tank-top shirt with khaki shorts and a pair of sandals, while the other, who was completely bald on top, wore a florescent blue silk shirt over his hairy, bloated stomach that read *Geno's Bar* in bright glitter, as well as a pair of dark blue shorts that covered his blackened knees.

He could tell that both men, much like others who dared to enter Millard's hovel, were astonished at just what they had entered into. Millard was well aware of his surroundings, as well as the fact that his own son was embarrassed to see his father naked before the world; he could see it written all over the young man's startled face.

With a back that felt as if it were ready to break in an

instant, he reared over and picked up his pants that were lying on the floor before sluggishly pulling them up and onto his legs.

It wasn't as though he were waiting for it, but the second he saw a glimmer of relief cross over his son's blushing face, Millard asked, "What the hell did you come all the way down here for?"

Beginning a stroll around the living room, the man replied, "We heard about the storm from mom. The news didn't seem to carry any coverage of it. We just came to see how you were doing."

Looking at his son's companion, Millard asked, "We?"

"Oh, sorry about that," Millard's son paused as he came back and stood beside his friend. "This is Bird. We work at the same bar together."

With an overjoyed smile gracing his chunky face, Bird extended his right hand and loudly said, "Glad to meet you after all this time, sir!"

Millard just strangely stared down at Bird's hand like it was diseased before grumbling, "Boy, I ain't deaf." Millard then looked over at his disgruntled son and asked, "Where's Brett at, Greg? Did ya'll see him outside?"

Greg frowned and said, "When did Brett get out of jail?"

"Aww shit, forget it." Millard snarled before scratching at his bearded face.

"Where's Shirley at?" Greg questioned as he rubbed his right hand over the seaweed feeling wall.

"Shit," Millard sniggered, "I ain't seen that dumb bitch since yesterday mornin'."

"Did she just up and run away?"

"Beats the shit outta me, boy," Millard irritably yelled.

Millard kept his eyes on both men as they both stood in the middle of the floor, gazing around from top to bottom and looking as though they had stepped into another dimension of sorts.

For the life of him he couldn't even begin to figure out why they bothered to show up at all, and for all intents and purposes, he wished they hadn't arrived, especially since Millard had a headache the size of a continent.

"Dad, what happened to your ceiling?"

"Boy, you know that roof has been leakin' for years." Millard yawned.

"I know that, but where did all of these imprints come from?"

Millard heaved himself from up off the couch and looked up at the ceiling in disbelief. In all the commotion from the night before, he couldn't recall hearing anything creep about on the roof, which didn't seem to surprise him one bit.

Shrugging his shoulders, Millard said, "Probably that stupid Shirley."

"Since when did Shirley gain two hundred pounds?"

"Looks like you have bears that can climb houses, now." Bird quipped with a hearty chuckle.

Millard heard the joke, but chose to keep his back turned to both the comment and the one who made it.

"I'm gonna go take a look." Greg said.

"You," Millard questioned with a snicker. "What the hell do you know 'bout roofs, boy?"

"I do a little construction on the side up in Queens." Greg declared proudly. "I'll be right back."

"Just remember, you don't weigh fifty pounds no more." Millard grinned back.

Greg paused before exiting through the front door. Millard could sense that his crack vexed the young man; the old man gave it not another thought.

"You'd be real surprised at all the things he can do, sir." Bird chimed in.

For a few unceasing moments, there was only the sound of Greg climbing up to the roof. Millard sat back down on his urine drenched couch and resumed his staring of the heavy man in front of him.

It wasn't the fact that Bird was fat that caused Millard's inquisitive adrenaline to go wild; rather, it was something a lot deeper and infectious.

"It sure does get hot down here. I guess it's true what they say, the south does have a different kind of heat." Bird mentioned as he stood impatiently in the middle of the floor, seemingly too afraid to sit down in a chair. "Judging by all the panties and condoms, it looks like you had a real good time in here last night, sir."

Millard said nothing; he just sat and studied Bird with an impish, joker grin on his face.

Bird's stout legs began to nervously tremble as he swatted at a mosquito that buzzed by his nose.

"Uh, Mr. Lang, what happened to your face?"

"Nuttin' much," Millard shrugged. "Sometimes, I get folks runnin' around here in my yard, tryin' to get into my house. Man's gotta do what he's gotta do. We old folks don't heal as fast as you youngens. Tell me somethin', Bird, what kinda name is that?"

"My real name is Barry, but for some reason or another everyone at Geno's calls me Birdie, Bird for short. I don't mind though, I think it's kind of cute."

"What kinda bird do you take after the most?"

"I beg your pardon, sir?"

"Ya heard me," Millard sat up. "When ole' Greg was little, he would flutter and twirl around here all the time. I called him a little hummingbird. His mama hated for me to call 'em that, she said that it hurt his feelings."

"Oh really," Bird's eyes opened wide. "Well, Greg has told me a lot about you, too, Mr. Lang."

"Is that right, boy," Millard asked, listening like an attentive soldier.

"Yes, sir, he said that you were a real hard ass, if you don't mind me saying so."

"No, I don't mind." Millard continued to cheese from ear to ear. "Tell me somethin', how did you two meet up? They got bars up there for you folks?"

"You folks," Bird questioned, nearly choking in the process.

"You know good and well what folks I'm talkin' about. You homo folks up yonder in New York."

"Mr. Lang, I don't know what you're talking about, but—"

"Look at ya, you're sweatin' Crisco, son." Millard smiled as he buckled his overalls. "I hear about all the stuff ya'll do up there, all that faggety chains and whips shit."

Bird began to pace the floor, he could have walked outside, but it seemed that he couldn't bring himself to pull open the door.

"What's the matter with you, big fella? You look like you gotta pee or somethin'."

Bird stopped rambling about and said, "Mr. Lang, I really do wish you hadn't said that, times have changed, and—"

"Say what things, Tugboat? Say the truth? Boy, please, you fags come outta nowhere and expect the whole world to rollover for ya'll."

"Mr. Lang, let's just try and talk more civilized here."

"Nigga, please, you all need to be put out of your damn misery. You all make me sick!" Millard's eyes rolled.

"Mr. Lang, I have stood here and tried to be patient, but I can't take any more of this!" Bird screamed as tears started to drizzle down his sweaty face.

"The truth hurts, don't it?" Millard smirked. "Are ya gettin' mad, boy? You wanna hit me, don't you?"

Millard sat and watched as Bird balled up his right fist. It was almost as if the old man were expecting, or wanting it at that point in their meeting.

"Hey, dad, did you know that…What's the matter, Bird?" Greg asked as rushed back through the front door.

Wiping tears from his eyes, Bird answered, "I just want to go, now, Greg, that's all."

Looking back and forth from Bird to his father, Greg urged, "Wait a minute, what happened?"

"I'm ready to go back home, that's all!"

"Does he cry like this all the time?" Millard inquired with his crafty grin still pasted on his ruddy face.

Greg took one hard look at his father before wrapping his arm around Bird and saying, "Why don't you go out to the car? I'll be there in a few moments."

Without saying one more word, Bird stormed out the open door. Millard didn't even clinch himself as he and his son stood face to face, all alone.

"What happened, dad?" Greg impatiently exhaled with his hands on his hips.

"Whaddya mean 'what happened?' Millard tossed up his hands. "Me and your friend was talkin', and next thing ya know, he just starts ballin' and cryin'.

"If Bird cries then it's for a damn good reason."

"Well, I guess now was a good enough reason as any, boy."

"First off, I'm a twenty-eight year old man, not a boy!" Greg sternly pointed out. "Second, I know you. You said something to him to set him off."

Millard sat back, staggered by his son's brazenness. He realized that Greg wanted to lash out in the worst way, but it was up to Millard as to just how much of the backlash he would actually allow.

Right then, Millard's hyena grin vanished before he

squared his eyes and asked, "Tell me somethin'…boy, why did you come down here after all these years?"

Greg paused for a few seconds before staring down at his father and saying, "I asked myself that same question on my way here. I visited mom over in Gulfport, just to see how she was doing after the storm. When I told her that I wanted to visit you, too, she thought I lost my mind. Then she said to" 'try not to get infected. Who knows who or what your father has been with lately?' "That one made me laugh."

"Your mama was a damn joke herself." Millard sneered.

"I would have called, but you still don't have a phone in this shed you call a home."

"Well, as you can see, I'm doin' just fine."

"I can see that, and I can also see that you still love to stir the pot, too."

"Look, all I said to the nigga was some stuff about some bar he works at, and then outta nowhere, he just busts out cryin' like some gal."

"That's a crock and you know it!" Greg suddenly exploded. "You said something else, didn't you?"

Giggling, Millard said, "Oh yeah, I reckon I did say a little somethin' about how you and him met up, and where all you homos hang out. But other than that, I was cool."

"You just happened to mention something about us homos? You mean to tell me that after all these years you're still on that boat?"

"Well, I know that you and the Birdman sure are."

Frustrated, Greg said, "You wanna know what the problem with you is, dad?"

"No, boy, why don't ya tell me?" Millard responded in a confrontational tone.

"You don't want to change. Yeah, I'm a fag. Hell, me and Bird fuck like a couple of hippos every other night. As a matter of fact, we fucked back in Tennessee on our way down here. Hell, were even thinking about going up to Canada and getting married."

Millard squirmed about in his seat; his face was twisted, as if hearing every detail of Greg's personal life made him sick to his stomach.

"I never asked you for a thing in all my life. When you found out that I was gay, you ran and told just about everyone in town. You just don't know how bad I wanted to kill myself that day."

"Then why didn't you?" Millard frowned. "Rather death than to live like that! Hell, you might as well go fuck a dog up the ass if you're willing to stick your thing up another man's hole, you'd probably get the same feelin' regardless!"

Greg angrily advanced towards Millard with blazing red eyes. Millard, who remained seated, watched every move his son made, like he was expecting it. "C'mon, you wanna jump? Then jump, dammit!" The old man yelled as he held tight for the next eventual move.

Greg stopped right where he was before smirking and asking, "That's what you want, isn't it? You want to fight a fag so bad, don't you, even if that fag happens to be your own son?"

In a sullen voice, Millard said, "Boy, you stopped bein' my son the day I caught you suckin' Terrence Colby's dick down at Claymore's years ago."

Millard could both see and feel his son's blushing anger; he realized that Greg wanted to tear him apart and not look back. In all honesty, there wasn't a single bone in Millard's body that wasn't prepared for a physical beat down. He was still feeling the raucous effects of his "good time" from the night before, but everything he had always wanted to say to Greg after so many years had at last been said. Greg could have wailed all over him at that point, the old man had at last made peace.

Greg put his sweaty hands on his hips and said with a lone tear drooling down his face, "I'm such a naïve son of a bitch. When I heard on the news that Mississippi was hit by some violent storm, I thought to myself, just maybe, one of these godforsaken storms would somehow change you. You wanna know what's even funnier? The news never once mentioned anything about Sullinger, it was like this damn town didn't exist, or maybe they heard someone down here was still alive."

"Nigga, shut that bullshit up and—

Right there, Greg turned his back on Millard and began for the door, but not before stopping midway and blurting out, "Oh, by the way, you might want to check out you're roof, looks like you got a bear problem around here after all…Millard."

At that, Greg opened the door and simply walked out.

With as much festering rage boiling up inside, it took only a matter of seconds for Millard to let it all just burst wide open.

Jumping up off the couch, Millard yelled at the door, "Yeah, get the fuck outta here, and don't ever come back! You're just like your fat ass mama, always runnin' away! You can kiss my black ass, motherfucker!"

Once he could hear Greg's car rip out of his yard, Millard began for the door, but before he could even place his hand on the knob, a sudden jolt caught his stiff body. It was so jarring that it caused him to stand and quiver.

In his brain, Millard wanted to go outside and scream some more, but all his body was able to do was shake like a leaf, as if he were stunned out of nowhere. All that kept replaying in his head was his argument with Greg. They had fought before, but never had the old man heard his son so bold and revealing. He had been cussed out so many times before by other people that the words they would use became nothing more than baby gibberish. But there was something different about Greg's words that seemed to sear right through his iron skin. All of the sudden, the word "fag" didn't seem to carry with it the usual jocular relief that he relished so much.

"Fuck that nigga," Millard grunted before buttoning his overalls and swinging open the door with a violent force, slamming it shut behind him.

It was the customary hot and hazy morning that Millard found himself blundering out into. With his boots already seated on the porch, all he had to do was reach down, slip the muddy pair of worn out shoes on and he was ready for the day.

Before he could even step down off the porch he recalled what Greg had mentioned about the roof. While rare, bears making their way down from out of the mountains and into human communities was not as uncommon as most would probably believe for Sullinger. But to have one wander into his yard after sixty some odd years was out of the ordinary, and not to hear Shirley make a fuss over it was even more unsettling.

Millard shuffled his way around to the side of the shack to find the brown ladder that Greg was using leaning up against wall. The same toxic odor that he had sniffed the day before inside the barn was still lingering about. The more he smelled, the more he could tell that the stench was originating from the roof itself.

"Don't tell me that dumb ass gal done got up there and shit all over the damn roof, with her crazy self." Millard sighed before sniffing into his overalls just to make double sure that the odors weren't coming from him by any chance.

Millard stepped onto the first rung of the ladder and began upwards. He didn't get halfway before he was abruptly stopped by the vulgar sounds of booming music that filled the country air; he looked back and watched as a red Cadillac blasted down the road and past his property.

Loud cars weren't anything new to Millard, but it was the sound of the car itself that caused him to take a sudden, sharp notice; the car's engine sounded like a tank were rolling through town.

Like a mad man, Millard immediately got down from off the ladder and hobbled over to his truck, the roof would have to wait.

The keys were still lodged in the ignition, courtesy of an absentminded Brett, Millard paid it no attention, he just cut on the vehicle and stepped down on the gas as hard as he could; even his bout with Greg had become nothing more than a whisper of a memory.

He knew that he wasn't going to get much speed with all the mud that was still on the roads, and yet, that still didn't stop Millard from tearing down the thoroughfares as though he himself were the one being chased.

CHAPTER 8

The high that Millard was infected with both the night before and that morning had all but worn off after his spat with Greg; getting rid of hangovers was child's play to him. The heat slowly started to clear his smoggy head, making his swollen vision clearer and more focused with every bump that his truck bounced upon on the road.

After about two miles, Millard could see the red Cadillac in front of him as clear as day. The shade of the woods to the side of the road provided enough darkness for him to notice that there were five persons all huddled up together inside the famed vehicle. The individuals inside the car were all male; three had cornrows while the others wore wild, unkempt afros.

Millard's truck was twenty feet apart from the car, so that only meant that it was time to act, and act quickly. He reached over into the glove compartment and pulled out an already loaded Saturday night special.

After an entire year of playing the cat and mouse game, Millard was planning on the ultimate finale for his "getaway boys". Unlike in past instances, there would be no talking and exchanging foul words, with the perfect precision and timing, tires would be blown out, young men would be fleeing for their lives. That would be Millard's plan, for the time being.

The last thing Millard wanted was to alert the brood to his presence, not yet at least. He wanted his wrath to be sweet and cold, something that would have them going home telling horror stories of their experience with the old man for years to come.

With every road that was passed the more Millard realized that they were nearing the town's one and only railroad track, a completely different path that caught him off guard. It was the 9:15, right on schedule, and the roar of the engine and the blaring whistle could be heard for miles away, twice a day.

The two red and white colored blockades lowered, but to the car ahead, it was as though not one of the passengers heard or saw anything in terms of a locomotive coming their way as they just casually drove in between and through the blockades.

The second Millard approached the tracks the train was already passing through. Instead of trying to outrun the mighty machine he slammed on the brakes and cursed a yellow streak with every boxcar that loudly rolled by.

There was no other way around the train, and by the time the thing had fully passed by, his prey would have already arrived at their bi-monthly destination. All Millard could do while waiting was ponder on how he was going to dispatch his brand of pain and punishment on the five young men.

As infuriated as he was at that gut twisting moment, Millard, out of the blue, took notice of something quite surprising, something that he didn't comprehend at first; usually there would be only four young guys that would arrive, the fifth was brand new to him.

Millard reached back into his glove compartment and snatched out his rusty pair of brass knuckles, the same knuckles he purchased for five cents back when he was only eleven years old from the Jackson County Fair.

His slid the steaming hot piece of metal through his arthritic right fingers and gripped as tight as he could. In his left hand was a gun, on the other, a pair of brass knuckles; a whole different kind of warfare was at last going to be waged.

* * *

After ten and a half minutes of mind-numbing waiting, the train at last finished its pass. Even before the bars could be raised, Millard zigzagged through the barriers and continued on his way down the road. He didn't have to worry one bit about his buddies making a quick getaway, they, much like him, had all the time in the world.

Minutes later, Millard arrived at a rundown trailer park community. The fact of the matter was that even before the storm days earlier, the park was still a shantytown. Some mobile homes were still turned over onto their sides, while others had their roofs completely shredded off like sardine lids.

As Millard pulled into the park, he could still hear the booming music from the car; the tiny community honeycombed like a maze, but finding the vehicle was as easy as finding an elephant inside own his shack.

Millard sped his truck through just about every open space available, almost knocking residents over like rodents. The bumping noise increased the deeper he made his way into the community until at long last, just from out of the corner of his right eye, there sat the shiny, red Cadillac parked in front of a rusty, navy blue mobile home.

The old man stopped his truck and put it in park before jumping out with his gun and brass knuckles. The car still had three bodies seated inside, and thanks to their loud and obnoxious music, not one of them could hear Millard brazenly stampede behind them.

With his gun pointed to the driver's temple, Millard commanded, "Turn that shit off right now, boy."

Without saying a word, the young black man switched off the radio before fretfully glancing over at Millard.

"Man, c'mon," the boy shivered. "Do we gotta go through this shit again?"

The other two in the back seat sat still and quiet as if their lives depended upon doing so. Without the music blaring, Millard could hear yelling and cursing coming from inside the trailer.

Still holding the gun to the driver's head, Millard said, "I saw five of you little niggas in this car. Who's the fifth?"

"Man, he's just one of our boys!" The driver stuttered.

"Just one of your boys, huh," Millard grinned. "Well, let's just see how your boy likes me."

Millard turned and stepped towards the hollering trailer with his gun cocked and ready, and since the door was already unlocked, there was absolutely no point in knocking.

"Get the fuck away from her now, motherfucker!" Millard yelled in an almost animal-like pitch as he pointed his revolver at the two men.

Courtney, with tears streaming down her face, ran over to her chubby twin boys who were both huddled in a corner shaking and crying.

"What the fuck, old man?" A slim built, brown skinned man with cornrows hollered. "Why you gotta keep doin' this shit? Don't you know when to mind your own fuckin' business?"

The other man was a tall, dark skinned mountain of muscle. He, like his comrade, wore a white tank top shirt and clean cut cornrows. His sweaty muscles glistened in the gaping sunlight from the window beside him. He didn't say a word, he didn't have to, he stood by and allowed his thuggish scowl to do all the talking for him.

"Look, man, just put that gun down and let me talk to my girl and kids." The slim man calmly appealed. "This ain't got nothin' to do with you."

Millard reared back and pointed his weapon directly at the young man.

"My partner said he wants to talk to his girl, old man." The muscular gentleman spoke up as he boldly advanced towards Millard.

All it took was one step from the man, and with one simple pull of the trigger, Goliath was floored. Like a newborn baby, the man bawled and cried out in pain at the gunshot wound to his right knee. Courtney and her two boys screamed in terror.

"Motherfucker shot me!" he bawled as he grasped his bleeding knee.

The slim man, with his hands in the air, desperately urged on, "Just put the gun down, pops!"

Millard stepped towards the man, and with his brass knuckles he punched him square in the nose. "Get your sorry ass up and outta here before I kill ya!" He hollered as he unhinged the man's cornrows enough to where he could grab a few strands for dragging purposes.

Millard pulled the man out of the trailer, the blood from his injured nose left stains and puddles along the way.

Once he tossed the fellow out, Millard went back inside to retrieve the other invalid, he didn't even try to unravel his braids, instead, he just kicked him along like a heavy body bag until his carcass fell out the door and onto the ground outside.

Once the riffraff had been disposed of, Millard did something that he didn't want to do, something that he knew full well he shouldn't have done. He looked back at Courtney and her boys, all three were still crowded in the corner, crying and waiting for the entire incident to end.

Ignoring the boys, Millard couldn't stand to look Courtney in the eye, but his petrified eyes couldn't tear themselves away from her horrified face. She didn't even look like herself at that point.

Fed up, Millard turned and stormed outside. Onlookers gazed on in their usual weary manner as they did every other month. If they had one thing to be proud of it was that their trailer community had to be the liveliest in the state.

Kicking and clawing, the gunshot victim wailed, "Motherfucker, I'm from Detroit! West 12th Street, nigga!"

"I don't give a damn if you're from the crack of my ass!" Millard screamed back as he continued to kick him along to the side of the car.

The skinny man got to his feet and attempted to launch an attack against Millard from behind, but the old man was used to all the sneak tactics; whether it came to protecting his homestead from intruders, or to clearing the mobile park of useless garbage from Detroit, Millard was learned in all the tricks of the trade. So when he spun around and punched the man square in the jaw with his brass knuckles, that let the young man know that some old folks weren't that old at all.

"Get up," Millard shouted as he hoisted the man to his feet and stuffed him into his own car. "Get you asses outta here, now!"

The remaining three fellows in the car looked on in absolute disbelief, all they could do was sit and brace themselves for whatever strike would come next.

Millard walked back and helped Goliath to his feet. It seemed at first that the act was being done so out of compassion, but the instant the old man kicked him face first into the side of the car and eventually inside the vehicle, compassion was nothing but an afterthought.

"And I ain't forgot about ya'll either!" Millard said as he

approached the driver with a fist to the mouth and the other two in the backseat with open handed slaps across the face and heads. "Now, get the hell outta here! And if ya come back again, each of ya is gonna get a bullet in the ass!"

The driver wiped his mouth clean of blood and started the car, he then backed up and ripped right out of the trailer park.

Millard stood in front of Courtney's mobile home with a curt grimace on his sweaty face, admiring his handiwork. He could still hear the young lady and her boys crying inside their trailer as residents of the park stared Millard down as if he were just as bad, if not worse, than the thugs he disposed of.

There weren't any smiles or sniggers amongst them as in times past; instead, there were looks of disgust and fatigue. Millard gawked from his left, to the right, and from front to back. There were people surrounding him, he could feel their cold eyes bearing down upon him.

He looked down at his bloody right hand which still had on the brass knuckles. A little Hispanic boy stared oddly at the old man as tiny drops of blood slowly dripped off the knucks and into a puddle of water right beside him.

Millard haughtily swaggered his way back to his truck, rolling his bloodshot eyes along the way at everyone who seemed to look down on his vicious behavior.

Once he was inside the truck, Millard placed his gun down on the passenger's seat and wiped the sweat from off his forehead.

"Damn heat, liable to kill somebody soon." He casually muttered to himself as he put the vehicle in reverse and backed out of the trailer park.

He couldn't help but to do so, but for a few fleeting seconds, Millard happened to look into his rearview mirror at the crowd that he had left behind. Not one of them, it seemed, could take their eyes off of him.

CHAPTER 9

Millard didn't return home for another hour. Two bags full of food and beer tucked securely underneath his armpit was as treasured as all the gold on earth.

Millard never bought any food in town, he either shot deer and rodents or took his bi-weekly trip to Jackson. He had a paranoia about Sullinger food; 'if it was grown or bottled in Sullinger, Mississippi, don't bother waking up the next morning,' he always said.

He pulled his truck into his yard, and with his two grocery bags, he got out and began for the house.

First, his duel with Greg, then the showdown with the Detroit clan. It wasn't even the midday and he was already flushed and worn out as if he had worked a thirteen hour straight shift.

There really wasn't all too much for a person to do in Sullinger except hunt or hang out down at the supply store and drink beer all day long. Most residents, mainly the younger crowd, would take off for Jackson if excitement was what they craved.

For the vast majority of the residents of the town, life after the fiberglass exodus did more harm than good; no more paychecks, no new businesses, and just as bad, people were leaving the town for greener pastures.

As for Millard, a person who couldn't stand the sight of another human being, the confines of his dilapidated farm was all the companionship he longed for, that and Shirley. He decided a long time ago that if he didn't have Shirley or his home, then he would rather just dig a hole for himself and lie in it until his eyes decided not to open anymore.

As he drew closer to the front door it donned on him to investigate the roof once more. He wanted to resume his search for his dog, but the very notion that a bear or whatever had made its way up onto his roof without him even knowing it seemed to take front stage before any and everything else.

He sat the two bags down onto the porch and walked around to the side of the house where the ladder was left earlier. The rancid odor that he had taken notice of for days was by then a faint trace in the wind, the only aroma that seemed present was that of his own body stench from the night before.

The second he reached the roof, Millard expected to see huge bear claws or some other sort of wild animal markings, but instead, what he witnessed with his own two eyes was something that not even he was expecting. The markings resembled those of an animal, but what kind of animal was the real mystery.

Millard carefully climbed onto the blazing hot roof, cautiously taking into consideration that it was about as stable as straw. He then used his index finger to scrape at the strange claw marks. There were exactly six footprints that he could spot; all six had only two sharp, twenty inch long toes. It was apparently a heavy beast because it left a five inch deep dent with every step that it made on the roof.

With all the crazy happenings ever since the storm he knew full well that whatever had annexed his yard had to be beyond supernatural. He couldn't recall ever seeing a ghost leaving footprints, and it wasn't a figment of his imagination either.

Just as Millard was about to investigate further, the glimmering sun forced him to shade his eyes with his left hand, which in turn caused him to look over and down to the side of the house. Without the brightness of the sun blinding his vision, he was able to see yet another unexpected sight.

Dizzy and disoriented, Millard lost his footing and dropped down to the ground in a heap right next to both dead halves of Shirley. The height from the roof to the ground was no more than eleven feet; most people would have cried out in pain after falling from such a height, but Millard never let out a single scream.

He crawled over to the bloody, mosquito infested carcass with a wild-eyed glaze plastered all over his face. He gathered both limp ends of Shirley and placed them carefully in his lap. Her long tongue dangled from out of her foam rimmed mouth. Millard tried to roll it back in but he found that he couldn't keep her jaws closed shut.

He could tell that she had gone into some kind of shock before her mutilation; the old man could sense that his only friend suffered before dying.

Millard lied down on the mud coated ground and morbidly held tight both ends of Shirley in his bosom like he were coddling a baby. He recalled the day he found her in the woods, lying half dead next to her siblings.

Not one tear bothered to swell up in his eyes. Not a whimper or a sniffle could be heard. Millard knew what was responsible for her death, his eyes stared ice spikes at the barn ahead of him, but all he sought at that moment was loneliness as the merciless sun beat down on both of them.

His lips quivered as his eyes gazed blankly into the hazy sky.

CHAPTER 10

He felt a poke, something of a pinch or two while wallowing in his muggy slumber. Even in his altered subconscious, Millard was aware that he was asleep; however, once the voices started blaring out in his head, he began to realize that whatever dream state he was residing in was rapidly beginning to get on his last nerve.

It was a female voice shouting at him. The voice sounded both frightened and garbled, like it was underwater. Millard tried to open his eyes, but the harder he attempted, that was all the more his eyelids wanted to stay closed.

"Baby, wake up," the high-pitched voice urged on. "Wake up, Millard!"

Not even the shrillness of the voice could seem to awaken Millard, he was entirely too cemented in his inertia to arise.

Soon, just when it seemed as if Millard couldn't sink any deeper into sleep, a sudden series of what felt like slaps across the face caused his eyes to suddenly pop wide open.

Millard violently coughed his way into conciseness; he immediately placed his hands on his bosom to see if Shirley were still lying peacefully on top of him.

"Get outta the way," he slurred loudly as he sat up and

looked around until he spotted Shirley's rotting flesh just a few inches behind him.

In a frenzied manner, Millard picked up both halves of the dog before carelessly cradling them in his arms while scanning to his front and back as though he were under some kind of surveillance. He couldn't even look down at his beloved friend who by then was beyond bad smelling as flies swarmed about both their faces.

Millard's young lady friend stood before him speechless with the most startled and spaced out expression on her blushing face.

Millard staggered from the side of the house to the porch where he sat down on the steps while continuing to hold Shirley in his arms. When his eyes were able to focus upon his surroundings, he spotted his lady staring down at him in a disgraceful fashion, like she was ashamed to be near him.

He watched closely as her accusatory eyes gazed at him while she paced back and forth like a disappointed parent. As soon as she was done marching, the young woman ever so slowly turned and skittishly approached Millard like he were a time bomb she was afraid to go near.

"Millard...Millard, can you hear me?" She shook while pulling a dirty, dried up tissue from out of the pocket of her hip-high blue jean shorts and wiping the sweat from off his forehead.

Millard wasn't too far off base to know that his lady friend was standing in front of him. He knew that she was scared to death, and he also realized that whatever had destroyed his dog could very well be after him soon enough. Millard wasn't one to wait around for death to arrive, if it wanted him, then it didn't have too far to search.

"Millard, what did this?" The woman frantically asked as she continued to rub his sweaty head with the tissue.

Millard didn't respond, he just got to his feet, and with both ends of Shirley in his arms, got up from off the porch, dropped the animal to the ground and began digging into the dusty earth with his bare hands.

"Millard, what did this to Shirley?"

The old man persisted in his digging expedition as though his two hands were shovels. He could hear what the woman was saying, but there were no words to describe what happened to Shirley, especially since he himself had no clear clue as to what exactly took place.

But there was always that one lingering spark of speculation in the back of his brain that kept him quiet about his unusual visitor in the barn. He couldn't even turn around to look back.

But it appeared the more Millard ignored her that was all the more impatient the young lady became. She folded her rail-thin arms and sternly asked, "So…where did you get that smell from? Were you fucking another woman again?"

Millard couldn't stand to be questioned, especially by a female, but her blatant attitude still could not deter him from burrowing deeper into the ground.

"I asked you a question," she persisted. "Did you fuck another woman? I smell pussy all over you!" She angrily shouted as she nudged Millard on the back of the neck with her knee.

By the time Millard was finished digging, he ended up with a two foot deep hole right in front of his own house. He then rose to his feet and somberly went over to pick up the pieces of Shirley.

The young woman then got directly into Millard's face and screamed, "I want you to answer me, dammit! Did you fuck another woman or not? What did this to Shirley? What's happening?" She hysterically yelled before slapping both ends of the dog from out of Millard's arms.

Like a light suddenly coming on inside of Millard's head, he grabbed a hold of the woman's neck and proceeded to strangle her down to her knees. Usually, whenever he became physically abusive with her he would be cursing a storm the whole way through while slapping her across the face, but at that instant, he remained silent. With his lips pressed together, he only grunted as his dirty hands gripped tighter around her neck until she was no longer able to breathe.

Millard then unlocked his angry, powerful hands from around her neck before yanking her back to her feet and yelling, "You listen to me, motherfucker, I don't answer to you! I don't answer to no one! You understand me?"

Coughing and wiping tears from her eyes, the woman didn't have the strength to utter another word.

"I said, do you understand me," Millard hollered as he popped her right across the face with his open right hand.

"Yes, Millard, I understand," she relented, holding her face in pain. "Please…don't hit me again!"

Millard shoved her aside before turning and staring irately at the barn ahead of him. His eyes were red and pain stricken, he knew that it was still in there.

Just hearing his lady gag on own her saliva made him sick to his stomach. Millard spun around and yelled, "Now, you get your ass outta here before I—

But before he could even say another detestable word, a dusty, maroon colored Astrovan came barreling off the main road and onto Millard's property as though it were shot out of a cannon.

Both Millard and his lady awkwardly looked on as the wild driving vehicle, full of whooping and hollering young white men came directly towards them at top speed.

Out of instinct, Millard grabbed a hold of the young woman's left arm and pulled her from out of harm's way before falling face first down to the ground.

The van stopped right in front of them both. From out of the side of the already opened sliding door appeared a bald white man with a thirty-eight gripped in his right hand.

"I heard about what you said to my granddaddy the other day, coon!" He screamed while waving his gun in the air. "Now, you're gonna get your ass beat!"

Millard got up from off the ground and boldly yelled, "Then get your asses outta that there van and come get it!"

"Millard, no, come back here!" The young lady urgently screamed as she pulled on Millard's right arm.

The same young man that had the gun stepped aside while another white man with an already lit bottle of malt liquor with a cloth stuffed inside appeared. The man tossed the flaming bottle at the shack, just missing both Millard and his lady.

Soon after the first bottle was pitched, another burning Molotov was hurled, which ended up landing near the porch.

"Whatcha gonna do now, ya nigger," the gunman sneered. "Run his black ass down!"

Millard's lady yanked her man out of the way of the van before dragging him over to his truck that was only ten feet away.

Millard wasn't accustomed to running; if it were just him then he would have taken on every person inside the van. His old house could have burned to the ground and he would have ended up a bloody wreck, but at least he would have gone down fighting, just the way he wanted. But for inexplicable reasons that he couldn't explain, he allowed the woman to push him into the passenger's seat before she ran over, hopped into the driver's side and tore out of the yard like a crazy woman.

Millard held on to the door handle as the young lady careened down the road with the van close in behind them.

"Why can't your truck go any faster than this?" She squealed as her little feet pressed down as hard as they could on the gas pedal.

The old man didn't know how to respond at that lighting moment, he felt as if he were being carried by some Hollywood stuntwoman considering the insane method of driving his friend was conducting.

"They're still on us!" she screamed as she spun the wheel from one direction to the other. "Where should I go, Millard?"

Millard turned to look back at the van behind them. He knew why they were after him, but he honestly couldn't have cared less. He reached into the glove compartment and pulled out his revolver.

"What are you doing," the young woman screamed.

"What the hell does it look like I'm doin'? I'm gonna blow their damn heads off!" Millard hollered back as he rolled down the window and pointed the gun directly at the van in the hopes of getting off the perfect shot or two.

Both vehicles roared down the dusty road at speeds well over a hundred mph. From a clear distance a person would have thought that both truck and van were racing one another.

"I could cut through the valley and try to lose them on the—

The woman's words were cut short by a sudden pop which was eventually followed by the explosion of a tire that caused her to lose control of the truck and zigzag down near a creek where a group of children were already playing and swimming.

"Stop the damn thing, gal, before we wreck!"

"I can't," she gasped, "I think there's something wrong with the tire!"

Unable to control both the steering wheel and brakes, the woman had no choice but to allow the truck to veer off the road and into an embankment.

"Are you alright," the girl cried as she tried to get out of the truck.

"Get the hell outta here before I kick your ass!" Millard shouted before opening the door and getting out with his gun pointed and ready to fire at the approaching van that by then was only a few yards away from his truck.

Millard feverishly watched as the four young white men, two dressed in white undershirts and two without, all climbed out of the van and ran down the hill towards him with furious rage. Millard glanced back at the children who had ceased their summertime activities to view the shocking melee from across the creek.

In total, there were seven little children in all, two black girls, one white girl, a Hispanic boy, two white boys and one black boy. Millard always figured that the only way a child could ever learn about cruelty in the world was to see it first hand, right before their virgin eyes.

Without hesitation, the old man turned back around to the four white men and pulled the trigger on his revolver, only to discover the chamber was dead empty.

"Come here, ya nigger!" One of the attackers shouted before tackling Millard down to the ground and beating him from head to toe. Soon, the other three joined in on the assault, all pummeling the old man until his entire face was a crimson soaked collage.

"Stop it, stop doing that!" The woman screamed as she ran to Millard's aid.

"Hold that spic bitch back!" The leader of the pack yelled before pulling a rope from out of his back pocket and tying Millard's ankles together with it. He then dragged him down to the creek's edge, not once giving a second thought to the old man's head that was bumping into the sharp rocks along the way until they reached the edge where they dunked Millard head first into the warm water.

"String 'em up," one of the attackers gleefully hollered. "String that sum bitch up!"

At that point for Millard, the current violent events slowed to a creeping crawl as he tried to grasp for any glimpse of air that he had left in his collapsing lungs. He could hear both the men above hooting and laughing over his lynching, as well as his lady screaming for mercy.

Soon, rain began to pelt into the water; it was as if God were shooting bullets into the stream, directly at Millard.

Gradually, the air that he was trying to clench was evaporating with every painstaking second that passed by. He had no final thoughts or remembrances; no one was worth that much to him to be recollected upon for one last time.

The air was gone, his brain was drying, and all that was left was for his eyes to close one final time. But somehow it was his eyes that managed to remain open for just five seconds more. For some people at the doorstep of death, those final seconds mean everything in the world, for Millard, it meant that he got the opportunity to see what resembled a blurry glow that came swimming directly at him like a launched torpedo.

To Millard, it looked as if the swimming blur was about to devour him, but he looked on in curiosity as it blew right past him before leaping up and out of the water.

After a few seconds the laughing and gleefulness of vengeance from above turned into guttural screaming and yelling for dear life as the once blue water shockingly went red.

Being submerged seemed like living in eternity as far

as the old man was concerned. Surprisingly he was still conscience, the noises from above were fuzzy, but Millard had somewhat of a clue as to what was taking place. His brain at that moment was too confused on just what it wanted to do, see what had happened on the surface or remain under and let death snatch him to another world.

Ever so slowly, Millard could feel the rope that had his ankles bound being pulled backwards. Gradually, the suffocating weight of water soon gave way to what felt like air as the raindrops slapped him across the face.

"C'mon, baby!" The young woman frantically screamed at the top of her lungs as she tried her best to drag Millard's body onto the dry ground.

Millard could feel his friend beat and pound on his chest like she were trying to finish the job the other four started. He felt her mouth meet his as she attempted to breathe air back into his watery lungs once more.

The more she beat on his chest that was all the more he wanted to throw up. Millard sat up and spat out a torrent of both water and blood on the ground before regaining his senses and looking around at the valley and the numerous torn body parts that were strewn all over the wet grass.

"Where did those little cunts go to?" Millard continued to spit.

At first, his lady appeared utterly speechless; even in the warm rain that poured down from the sky her face looked flushed, like she had witnessed the most wicked occurrence in her young life.

With her jaw trembling like she were cold, the woman stuttered, "They're all gone, honey."

Millard gazed all around, even behind him to see that the children that were once on the other side of the creek were gone. Once he was through scanning the area he stared forward at his attackers' van that was smashed as if it were hit by a train.

"Who came and got 'em? Did ya shoot 'em all?

"No...something came and got them."

With blood in his eyes Millard turned around once again to see the entire creek full of blood and a headless body floating in the water.

He chocked, "What the—

"I don't know what it was...I couldn't see it." The girl muttered on as though she were locked in a trance. "It just tore them all apart, one by one. It all happened so fast."

All of the sudden, out of Millard's right ear arose what sounded like heavy footsteps approaching in front of them both.

"Shh...I hear something," he whispered.

"I hear it, too."

Both Millard and his lady sat and listened closely at the crackling grass ahead of them. Millard looked forward but could see absolutely nothing or no one but the falling rain.

"C'mon, get up," she hollered as she tried to pull Millard up by his limp shoulders.

"Shut up and be still," Millard strongly commanded. "Just be still!"

She did as ordered and sat holding Millard in her arms as the mysterious footsteps drew nearer. Millard could hear his friends' heart beat against her chest. Both her hands and arms were shaking incessantly. He tried to restrain her the best he could.

The footsteps eventually stopped right in front of the two. Millard could feel a heavy, brooding presence in front of him. It felt cold, winter hard cold.

"Millard, what is it?" The woman shivered as she looked up at the sky.

"Shut up…just shut up." Millard whispered while staring off into the quiet and desolate valley ahead of him, hoping to grab at least a brief glimpse of whatever it was that was breathing down on them.

Growing up in the country, a person tended to become familiar with many odd sounds, Millard was somehow able to recognize the noises of what sounded like claws scraping back and forth in the grass in front of him, razor sharp claws, like a bear or raccoon.

It stood right before the two; the old man could hear it breathing, like a loud truck's engine turning over.

"Oh, God no," his lady screamed out in terror before crawling away from Millard.

"C'mere, gal, and stay still," Millard said as he reached over and tried to hold her in place.

"It touched me!"

"Just be still…be still for a moment. It may not kill you." He desperately whispered into her ear.

The two somehow managed to remain quiet long enough for the creature to eventually turn and meander away in the opposite direction.

"C'mon," Millard gasped as he struggled to his feet. "C'mon and let's go."

"Millard, where are you going?" The woman yelled before getting up off the ground and chasing after her man.

In the pouring rain, Millard slurred, "Where the hell does it look like I'm goin'? I'm takin' my black ass home!"

"Was that the same thing that killed Shirley? Is it a ghost, Millard?"

Millard never bothered to reply to her question, he just kept on lurching on in a chaotic and uncoordinated fashion like he was drunk. The beating combined with his attempted drowning caused his motor skills to function improperly.

As soon as the drenching rain let up, the sun almost immediately began to peek through the dark clouds, leaving a bright rainbow over the horizon, and the four young men lying dead in the valley.

Millard trampled onto the mud sodden road. He was still alive; the man had taken one of the worst beatings of his life, and yet he was able to attempt to carry himself home. He just passed it all off as dumb luck.

Trying to keep up with the old man, the lady breathlessly asked, "Millard, what about your truck? You just can't leave it here!"

Millard trudged on as if there was absolutely nothing or no one behind him.

Chapter 11

A lmost a half an hour later, Millard and his girlfriend arrived back at his house. Millard tripped and staggered towards the safe haven of his hovel as his friend helped him step past a partially buried Shirley on his way to the porch. She then kicked open the locked front door and hurled the man onto his couch out of exhaustion before finally sitting her tired self down beside him in heap. It was as though both had individuals had just run a statewide marathon that no one cared to win; Millard had developed a serious case of cottonmouth as his sore body throbbed in excruciating pain.

Millard happened to glance over at his lady whose face was saturated with sweat as she huffed and puffed. He had realized that through the years she had become accustomed to seeing him beaten down, but there was still the grotesque matter of Shirley, and the happening down at the creek that he knew she would never rebound from for as long as she lived.

Millard wearily watched as she got up from off the couch and slugged her way to the bathroom. His bludgeoned eyes could barely make out the blackness of the wall in front of him.

He hadn't dismissed what happened back at the creek. He was fully aware that Leon would be on his way over sooner than later to question him on the deaths of four white men, and unlike in times past, there would be no chance he could argue his way out of a murder rap that seven children all witnessed with their own eyes. It didn't matter if he was the one doing the killing or not.

Suddenly, and from out of nowhere, Millard's already stiff neck spun around to the sound of running water in the bathroom. Like it were on fire, Millard hopped up from off the couch and lumbered into the bathroom to find his friend drawing a hot bath, in the tub, of all places.

Outraged at what was happening, Millard hollered, "What the hell is you doin', gal?"

"I'm making you a bath, Millard." She quietly replied while taking off her shirt and wiping her sweaty face in the running water.

The old man quickly scampered over, and while twisting the faucet he said, "Turn that shit off and get over here!"

"Millard, look at you, you're a bloody mess. Your face is all tore up, and—

Refusing to listen to anymore of the woman's ardent pleas, he snatched the young lady by the arm.

"Oww, Millard, that hurts!"

"You know good and damn well I don't use no bath water!"

"But we need to take a bath, especially you, you smell worse now than you did when I came over here earlier!"

"Don't you mind how I smell, just leave that water alone! Ya hear me?" He hollered into her face.

"No, I don't hear you," the woman fought back. "Did you see what happened today? Did you see all of that, Millard? No, you didn't see it, you were underwater the whole time!

And all you can talk about is the fucking water? Everyone is dead, so is Shirley! We gotta tell Leon!"

"Don't you go tellin' nobody nothin'!" Millard roared as he restrained his lady friend.

"But what about—

"Don't worry 'bout that."

"Whaddya mean, don't worry? Ray Roberts' grandson and his friends were all killed! Doesn't that mean anything to you?"

Millard simply shrugged his shoulders and said, "Shit, better them than me! Those little bastards tried to kill me! Fuck them!"

"But what do we say when someone asks about it all?"

Millard relinquished his painful grip from his lady before wrapping his arm around her shoulder in a consoling fashion while whispering, "You worry entirely too much, gal. Everyting is gonna be alright. Those youngens that were there at the creek is probably gonna say they saw a gator or somethin', so let 'em. Remember when I told you about that gator in the creek from years ago?"

"Millard, this thing was invisible! Do you know what that thing was? I think it was on top of your barn the other day."

"I don't have a damn clue, and that's exactly why we ain't tellin' Leon a damn thing, because we don't know a damn thing."

With the most sorrowful expression on her pitiable face, the woman cried, "Tell me the truth, Millard…just tell me the truth."

"I am tellin' the truth!" Millard yelled out before catching himself. "I mean, I am tellin' the truth…sweetie. Why is you cryin'?"

"Because I'm scared, Millard, that's why." She whimpered. "Why didn't it kill us, too?"

"Shit, are you complanin' that it didn't kill us?"

"No, but if it did what it did to Shirley and those guys, then what's stopping it from killing everyone else in town?"

"As far as I'm concerned, this whole town can go back to hell where it came from. Now…calm down and get to your knees."

Hopelessly shaking her head from side to side, the woman whined, "No…I can't do that, not right now."

With a phony, cavalier-like grin on his beaten mug, Millard softly kissed her on the forehead before whispering, "C'mon now, just go down while I unzip my pants. Everything is gonna be okay, just go down real slow."

The young woman said nothing; she wiped her teary eyes clean before reluctantly kneeling down to the mildewed floor and waiting as Millard unzipped his pants and whipped "it" out before her.

He knew that she wasn't in any mood to give him pleasure, much like he was in no mood to receive it, but it was all he could think of doing at that time to try and cope.

CHAPTER 12

The following morning

The brown and white station wagon rolled down the dirt road slower than usual. The two white, male passengers inside could never stand to stay in town any longer than they had to. On occasion, if they needed something and didn't have the time to head up to Jackson, they would run in and out of Mikey's diner or just do without completely. But on that day, the day after, they had no other choice but to make an untimely visit into Sullinger to settle.

The driver, with his thinning grey hair flapping in the passing breeze, was a man in his mid to late fifties. There laid upon his dull face a sort of miserable appearance, as though he was nearing the thralls of letting loose his breakfast on the floor beneath him.

Every other second he would glance over at his young partner whose head stuck out the window like a dog that was going to the park to play. He could see that the young fellow's eyes were closed, like he was in a sort of methodical deep thought.

The driver wanted to say something to his comrade, a word or two that would give him at least a brief respite from his current anguish, even if no one had the same words for him.

The driver realized that he was nearing his undesired destination, that was when he felt the need to look over at his partner and just stare for a few seconds more before eventually attempting to open his salty mouth.

"You don't look too good there, Jim. You look kind of sick, if you ask me."

Jim awakened from his trance and looked over at his comrade with a pale face. "I think it's getting hotter here." He mumbled. "It's been that way ever since the storm."

"Yeah," the driver mumbled back, "that's this tropical weather for you."

"So…have you thought about what you're gonna say to the sheriff yet?"

Without warning, the driver veered off the road and stopped the car before jumping out and throwing up all over the ground. The last thing he wanted was to let his young protégé see him lose his faculties, but it was beyond his control.

He could hear Jim walking over behind him like an oncoming dark cloud hanging heavy over his head.

"So, uh…is there a particular script that you use for this situation, Steve?" Jim carefully questioned.

Still coughing, Steve said, "Give me a break, kid, I just got through hurling my fucking guts out. Besides, why do I have to be the bearer of bad news?"

"Because, you've been doing this a lot longer than I have," Jim replied with a jocular tenor in his voice.

"I see," Steven said as he wiped his mouth clean and turned to the rear view mirror to shuffle his hair from side to side. "Truth is, you can't rehearse for something like this. I've been down here in this pit of a town for seven years and

I still haven't gotten used to the heat, the smell or even any of these braid dead, country numbskulls. And to think that something like this could happen is…sickening. Nope, you can't rehearse this stuff; you just do it and hope the outcome turns in your favor."

"You think we should call Brooks in on this one?"

"No, not yet at least," Steve replied as he turned to Jim with his hands in his pockets. "Let's just let things marinate for a few days, we should be able to take care of it without any more incident. It's a small town, out of sight. Hell, the local news didn't even mention this place after the storm, that's how insignificant this berg is."

"You're kidding, right?" Jim's mouth hung open. "You actually believe we can handle this on our own?"

Rolling his eyes, Steve said, "Don't get me a headache, kid."

Jim turned his head to the road beside him and mused, "I don't think I've seen another human being for miles."

"The less the better as far as I'm concerned," Steven grunted before pulling himself away from his own reflection and getting back in the car.

"I guess it's too early to ask for a reassignment, huh?" Jim asked as he hopped back into the vehicle.

Steven just shook his head from side to side like he was amused somewhat with his partner's inquiry. For a few brief seconds there bubbled in his stomach a calm relief; that same relief quickly vanished the instant he pulled back onto the road and continued on.

*   *   *

With simultaneous sighs of both grief and trepidation, Steven and Jim reached the sheriff's station a whole lot sooner than expected. Steven rolled the station wagon into the lot and parked next to a red tow truck.

They both got out of the vehicle and dragged themselves towards the small building that was shaped more like a church with a steeple on top than a police station.

Steven looked over at his partner who was still wearing a pale white stare on his face, but was also walking with a determined stride, possibly to impress his senior. Steven admired the young man for his boldness; he desired the same solid resolve for himself at that instant more than ever before.

The second Steven opened the entrance door both he and Jim were immediately bombarded by the rowdy barking of an old man screaming furiously at the sheriff who was standing behind a long desk.

"I don't care if he is your cousin, Leon, you need to do somethin' about that man or someone else in this town is gonna get killed!"

Sheriff Leon slammed a ring of keys down onto the desk beside him before shouting back, "Ray, you know good and well that Millard didn't kill Kenny or any of those other boys!"

"Well somethin' sure as hell did! My grandboy was torn to pieces! Both his mama and grandmamma are cryin' themselves half to death back at home! I want answers!"

"I'll tell you the same thing I've been tellin' everyone else, were doin' the best we can in this here situation!"

"Well ya sure ain't doin' enough, Leon!" Ray furiously screamed before turning and blasting past both Steven and Jim on his way out the door. But before he exited, Ray paused and turned to the sheriff weeping, "And they died in town, Leon! They died here...of all places!"

Steven watched as the old man bolted out the door, cursing the whole way along. From there he turned and approached the desk where the sheriff was using a wet rag to wipe the sweat from off his face and neck. Steven could tell by the unbuttoned shirt and stressed out look all over his face that the sheriff was about as stretched thin as he could possibly be.

With a deep sigh, the sheriff asked, "What can I do for you fellas?"

Clearing his throat, Steven said, "Well, Sheriff, my name is Steven Winemore, and this is my partner, Jim Livingston. I'm not quite sure how to start this off, but…I, uh. You see, we—

Steven could sense that Leon was entirely too busy and caught up in his own dilemma to pay even the slightest attention to both him and Jim. The sheriff was rooting around for a ringing telephone while trying to keep his sweaty body cool with a rolled up newspaper that he was fanning himself with.

The second Leon found the phone underneath a pile of papers he immediately snatched it up and answered, totally ignoring his two guests in front of him.

Steven listened carefully as the sheriff tried to get the loud person on the other end of the phone to calm down. He could hear that it was a woman and that she was about two seconds away from jumping through the phone, until Leon, frustrated and to his boiling point, slammed the receiver down and looked back up at both he and Jim.

"C'mon now and spit it out, son, I'm a busy man!" Leon impatiently yelled before walking over to a file cabinet and pulling out a manila colored folder.

Still trying to find the proper words to say, Steven once again opened his mouth. "Well, Sheriff, you see—

Slamming the folder down onto the desk, Leon roared, "Listen here, I ain't got no time for double talkin' or half steppin'! My phone has been ringin' off the hook ever since yesterday, and folks keep comin' in here worryin' about some shark or gator! And on top of all that, some folks still don't have a lick of power in their homes ever since that storm the other night! Now, either hurry and state your business or be on your way!'"

Completely numb, Steven puffed out his chest and simply uttered, "Sheriff…we know what killed those young men yesterday."

Leon, right then, stopped cold dead on a dime before slowly turning to face Steven who had turned a deeper shade of white all of the sudden.

The sheriff leaned forward before slowly stating, "You wanna run that by me again, sir?"

"I said, we know what—

But before Steven could get another word out, Leon instantly put up his right hand and said, "Ya'll c'mon in here, right now."

Steven and Jim looked over at each other before marching in behind Leon into his office. The sheriff waited until both men were inside before slamming the door shut. To Steven, it sounded like a jail cell locking.

"Ya'll have a seat." Leon commanded as he sat himself behind his desk and motioned for the men to sit in the two chairs in front of the desk.

With the exception of a little white, plastic fan that sat behind Leon, there wasn't a sound inside the tiny room for nearly a whole minute.

"Now, did I hear you say that you know what it was that killed those boys?"

"Yes, sir," Steven hesitated. "It's kind of hard to explain, but in order for us to tell you what it is, we'd have to have complete anonymity from you."

Leon scrunched up his face, looking as if he were somewhat confused at the word that was just tossed at him.

"Anonymity, it means—

"I'm fully aware of what the word means, what I'm having trouble with is why it has to be a secret."

"Well, Sheriff, you see—

"Hold on a second," Leon hastily interjected, "let me tell ya'll a story, if I may. Back in 1909, a baby great white swam its way into Claymore's Creek from the Mississippi River. Of course this was way back when the creek was full of salt water. It bit one fella's leg completely off. He bled to death only because no one could get him to the hospital in time. Then, back in 1968, an alligator got into that same creek; bit ole' Tyler Wade in the stomach. Till this day, the man still has trouble digesting food. Now…yesterday, four young men were torn limb from limb, down at that same creek, and you mean to tell me that you know what it was that killed them? Because the youngens that were down there yesterday say that it was another gator."

Perplexed, Steven made his own crooked face before asking, "I'm sorry, Sheriff…youngens?"

"Kids, man, kids," Leon irritably replied.

"Wait a minute," Jim suddenly intervened with a hint of awe in his tone, "you mean to say that there were children present when this all went down yesterday?"

"That's right, 'bout seven of 'em. Folks go down to the old creek when it gets hot; nothin' out of the ordinary. Of course, when it comes to kids, they could have seen anything from a gator to Batman."

"I can assure you, Sheriff that this was neither a gator nor shark attack, and if we could perhaps take a look at the bodies then we would hopefully be able to explain this whole situation in more depth." Steven said.

"One thing at a time, fellas," Leon sank in his seat. "First off, tell me what this thing is supposed to be."

Steven swallowed for a brief moment, trying in earnest to give himself enough time to conjure some semblance of rationality. "It is...something else." He murmured.

"There ya go with the dang double talkin' again!" Leon suddenly shot back. "Who are you two anyways? Neither of you sound like you're from around here," he shrugged as he sat back in his creaky wooden chair and folded his hands together.

"We represent a very secretive branch of the U.S. government, Sheriff." Steven carefully articulated. "I, myself, have been here in Sullinger for the past seven and a half years; my partner here just joined me last year. You'll have to bear with us for a moment, Sheriff, because what I'm about to divulge will not sound coherent at first."

"I'm listenin'," Leon lazily replied, still leaning back in his seat.

"Eleven years ago, along the Mexican border, U.S. Marines happened upon a very unique find. So unique in fact that it really doesn't have a name, just a classification number. Before it was eventually captured, it managed to kill twenty-three soldiers with its bare hands. We knew that with Mexican officials swarming around that we weren't going to be able to keep it under wraps for long. That's why we came down here to Sullinger."

"Why Sullinger, of all places," Leon questioned with a sharp eye pointed dead at his two visitors.

"Sullinger is the perfect place. Thin population, dispersed land mass, it's pretty damn hard to find on a map."

"Well, if there's one thing Sullinger is famous for, among other things, is that it's nearly impossible to locate. I don't think ole' Sullinger is even on the map." Leon smirked.

Steven continued, "This thing is incredibly powerful and resilient as hell. We've actually attempted to kill it on numerous occasions, but with no such luck. Soon, we eventually gave up and decided to contain it in the hopes that our scientists could study it, perhaps gain some useful knowledge from it. But of course, everything was fine up until the storm the other night. When Jim and I awoke the next morning, its containment unit was ripped wide open. The rest is history."

With an abrupt grin, Leon slugged his way up in his chair and said, "Hold on, let's just say for one second that I'm some backwoods, hayseed, colored boy that doesn't know his right foot from his left. Do you both except me to sit here on my fat ass and believe that whatever killed those boys yesterday was some…monster?"

"Sheriff, time is of the essence." Jim unexpectedly chimed in. "Something seemingly indestructible is on the loose in this town. We don't have any more time to waste."

With a thousand yard stare pointed straight at Jim, Leon dragged out, "Only God is indescribable, son."

"With all due respect, Sheriff, it looks like God has finally met his match."

Steven sat and watched Leon's sullen eyes stare on and on and both him and Jim. He could sense that the man wasn't for one moment buying the story that was being thrown at him so diligently.

"So, after all these years you two still don't know what it is?"

"We really don't have a clue, sir." Steven said. "When our people stumbled upon it, the thing was apparently sleeping at the time. They just took advantage of a priceless situation."

Leon suddenly jumped up out of his seat and screamed out, "Priceless situation? This thing that you're speakin' of just killed four boys yesterday! Four boys that just graduated from high school a month ago! Now, you and the government had darn well better come up with a better excuse than that, because I don't think any of this is funny in the least bit!"

"Neither do we, Sheriff." Jim stuttered. "We've seen firsthand what this thing is capable of, which is why we're confused as to why it spared those kids."

"Sheriff, I assume you've see the bodies?" Steven asked. "Were they torn in half? Were their faces shredded into pieces? Were their bodies cut wide open?"

Flabbergasted and out of breath, Leon opened his mouth and began to push out what sounded like words. "Yeah… yeah, they were."

"Then as you just explained, this is far from funny. I think you'll agree with me when I say that we need to work together on this and damn fast, because something is extremely curious about this whole situation we have here before us."

"And what's that?"

"In the past, this creature has never hesitated to kill any and everything in plain sight. We're wondering why it hasn't wiped out every living being in this town as of yet."

"Sheriff, would it be okay if we took a trip to your county morgue and viewed the bodies?" Jim humbly requested.

Leon stood with a dry expression on his face, trying to crack a somewhat courteous grin. "Uh, sure, come with me."

At that, Leon escorted his visitors behind the station where a small brick shed sat all alone, covered in a cluster of withered bushes.

Covering his nose, Steven gasped, "What is this?"

Without looking back, Leon took a collection of keys that were hanging from a large ring from out of his hip pocket before unlocking the steel, air tight door. "It's our morgue, my friend."

The very instant the door swung open, the striking odor of rotting corpses, as well as a freezing cold snap, slapped all three men across the face with such a force that it was dizzying to the senses.

"You can't be serious." Jim frowned as he held his nose in repulsion.

"I'm afraid so, young fella." Leon said as he led both men inside. "Sullinger ain't no big city, in fact, it's barely even a town. We have to share Jackson's zip code. We don't have a big time budget that the rest of the state has, so we make do with what we got."

Trying not to lose his breath, Steven suspiciously questioned, "You mean to say that you somehow keep all your dead in here?"

"We don't keep 'em in here forever, of course, we make 'em up for their funerals and then bury 'em. We just keep this place for the strange deaths, like the ones from yesterday."

"Do you get a lot of strange deaths around here, Sheriff?"

"Sir, you're in Sullinger, Mississippi, that right there is strange enough."

All three men stepped into the structure; the place was no bigger than a school classroom, complete with ten steel gurneys, four of which were occupied, all draped under white sheets.

"How are you keeping it cold in here?" Steven asked as he approached one of the gurneys.

"Ya hear that motor in the back?" Leon pointed. "That's the generator that runs twenty-four seven. Without it—

"We get the picture, Sheriff." Steven adamantly replied.

Leon walked over and somberly presented one of the four murder victims. "This one here is Kenny; he's the grandson of the fella ya'll ran into a while ago." He explained as he pulled back the white sheet just enough to where they could see the young man's face.

Steven looked down in white knuckled fear. It wasn't so much that he had never seen a dead body before, rather, it was the notion that he had dropped the proverbial ball that gripped him to a near stroke stage.

"Can we see the rest of him, Sheriff?" Steven gasped.

Leon pulled the sheet completely off the boy. The moment his entire mutilated carcass was revealed, Steven closed his eyes for a few seconds before opening them again.

The young man's skin had already turned pale. The menacing closed eyes that looked as though they could open at any second. It was a scene all too familiar.

"Tore 'em right in half, just like ya said." Leon sighed. "We weren't able to find his other body parts yet."

Steven, too, belted out a wistful sigh before saying, "And you never will find it, Sheriff. It's rare for it leave anything behind after a kill."

"You described the other murders pretty well. Does it kill like this all the time?"

"Pretty much so, sir, it doesn't discriminate." Jim remarked.

"Sheriff, would it be too much trouble for us to travel to the scene of the crime?"

"No trouble at all, it'll get me away from the phone for a while."

Before being led out of the morgue, Steven couldn't help but to grab one final look back at the young man's corpse. All that was left of him was a head and torso, not even his arms were attached. Suddenly, his chosen career path as a government agent didn't seem as intriguing as he had hoped.

* * *

No more than ten minutes later all three men arrived at the old creek. If there was one place on earth that resembled death in its purest form, it had to be Claymore's Creek the day after a sadistic massacre. No human or animal could be seen or heard down and around the arid valley that lazy, hot morning.

Steven followed both Leon and Jim down the hill that led to the creek. He could see the water that was still red with blood from just a few yards away.

"Well, here it is, fella's, where it all happened around ten till eleven yesterday mornin'." Leon announced as he stuffed his hands into his pockets. "Yep, I can remember years ago, there was a little corner store that old man Claymore owned just up yonder there. But when he passed on, his son had the place tore down. I remember when I was a youngen, we'd come down here and swim all day long on these hot summer days, and then go up to 'ole Claymore's to buy five cent popsicles." He fondly reminisced while leading his guests down the embankment.

Ignoring Leon's recall moment, Steven, with Jim close on his heels, ventured further down the hill until he reached the creek's edge. He then knelt down and dipped his right hand into the cold water, sloshing it back and forth. Once he was through splashing about, he looked up at his partner and shook his head up and down while shielding his eyes from the berating sun.

"Ya'll find somethin' down there?" The sheriff called out as he waddled down towards their direction.

"No, sir, nothing at all," Steven shouted back as he stood and wiped his wet hand dry on his pants. "Sheriff, I was wondering, just what was happening before the murders took place? I mean, what type of situation was going on at the time?"

Appearing as if he were trying to giggle, Leon said, "Well, I gotta go by what the kids told me. They said that they was down there playin' in the water when Millard and the boys' van were chasin' each other. Next thing ya know, Millard drove his truck down into that there ditch and Kenny and his buddies started to beat 'ole Millard. Then they tied up his legs and dunked him into the water. And that's when they say something came out of the water and pulled Kenny down under. Well, after awhile, the youngens said that somethin' just started killin' everyone around, and that's when they ran off. When me and my deputy got here, there were four dead bodies, a busted up van, and Millard's old truck just lyin' around."

"Who is this Millard person?" Steven asked.

"Millard's my cousin; our mama's were sisters." Leon answered. "Yes, sir, I just thank the good Lord that none of the little ones was hurt. They ran just like they were supposed to."

"Have you questioned your cousin yet, Sheriff?"

"I talked to both him and his girlfriend yesterday when me and my deputy took his truck home. Millard said that he didn't see anything because he was underwater. As far as his girlfriend, she said that it was a ghost, but that girl is about as crazy as a pet coon if ya ask me."

"Sounds to me like these guys were trying to lynch your cousin, Sheriff." Jim speculated.

Leon gave an offhanded smirk before explaining, "I don't want you fella's to think that sort of thing goes on down here all the time. But, to be honest, and I hate to admit it, Millard kinda had it comin' to 'em. He's got a real bad reputation 'round these parts."

"What's his girlfriend's name?" Steven questioned.

Leon scratched his head before answering, "To tell ya'll the truth…I don't have a darn clue what that child's name is. Millard just calls her gal and she always comes runnin'."

"So you mean to tell us that the creature spared both your cousin and his friend?" Steven's eyes sprung out.

"That's right," Leon shrugged.

Shaking his head in stunned disbelief, Steven chocked, "I…I just have to talk to these people, Sheriff, if that's possible."

Leon stood back for a few seconds with a jolted expression of his own printed on his sweaty face. "You wanna go talk to Millard?" He stammered.

"Is there a problem?"

"Let's just say that 'ole Millard doesn't take too kindly to folks comin' 'round his yard. Besides, he was beaten pretty badly yesterday; I doubt he'd even wanna talk to me right about now."

"We wouldn't be there too long, Sheriff."

"It's not the duration of your visit that's the problem as it is the visit itself."

"Well, Sheriff, it's of great importance that we speak with the gentleman. The specimen leaves no survivors; it would have killed those children had they not ran away. Any information your cousin could give us would be invaluable." Steven persisted.

Appearing hesitant at first glance, Leon gawked around the valley before saying, "Well, I can give you directions to his farm, or what's left of it. He don't live but a few minutes away from here anyways. But I warn ya, don't come back cryin' to me with your tails tucked in between your legs after you've met 'em."

"Is he that bad of a person?" Jim smiled from ear to ear in a jocular manner.

"I wouldn't be too worried about Millard right now if I was you two. I got a killer in my town, and I wanna know how to stop the darn thing." Leon seriously stated as he took his pudgy hands from out of his pockets and folded them in a royal-type fashion while staring deep into his visitors eyes.

Steven stood and stared right back at the stoic man whose southern comfort mannerisms oft times amused him to where he wished both he and Jim had visited in-town more often.

"Not much happens 'round here," Leon continued. "We get the occasional drug dealer every so often. Moonshiners. Sometimes Old Lady Collins may forget to take her medication and we have to find her to make sure she ain't botherin' the school kids. Other than that, Sullinger is a nice place to be. But when I get four people torn to shit by God knows what, and all you two can tell me is that it escaped from some containment unit, I tend to get a little nervous. Now, do I believe in monsters? Well, it depends. But I do believe in what I saw down here yesterday, and I do believe that it was no gator that killed those boys. I don't care who they beat up, nobody deserves that kind of death."

With a stone face of his own, Steven stepped forward and placed his left hand on Leon's shoulder saying, "Sheriff, I say this to you as one man to another, I'd evacuate this entire town if I were you, right now."

Leon cracked a somewhat whimsical smile before glancing behind him and asking, "Are there any more of these things runnin' around?"

"We don't know, sir." Steven turned away. "We have scientists that come down here four times a year and study it. They believe it to be something possibly left behind from the prehistoric era, but—

"That's not what I asked you." Leon forcefully clarified. "I need to know right here and now if there are any more of these things?"

Steven swallowed and looked up to the cloudy sky for more time to conjure a response. Soon, after so much stalling and procrastinating, he looked Leon straight in the eye, and with every muscle in his jaw, he opened his tasteless mouth and uttered, "No, sir, this is it."

"Good, I only got one deputy." The sheriff sucked in his gut before marching back up the hill. "C'mon, I'll take you fella's back to the station so you can get your car."

Steven and Jim had nothing to say to one another, they couldn't even look the other in the eye at that point as they followed the sheriff.

"Oh, I just wanna make somethin' perfectly clear before we head back." Leon suddenly paused. "Once we catch this thing, I want you two, and it, out of this town. Don't take any offence, I like you boys, but you brought the devil down here, and I want 'em out of my town yesterday. Sullinger ain't no place for the government to be sendin' its trash. And you can tell Mr. George H. that Sheriff Leon Collier said so. Ya hear?"

Steven glared strangely at the sheriff for a few moments, trying to make sense of his last sentence before he tossed up his hands and humbly remarked, "Yes, sir, Sheriff."

As the three made their way back up the embankment and to the squad car, Steven couldn't help but take one last look back down at the creek before heading off.

The man stared on and on at the calm, crimson water before his eyes caught sight of something that resembled clothes. Eventually, after so much hard staring, Steven was able to make out the shape of the object in question.

His motionless face remained immobile as he watched the two legs that were still clothed in their respective pants at last wash ashore.

There was nothing he could say at that juncture, even to the sheriff who had already started the car's engine. Steven pressed his lips together as tight as he could before clinching his fists and resuming his walk to the cruiser.

CHAPTER 13

Much like a hunk of festering meat, Millard sat on the edge of his bed with his hands lying in his lap, just staring. From the comfort of his bedroom, the man had a straight ahead view of his barn.

There really wasn't much for the old fellow to say that morning; all he could do was keep his brooding eyes locked on the wretched old barn house in the hopes that his newfound guest would make a sudden appearance.

With about as much energy as he could gather, Millard looked back at his lady who was fast asleep on the other side of the bed with the white sheet covering her naked body. The small fan that sat on the dresser blew her hair up and down and from side to side.

Once he was done glossing her over, Millard managed to lift his stale feeling body up off the bed, buckle his overalls and carry himself out of the bedroom.

He lazily stumbled out of the house and onto the porch. His face was a swollen collage of cuts, bruises and bandages that were wrapped around his chin.

The second he stepped down from off the porch he immediately paused right next to the makeshift grave that he finished burying Shirley in the night before, right next to the porch steps. The man just couldn't bear to see her long tongue spewed out of her gaping mouth a moment longer.

It was rapidly closing in on noontime and the old man was still drowsy; he had been awake since four a.m. He wasn't exactly losing any sleep over the deaths of the four young men that attacked him; rather, it was their attacker that had him unsettled.

He kept on asking himself why it killed Shirley and the boys and not him. And most of all, why it chose his homestead to roost. It was all his overloaded brain could seem to ponder upon.

He knew it was still in the barn, he had heard it all night long rustling and scattering about like a rat trying to scratch out of a burning building.

Millard could hear his friend begin to stir and moan herself awake inside. It was incredibly rare for her to stay the night. The only reason he had her stay was so he could keep her from running around town and telling everyone her insane side of what took place the day before. What she told Leon was enough to make anyone go up the wall.

Millard didn't really care about how frightened she was by the whole incident, all he wanted was for her to keep her mouth shut completely on the subject, or at least until he was able to get a stranglehold on the matter himself, and if that meant keeping the young lady at his homestead for an extended amount of time, then so be it.

Just limping from his house to the barn caused Millard to break out into a soupy sweat. He was amazed at how Leon just took him and his girlfriend's stories and ran with them without question. He realized that Leon wasn't all too dim, and after seeing four mutilated bodies strewn all over the hillside, Millard knew that more questions would be coming his way sooner than later.

Millard stepped into the icy cold, stench ridden barn and aimlessly strolled about in the hay, looking up at the loft and around at the various tools and broken down, rusted machines that he had stored within the old structure.

Millard Lang was a lot of things, but naïve wasn't one of them, he knew that he was dealing with something that no one in their right minds could or would want to understand, and his own common sense was far too frazzled to try and figure out just what he was getting himself into.

But out of everything that had recently taken place, the one occurrence that kept on dancing about in his head was the night of the storm. He recalled being knocked down by what he thought was the burglar's partner. He remembered the cold, wet hand that shoved him out of his own loft.

Inside, Millard knew far more than he was willing to tell anyone else. All that was left was for him to admit to himself that there was a rational explanation to it all.

As cold as it was inside the barn Millard had to convince himself over and over that it was blazing hot, that the smoke that was blowing from out of his mouth every time he exhaled was all in his head. He even tried with all his might to somehow persuade himself that Shirley was still out in the pasture running and barking herself half to death as she usually did on summer days.

Millard took another gander up at the foreboding loft. The bright sun that was ducking in and out of the clouds managed to cast down a dark shadow on just about every corner.

The old man wanted to go up, but there was something keeping his feet from moving, almost as if an ominous force wanted him to stay stuck in place. He could feel it up in the loft, like a huge beast prowling about.

"Hello," Courtney all of the sudden called out as she cautiously stepped into the barn.

Millard spun around at that split second, not knowing exactly just how to react. Her very presence there was so unexpected that his heart just began to beat at a dangerous pace.

"I uh…I didn't hear your car pull in." He stammered as he stuffed his hands into his pants pockets and locked his wobbly knees so they wouldn't shake.

She was clothed in a white t-shirt that read *Jackson State*, and a pair of tight blue jean shorts and flip flops. It wasn't exactly the way Millard wanted to see the young lady, but her attire was the furthest subject from his mind at that moment.

"I'm sorry if I scared you," Courtney said with a straight, composed face, "I guess you were in deep thought."

Clearing his stuffy throat and glancing every other second up at the loft, Millard asked, "So, what brings you here after all these years?"

Taking a few steps deeper into the barn, Courtney answered, "I heard about what happened yesterday down at Claymore's. Looks like Ray's grandson and his buddies did a solid on you."

Shrugging his sore shoulders, Millard replied, "Shit, it ain't nothin' new. I don't care nothin' about them."

"You should see the roads, they're all quiet. Folks are too afraid to even talk about what happened yesterday. A lot of people are saying that we got a killer gator in town."

"Shoot, damn gators always seem to find a way here somehow. They get lost and need a place to stay for a while or so." Millard tried to explain while keeping a still face.

There sat a general unease in the frosty barn as the two stood feet apart from one another, both seemingly trying to keep their distance from each other.

"Well, I'm just glad that you're alright." Courtney mumbled. "I also stopped by to finally say… thank you."

"For what," Millard frowned.

"For taking care of Tyrone…again," Courtney hesitated. "I know it's long overdue, but, thank you all the same."

"Well, you'd think the nigga would have learned his lesson after all this time."

"You know that he'll be back soon, and in more numbers than before."

Chuckling as though he were amused, Millard cunningly replied, "Well, August is almost here, and I ain't goin' nowhere."

Cracking a somewhat whimsical smile at Millard's comment, Courtney blushed and said, "The boys were pretty shaken up by it all, they've never seen a person get shot before, except on TV."

"Where are they now?"

"Rayshawn is out in the car, and Keyshawn is sick, so I left him with a friend of mine. Mikey let me have a couple of days off; I was on my way up to Jackson to do some shopping."

Millard suddenly stepped forward, nearly tripping over his own long and narrow feet just so he could make sure Courtney could hear him loud and clear. "Ya know, I was thinkin', maybe you and the boys should get outta town for a while."

"By the time Tyrone gets back down here again I'll have another address. I've been saving some money for another place."

"I ain't talkin' about Tyrone, I'm talkin' about…about somethin' else more serious than that horse's ass."

Courtney reared back and stretched another smile before saying, "I'm not afraid of an alligator, especially since I live in a trailer park."

"I'm not quite sure it's a gator."

Courtney momentarily suspended her response, but the discreet smile that usually followed was nowhere present. Just then her face morphed into that of a person ready to explode.

"You're concerned about me?" She snapped. "You know what really gets me about you, Millard? It's that after all these years you never once asked me how I was doing. Don't get me wrong, I appreciate that you ask about the boys, but you never ask me how I'm doing. And now, you're concerned?"

With a confused grimace on his face, Millard grunted, "Where is all this comin' from?"

"It's coming from twenty-three years of knowing that I have a father that lives in the same sorry town as I do and the only time I ever see the man is when my sons' father comes into town to get money from me!"

Millard stood in the middle of the barn puzzled and disoriented at what was taking place. He instantly realized that the words they were speaking were the most they had uttered to each other in their lives.

"What else do you want from me, gal?"

"First off, I'm not a gal, that's what you call your dog Shirleen or Sharonda or whatever her name is! Second, I never asked for your help in the first place!"

"Who else is gonna look after them youngens of yours?"

"You didn't even know their names before I told you a second ago, did you?"

"Girl, you're talkin' to a man who's forgotten more names than people run through underwear."

"Do you even remember my name?"

Agitated and running low on breath, Millard sighed, "Of course I remember your name. If I can remember your brothers' names I can—

"No, not my brothers, your sons!" she furiously shot back.

"Alright," Millard relented. "If I can remember my sons' names, then I can surely remember yours. Now, is that what you wanna hear?"

"Tell me something, why do you even care?"

Rolling his eyes, Millard groaned, "I ain't got no time for this, girl."

"Wait a minute, I wanna know!"

"Whaddya mean?" Millard hollered. "If I wasn't around then you'd be complainin' about that! Fuck, I swear, a man can't do no good by a woman!"

"I guess my mother would know that better than anyone, wouldn't she?"

"Your mama wouldn't give a man a chance to be a man! Every time I wanted to do somethin' with my life she stood in my way! That damn woman couldn't keep a man if her sorry life depended on it! But I'm sure she's filled your head with her version of our story, so what the hell does it even matter?"

With her blush red face boiling over, Courtney turned and began for the barn's entrance, but not before stopping midway and yelling, "Do me and the boys a favor and stay the fuck away from us from now on! I never once asked you for help and I sure as hell didn't ask for your life story, either! Oh, and as far as my mother telling her version of the story goes, she never told me anything about you and her, I always knew that you were a no good bastard to begin with!"

Courtney spun around only to get herself and her silver belly chain caught in a nail next to the door. The young lady was so angry that she didn't even notice the chain; she just ripped herself away from the nail and stormed out of the barn.

Before she could take two steps to her car, she paused to catch a glimpse of her father's lady friend who was standing on the porch steps. Millard stood in the barn and watched as Courtney glanced back at him with such fury in her teary eyes before she eventually turned and stomped her way to her maroon Chevette.

As if she were being chased, Courtney hopped in and created a whirlwind of mud torpedoes that splattered from one end of the yard to the other just trying to get off of Millard's property. Meanwhile, coming down the road in the opposite direction was Steven and Jim's brown station wagon that casually pulled into the yard just at the same time Courtney was leaving.

Millard, with his hands still lodged in his pockets and his ego hanging on by a thread, strolled cool and calm out of the barn and into his yard.

His mood was melancholy at best. It was by no means whatsoever the first time he had ever been cussed out, but for it to come from his own daughter was something that he had anticipated for years, and yet dreaded all the same.

"Good day, sir!" Steven called out as both he and Jim climbed out of the car and walked towards Millard. "My name is Steven Winemore, and this here is my associate, Jim Livingston! We were just wondering if we could have a few moments of your time!"

With his face pointed to the ground, Millard nonchalantly walked right past them both like they weren't there at all.

Trying to catch up to Millard, Steven breathlessly said, "Mr. Lang, we represent a very prestigious government agency, and if it's not too much trouble, we'd like your account of the creek incident from yesterday."

As though he were commanded to do so, Millard stopped only a few inches away from the porch steps before gradually turning around to face the man. His burning eyes only made the moment all the more tense and reviled.

In a slow, bitter tone he asked, "What the hell did you say, boy?"

Steven cleared the cobwebs from his throat and meekly replied, "Well, sir, as I just mentioned, we would like just a few moments of your time to discuss the events down at the creek yesterday."

"Mr. Lang, were you and your friend able to see the animal that killed those four men?" Jim intervened.

At that very instant, Millard's lady timidly stepped down from off the porch and past Millard on her way towards the two men. With quick precision the old man immediately caught her by the arm and yanked her back.

"Where the hell is you goin to, gal?" He irately whispered in her face.

"I'm going to tell them what happened, Millard." She whispered back. "They have to know."

"You shut the fuck up, you ain't got no right!" Millard blasted back as he looked up to see only one man standing in front of him. "Where'd your boy go to?" He asked Steven.

When the old man saw that Jim was making his way towards the barn he right away raced into the shack and through the living room.

"Mr. Lang, we really must talk about this! You can't even begin to imagine what we have on our hands here!" Steven urged from outside.

All the man's words seemed to do was incite more hatred inside Millard as he reached for his rifle that was lying on the kitchen counter.

"You and your friend had better get out of here before he comes back out!" The young lady screamed.

Like a charging soldier into battle, Millard marched right back outside with his weapon cocked and ready for combat.

"Millard, no!" the girl pleaded.

"Jim, get outta there!" Steven yelled like a madman.

With as much fury as he could assemble, the old man stormed past both individuals before making his way to the barn to find Jim skulking about the hay.

Without sounding any warning of any kind, Millard simply pointed his rifle at Jim's face and snarled, "Now, I'm only gonna say this once, get off my damn property before I blow your head down into your ass!"

Jim, with his hands held up high, slowly and warily stepped out of the barn while trying not to come into direct physical contact with the gun.

"Mr. Lang, you are making a very huge mistake!" Steven pressed on as he began for the car.

"I don't need nobody tellin' me nothin', and I sure as hell ain't tellin' nobody nothin', either! You faggots comin' 'round here, snoopin' around like ya know somethin'! Ya don't know shit! Now, get the fuck outta here before I—

"Mr. Lang, if you would just please give us a few moments, we could—

But before Jim could even finish his precautionary sentence, Millard shot a bullet at the station wagon, blowing out the back window. Without another word, both Steven and Jim jumped into the car before ripping out the yard, leaving only smoke in their petrified wake.

With tears in her eyes, the young woman hollered, "Millard, why did you do that?"

Millard stood and watched as she turned and ran back into the house. He didn't need to explain his actions to anyone; if he wanted to shoot the men then he would have, without a blink of hesitation. But even he understood that one more murder stemming from him would be the final nail in his already buried coffin. He chased after his lady and caught her sitting on the couch crying her eyes out.

"What the hell is wrong with you?" He asked as he sat down next to her.

"Why are you doing this, Millard?"

"Doin' what, gal" he tossed up his hands.

"Not telling Leon or those two guys about what happened! They may be able to catch whatever it is that killed those boys!"

"Like they know what it is! Hell, me and you don't even know what it is, and we were right there! Besides, I ain't gotta hear nothin' from nobody! Those cracker motherfuckers don't know no more 'bout what's happenin' than anyone else, and the last thing I want is for them or anyone else comin' 'round here lookin' at my yard!"

"But what about Shirley," she continued to sob. "What killed her and why?"

"Gal, I don't have a damn clue, all I know is that I'm still here."

"You always say that!"

"And I always mean it, too!" Millard arrogantly replied before standing up. "Now, c'mon," he obstinately commanded.

"Where are we going?"

"You'll find out when we get there."

Millard stood and waited as his fatigued friend wiped her tear soaked eyes before ushering her out of the house and to his truck.

"I don't know how much more I can take, Millard." She pitifully whimpered.

Placing his rifle in the back seat, Millard sighed, "Just be cool and it will all be over soon."

Before pulling away, Millard looked into the rearview mirror at the barn. He was still both perplexed and enraged at his argument with Courtney, but he had more tentative situations to attend to for the time being.

"Where are we going, Millard?" She pressed on, sounding as though she were too tired to even speak.

"You like rides, doncha?" Millard sneered. "Well, me and you, were gonna take us on helluva ride."

CHAPTER 14

A few simple moments

With red popsicle juice drizzling down and drying up on his chubby cheeks, Rayshawn nervously glanced over at his crying mother while she was trying to keep her balance on the road that she was racing down.

He wanted so much to ask her why she was weeping. He had heard her argue with her father earlier, a man both he and his twin brother really never knew up close. They were treated to vile stories, either from their mother, grandmother or townspeople; neither boy could fully comprehend that they could possibly be related to someone so wretched. But beyond all the fabled stories that they had been treated to for years, both Rayshawn and his brother were fascinated all the same, much like wanting to see a twister right before their eyes.

Yet, beyond all the captivating allure that surrounded a man he had yet to meet face to face, Rayshawn could not overlook his mother's urgent pain. He was more concerned about her well-being than he was about her careening from one end of the dirt road to the other like she was drunk.

Too afraid to set his sliver of a popsicle down into the

passenger's door hole, Rayshawn scanned the car from front to back in search of a place to discard what was left of the treat until he noticed a red laceration on his mother's exposed belly button.

"Mama," Rayshawn hollered out in horror.

"What the fuck is it, boy?" Courtney furiously screamed back.

"Your tummy is bleedin'!"

In a state of shock, Courtney looked down before slamming down on the brakes and coming to a complete stop in the middle of the road.

Rayshawn watched as his mom rubbed at the wound before she stopped and began crying all over again. The child wanted ever so much to help her, but he was having trouble trying to figure out just how to approach her on the matter.

Just then, Courtney stopped crying long enough to glance over at Rayshawn and caress his pudgy face with her shivering hand.

"Mama, did you forget your chain at that man's house?" Rayshawn innocently inquired.

Chuckling from her stomach, Courtney answered, "Yeah, baby, I think I did."

"Do we have to go back to that man's house again?" He whimpered.

Courtney sat for a few moments before rubbing her son's rough hair and handing him an endearing grin as to say she felt his anxiety.

Softly she uttered, "I'm afraid we have to, baby. Your grandma got that chain for my birthday last year. It really means a lot to me. But after we find it then we can go shopping."

"Can me and Keyshawn get water guns and more popsicles, too, mama?" The boy excitedly asked, nearly jumping out of his hot seat. "Michael stole our other water guns and put Kool-Aid in them to shoot at me and Keyshawn the other day."

Courtney sniggered, "Yes, honey, we can get water guns, too."

Rayshawn eagerly watched as his mother put the car back in gear and resumed driving down the road. A tingling chorus of joyful butterflies rumbled lightly in his stomach at the thought of not only getting to buy what he wanted, but also seeing that his mom was feeling better.

All of the sudden, going back to the mean old man's house again didn't seem so laborious to his young soul.

*   *   *

Courtney pulled her loud-motored vehicle into the yard and parked directly in front of the barn. Rayshawn noticed that the old man's blue truck wasn't anywhere in sight, which in turn gave him a sigh of breathtaking relief.

The second he saw his mother climb out of the car Rayshawn began to whine, "Can I come?"

"Yeah, you can help me look for it."

Rayshawn jumped out and joyfully followed his mother into the bone chilling barn house. Right away the boy plugged his nose with his fingers.

"Eww, mama, it smells like dookie in here!"

"It must be some smelly farm animal up in here." Courtney frowned. "How the hell does he keep this place so cool?"

Both mother and son searched through the hay strewn floor while enjoying the uncanny coolness they were amongst.

"Okay, I think I dropped it somewhere around here, so start looking next to the doorway."

Rayshawn knelt down and sifted through the hay, wanting ever so badly to please his mom by being the first to find her beloved chain.

"Thank God, here it is!" Courtney beamed as she picked up the silver chain from off the ground right near where the nail that hooked it was located. "Okay, c'mon and let's get out of here before he comes back."

"Mama, who was that woman that was on the porch," Rayshawn curiously looked up at his mom. "Was she that man's wife?"

Courtney twisted her lips and grumbled under her breath, "More like his hoe."

"Huh," Rayshawn squinted.

"Don't worry about her, boy, let's go." Courtney said.

Just as they both were about to exit, Rayshawn abruptly stopped to listen to the hay patch behind him rustle and crunch.

"What was that, a chicken?"

"It's probably that stupid dog of his." Courtney grimaced. "Now, let's go."

Rayshawn resumed his walk towards his mother and took her by the hand. As they started for the entrance, both mother and son walked right into what felt like an invisible, wet wall that was conveniently placed directly in front of them.

"Oh shit," Courtney screamed as she fell backwards to the ground, taking Rayshawn down with her.

"What happened, mama?" Rayshawn shivered.

Too stunned to reply, Courtney sat on the ground and gazed all around her surroundings. Rayshawn mimicked his mother's movements, exhaling cold smoke from out of his mouth.

Courtney then got up, still holding on to Rayshawn's

hand. As soon as they both began to march forward, something that felt like a hand unexpectedly shoved them both back down to the floor once again.

By then, the chill factor in the barn gave way to a drapery of heat that melted all down Rayshawn's face in the form of sweat as he looked at his mother's shirt to see it partially ripped open with four slices down the middle.

Courtney snatched Rayshawn's trembling hand and started to slide backwards. Rayshawn could hear what sounded like footsteps scrape across the hay towards both he and his mom.

"Get up, Rayshawn, and run!"

Confused and flat out scared to death, Rayshawn somehow managed to get to his feet and bolt for the doorway, only to be snatched from behind and thrown clear across to the other end of the barn.

"Oh God, no," Courtney hollered before getting up and running over to her boy.

Rayshawn found himself semi-conscience but surprisingly mobile. He watched as his mom raced over and hoisted his heavy self into her arms before attempting to take off for the entrance once more, only to be knocked down for a third time.

"Get away, go and get away from here!" Courtney screamed as she began kicking at anything that moved in front of her.

Courtney then cried out in pain as the unseen force grabbed her by her hair and effortlessly lifted her up, causing her feet to dangle precariously in the air.

Rayshawn immediately stirred from his blurred state to see his beloved mother suspended in mid-air. He helplessly watched as she looked down at him with excruciating tears dripping from her eyes.

"Rayshawn, baby…run." Courtney gasped for life.

Rayshawn was too petrified to move any further. Instead, he remained on the floor and allowed the old ghost stories that all the little children in town would tell flood into his brain. He remembered them all, from start to finish.

The longer his mother hung in mid-air, the more he could see a grayish right arm form from out of nowhere. The opposite arm suddenly appeared soon after, as well as four sharp and shiny claws. But that was all that seemed to materialize, two arms and claws.

Courtney again gazed down at Rayshawn who had yet to move an inch. She then grunted in a struggling, somber tone, "Rayshawn…don't look at me."

Just like that, the same right arm that had Courtney hanging by her hair saw fit to fling her entire body at least fifteen feet across the barn where she ended up crashing head first into a rusted, steel tool table.

When he was able to turn his head, Rayshawn saw his own mother lying upside down next to the table with her eyes wide open and a deep gash forged in her forehead. After at least a few seconds, her entire body began to convulse until foam spilled out of her mouth.

The boy couldn't take his eyes off his dying mother. The longer he lay sprawled out on the floor staring at her the stiffer his body seemed to grow. He soon discovered that he couldn't even move one finger.

After so much incessant and violent jerking, Courtney's dead body eventually went still. From behind him, Rayshawn's ears could pick up the sounds of the thing that had attacked both he and his mother. Ever so slightly, the frightened little boy turned his head only to see the same two abnormal looking arms before him.

Soon, he could feel its very presence lurk above him like

a dark cloud hanging over his head. The large being then began to hover over Rayshawn's body as though it were going to lie down on top of him.

Rayshawn had no choice but to lie his back down on the hay and listen to the faint grunts and growls of the beast that was beginning to materialize right before his eyes.

Even though it's entire body was appearing, all the child could see in front of him was a row of sharp teeth that resembled a lion or tiger's. The outright stench of the thing's breath was enough to make the boy want to pass out right there, but he held on, he held on to a fond memory of his twin brother waiting for his brand new water gun.

Rayshawn couldn't stop shaking, and no matter what, he could not open his mouth to scream for help; his throat was as dry as sandpaper. It was only his brother that he could image at that instant, the same brother that he wanted to see again more than anyone on earth.

Rayshawn kept his eyes open long enough to watch the beast open its pungent smelling mouth. He tried to catch his breath, but it had long since escaped him.

It remained all quiet both in the barn, and in the valley.

CHAPTER 15

Millard tore a ferocious path through the woods as if he were racing from God himself. The argument he had with Courtney, much like any other disagreement with anyone else, had all but vacated his mind, Millard had moved on. He didn't even want to hear the young lady's name, let alone talk about her; it just put a bad taste in his already sour mouth.

"Are you sure you can drive with your right eye swollen like that?" His friend asked.

"I'm drivin' just fine, ain't I?" He murmured with an attitude.

For at least two or three minutes there settled a bitter quiet in the truck before the woman's mouth opened. Millard could feel it approaching; right away his stomach began to quiver.

"I know you don't like talking about," she shivered, sounding as though her voice wanted to break, "but I really think you should have told those two men—

"Gal, if you don't shut the hell up!"

"What about Shirley? She's was your best friend."

Millard glanced over at the woman with a dry idiom on his battered face, and in a raspy tone he asked, "Just what the fuck do you know about best friends?"

The woman turned her head forward to the shadowy forest in front of her before learning over and wrapping herself around Millard's right arm like a snake. Then, with stars in her eyes, she looked up at the old man and said, "You know, you and I should take that trip down to the coast sometime soon. After all the stuff that happened lately, the both of us could use a vacation."

Emotionless, Millard snatched his arm from her loving hold, and with his eyes pointed directly on the path in front of him he frowned, "A vacation from what, gal? You don't work."

"But what about you," she haplessly protested.

"If I go to the coast then you'd better believe my ass if goin' alone."

"But we've been planning this trip together for years, and—

"Don't you worry, I'll be sure to bring you back somethin' nice. "Now, be quiet so I can think for a moment."

Millard heard her sniffing, but to him, that was all that it was, a mere sound, nothing for him to be concerned with all too much.

Just up ahead he could see the bright clearing, signifying that their wilderness trek was soon coming to a close, which didn't set his mind at ease one bit.

The instant the truck cleared the forest, a small white house could be seen in the upcoming distance. Millard's heart immediately dropped to his feet.

He stopped the truck in front of the rundown home and sat for what felt like countless minutes, viewing the damage that the storm had left behind just days earlier. A small part of the roof was completely gone and the tiny porch was leaning to its side, ready to fall completely apart the instant something or someone set foot onto it.

Wiping tears from her eyes, the young lady asked, "Why are we here?"

Clearing his throat, Millard responded, "I got somethin' to do. Now, you stay your ass right here in this truck and doncha move. Ya hear me?" He raised his voice.

"Yes, you don't have to yell at me, Millard!"

"You just stay in here; I got man's business to tend to." Millard snapped as he ripped the keys from out of the ignition and got out of the truck.

No sooner did he take two steps, an abrupt, sharp pain clutched his chest, causing him to slump over and onto the truck's hood.

"Are you okay?" The young lady asked from her seat.

Embarrassed and still in pain, Millard gawked around before looking back at his friend and panting, "Hush up! I'm fine."

Once the searing agony in his chest subsided, he assembled his bearings and resumed his task. He didn't even want to take a guess as to what just took place inside of him.

He slowly strolled towards the rusty hovel and right into the front yard where a German Shepherd that was tied up to an oak tree barked and snarled at him, trying its best to get at the old man. Millard carried on unperturbed as though the animal wasn't even there to begin with until he reached the front door and let himself in.

"What the hell is this shit?" A young, meaty black woman with pink curlers in her hair shouted as she got up from off the floor and faced Millard. "What is you doin' up in here?"

Millard just sidestepped the woman, and came face to face with a fully pregnant, younger, dark skinned girl who was seated on the floor eating a bag of *Doritos*. He reached into his left pocket and pulled out a wad of bills. "Take this and get the hell outta this town." He strongly ordered.

The old man tossed the bills at the girl like it was burning his hand. The girl, whose face was besmirched with pimples, alarmingly looked up at Millard as she counted the bills one by one.

"Old man, what are you doin' here?" A large black woman dressed in a multicolored robe yelled from her couch. "You got no business bein' here!" She continued to rant as she sat her pot of ravioli down onto the floor next to her and struggled to lift her girth from off the couch where she was planted.

"It's alright, mama." The pregnant girl said before looking back up at Millard and asking with the wad of bills held up, "Why is you givin' me this?"

"You just do what I told you to do and everything will be alright."

"You just can't come in here and have your way, you son of a bitch!" The other young lady said as she again stepped into Millard's face.

"Gal, if you don't get the hell outta my face I'm gonna knock you into next week!"

"I wish you would hit me! I'll get—

Before she could get another word out, Millard, out of pent up rage, slapped her so hard across the face that she fell down to the grimy floor.

"Welcome to next week!" He roared.

"You just don't come up in here and hit my child!" The mother shot back. "I never thought I'd say this to another colored person, but I can't wait till the Klan comes here and takes care of you once and for all!"

Unfazed by her tirade, Millard turned his attention from the mother and back to the girl who in turn stared back at him with a puzzled yet knowledgeable stare on her face. The sounds of *The Andy Griffith Show* playing on the small RCA television filled the room while Millard and the girl looked into each other's eyes; neither saying a word to the other. There were no words to be said at that point.

"This is three thousand dollars here." The girl rubbed her round stomach. "Where am I 'pose to go to?"

"I don't give a damn, just get the hell outta this town, and soon."

"And just where do you think you're goin', young lady?" The mother with a gleam in her eyes asked as she gawked deeply at all the hundred dollar bills that were stuffed in her daughter's right hand.

It appeared as if Millard's sudden intrusion didn't seem to matter all too much to the woman anymore.

The girl didn't reply to her mother, instead she continued to look up at the old man while rubbing her belly. A small and nervous grimace shined on her face.

The longer she gazed on the more Millard just wanted to leave. Without so much as a goodbye, Millard turned and walked out of the house, nearly tripping over the loosened boards on the porch while heading back to his truck.

"What was all that yelling in there?" His friend asked while slipping on a pair of dark sunglasses.

"Where'd you get those from?"

"My mama gave them to me for my birthday before I kicked her out of my apartment the other day. Aren't they pretty?"

Millard snatched the sunglasses from off her face before tossing them out the window. From there, he turned on the truck and ripped down the road towards the woods.

"My mama paid a lot of money for those!" She griped.

Without even glancing at her, Millard, said, "Well, next time make sure she keeps the damn receipt."

Millard didn't even notice the young woman angrily

cross her arms, he just kept looking back in the rearview mirror as the white house behind him grew smaller and smaller. He then glanced over at his weeping friend then back again at the fading house. As hard as he tried to relieve his mind of all the recent stress, there was always something else to keep weighing him down.

Just one more glimpse back at the house, and just like that, it was completely gone. Millard slammed his foot down on the gas as hard as he could.

✳   ✳   ✳

A few moments later, Millard arrived at yet another house. The home he stopped in front of was really no bigger than his shack, but it happened to be one of the few houses in town that wasn't touched by the storm.

Millard glanced over at his friend, and before he could even open his mouth the woman spoke up first, moaning and rolling her eyes, "I know, stay in the truck."

Millard confidently shook his head up and down and got out. The house was a shade of dark orange with the paint chipping away with every stiff breeze that mercifully passed by on such an inhumanly steamy day.

The screened in porch had two wide open holes carved into it, and just like his house the roof was slowly caving in.

Millard carried himself up onto the porch and had to pry open the front door just to let himself in. The instant he was inside the rampant odor of cat droppings and urine loaded his senses full-bore.

From just about every corner of the dank and diminutive living room scampered felines of all colors, shapes and sizes. The old man could have cared less if he had stepped on any of the cats or the dead mice and rats that the felines hadn't finished off completely; he just wanted to get his ordeal over with as soon as possible.

He made his way into a hot and stuffy bedroom to find an old, brown skinned woman with liver spots all over her hands and face sitting on her bed staring blankly out the closed window in front of her.

Her stretched out hair looked as if she had been electrocuted, and the odor of her own waste that was scattered all over the floor caused Millard's eyes to tear up from the toxicity. He was accustomed to the smell and squalid conditions, it was the woman's pitiful and befuddled face that seemed to humble him the most.

He stepped over pots and pans full of urine just to stand directly in front of the quiet lady. Looking down on the woman he knew that the repulsive odors were the least of his problems.

Millard then knelt down and stared deep into the old woman's expressionless eyes. She had a breathing tube that stretched from her nostrils to an oxygen tank that sat next to her bed. It took a while, but gradually her eyes connected with his. The longer she gazed upon his beaten face a quaint grin seemed to grow on her own wrinkled and worn mug.

Millard on the other hand had no smiles to give in return, he was a brutal man in many ways, and yet, merciful, in extremely small doses.

Before he could even allow the woman's sweet smile to overtake him, Millard reached over, twisted the metal oxygen valve off and carefully laid the woman down onto her bed, gently making sure her frail head fell peacefully onto her dusty pillow. He then stood back up and gazed down on the old lady's kindly face once more before closing her eyes with his hand. She made sure to take her amiable smile with her along the way.

Millard cleared his saliva filled throat while watching the woman convulse into oblivion. And that was that. Millard turned and simply exited the house the same way he entered. He made extra sure that the front door was locked before stepping down from off the porch and back to his truck.

"Why are we visiting all these houses today?" His friend asked. "Who lives in these places?"

Catching his breath, he replied, "Nobody no more, gal."

Chapter 16

Millard's lady had begged and pleaded with him for miles to stop by the local market to get something to eat, but it was as if she had no tongue at all because the old man never heard a single plea come from out of her mouth. His brain, along with the rest of his body, was as dead as a withered branch. Ever since encountering his unexpected and unwanted visitor nothing made sense to him.

He was used to having all the answers, and when he couldn't come up with an explanation to whatever problem confronted him then he would simply shove it aside. But at last there was something that he couldn't shake loose, and worst of all, he never saw it coming, and that humiliated him to no end.

"Can I at least go back to my place and get some bologna, Millard?" The young woman persisted.

Sighing heavy, Millard said, "We can get somethin' later on tonight. I need to take a nap."

"Can we go up to Jackson and stop by Hardee's?"

"I'll think about it, gal!" He irritably hollered out. "Now, leave me alone!"

As Millard rounded the corner that led to his homestead, all he could honestly ponder on was how much he didn't want to go home. All of the sudden, heading up to Jackson for at least a few days didn't seem so troublesome.

"You can't keep me here forever, Millard. Sooner or later I...why is Courtney's car back here?"

At the snap of a finger Millard awoke from his gloomy stupor to look at the Chevette that was parked right in front of his barn.

His jaws trembling, Millard mumbled, "I dunno, maybe she forgot somethin'."

"She can't be inside the house, not unless she just got back here now." The young woman stammered.

Millard parked his truck behind Courtney's car and got out. "You stay right there." He ordered before steadily marching towards the barn.

It was pure instinct as to why he thought of the barn first and not his precious house. There wasn't a human being alive that could withstand both the heat and stench inside his shack for more than a full minute.

Millard ever so lightly stepped through the barn's threshold and vigilantly stalked about with his eyes from one corner to other of the all too quiet structure.

The smell and temperature had remained the same, nothing seemed to be out of the ordinary, that is until he happened to look over and up at the loft to his immediate right. He began for the ladder.

"Oh my God!" the young woman screeched out in fright from the barn's entrance.

Stunned to a near stroke, Millard spun around and yelled, "I thought I told your ass to stay in the truck!"

When he saw the outright petrified appearance on her face that was pointed north, all Millard had to do was look up at the barn's rafters.

Both Courtney and Rayshawn's bodies were overlapped across one of the wooden beams up above.

Millard's young lady turned and vomited all over the ground before running away. Millard didn't seem to mind. At that moment there wasn't another force on earth that could tear him away from seeing his daughter and grandson dangling precariously above him like two pieces of dead meat.

It all took only a few moments.

Chapter 17

A n hour later found the old man seated Indian style on the floor of his barn. He sat, watched and listened as Leon, Steven and Jim all poked and prodded at the two dead bodies that lay prostrate before them like science experiments.

There was something stirring inside of him, it gnawed away at him like the beastly mosquitoes that infested the town on such scorching days. His will had dies years earlier, and his strength was all but depleted. All he could do was sit and stare endlessly on while his bottom lip hung low and his surly eyes brooded on at three men that had taken over his property. His eyes didn't have the nerve to look upon Courtney and Rayshawn.

Closing Courtney's still eyes, Leon stuttered, "Judging by the laceration on her head, I'd say she probably went into a seizure before dyin'."

"That's a good observation, Sheriff." Steven remarked while using a stick to scoop up some of the translucent substance that was covering Rayshawn's body from head to toe.

Frowning, Leon asked, "What is that stuff all over him? And what is that God awful smell? It smells like one of Millard's farm animals done gone and died up in here."

Clearing his throat, Jim said, "That smell is the creature's signature scent. It usually leaves a cold spell while it hangs about, but apparently it's moved on, considering the heat in here. As for the matter all over the boy, this may be hard to hear, Sheriff, but, the creature swallowed the boy and then… regurgitated him."

"Swallowed him?" Leon yelled out in shock. "Just how big is this damn thing?"

"No more than six-foot six or so. You see, much like a snake, the specimen is able to swallow its prey whole. Then, it somehow sucks out all the nutrients from its kill before bringing back up."

"And you've seen it do this before?" Leon asked.

"Yes, sir, once before," Jim hesitantly glanced over at Steven.

Leon rubbed his head, looking as though he were agonized beyond reproach. Every so often he would sneak quick glimpses back at Millard. "I sure hope to God Almighty that there's only one of these things, especially since it can become invisible."

Well, Sheriff, if only your cousin would have allowed us to search his property, then perhaps this could have been fucking prevented!" Steven screamed out in rage.

"Gettin' mad ain't gonna help anything." Leon said as he stood back up and headed for the doorway where a young white man who was adorned in a tan deputy's uniform was standing with a dejected glare on his pale face. "C'mon, son, let's get these two outta here." He sighed.

"Sheriff," the young man relented, sounding as though his voice wanted to break in mid-sentence, "I…I went to school with Courtney, sir."

Leon stood and stared at the man for only a few seconds with a sympathetic, almost drowning expression on his face.

"I know you did, son. It's alright. C'mon, let's get the body bags for these two."

"Yes, sir," The young man replied before heading back to the squad car.

Millard watched as both Steven and Jim glanced back at him one last time with nothing but disdain written all over their faces. Just as soon as they exited the barn, Leon came waddling back in and stood over Millard.

"Millard," he slowly uttered, "we're about done here. Would you like to take a look at the bodies before we pull away?"

But not one sound came from Millard's mouth; he didn't even budge a single muscle. He just sat on the hay, melting in bitter silence as sweat oozed from his forehead and mosquitoes buzzed around him.

With his hands trembling and eyes beginning to water up, Leon said, "Millard, I'll make sure that they get a good funeral. I didn't call Virginia yet, but I will as soon as I get back to the station. Me and Cornelia will take care of the other boy until she gets down here. I don't think I have the nerve to tell Keyshawn what happened yet. Maybe Virginia can explain to 'em better."

Millard could hear sounds, but they were those of Courtney yelling and cursing him out before storming away earlier.

Allowing tears to drip from his eyes, Leon wept, "Millard...if only you had told those men where this thing was then...then perhaps this wouldn't have happened!"

Still, the old man sat perfectly motionless, almost statue-like; not even his eyes blinked as a mosquito landed on his right eyelash.

"Well...you call me if ya need anything, anything at all." Leon wiped his eyes as he turned and walked out of the barn and towards his squad car. "We'll come and get Courtney's car later on. Ya hear?"

Millard watched as the deputy stuffed both bodies into individual black bags before being carried out. He then heard the sounds of cars pulling out of his yard and onto the road.

Once all was quiet, Millard Lang got up from off the ground and dragged his carcass to his house. He closed the door behind him and surveyed his lonely shack with bloodshot eyes. He couldn't explain to himself why after so many years of being alone that the sound of silence suddenly felt so empty and cold.

It suddenly became hot inside his house, even though it had been that way for decades. It was smelly, soggy and outright dreadful. After so long, he at last realized the ugly truth that so many others had revealed to him time after time.

He had to move, if he stood still any longer his legs would end up giving out and he would have collapsed to the floor like a sack of dry bones. He droned his way down to his basement, screwed in the light bulb that was dangling above his head and went straight for the tool cabinet ahead.

Millard opened one of the large doors and took out a month old, unopened bottle of Vodka. But before he could even unscrew the cap, a small tin box accidentally fell from off of one of the cabinet shelves and onto the floor.

He opened the bottle and took a long, gulping drag before kneeling down and picking up the dusty, red tin box. On the cover it read *Mississippi Crate & Steel* with a large building that dated back to 1912 emblazoned on it.

It had been years since he had last seen the box, and he actually forgot all about the thing until that minute. Before allowing his lazy curiosity to take a stranglehold on him, Millard took another swig from his Vodka bottle and unlatched the rusty old thing.

Inside were faded photos, some were in black and white, while others were in full grimy color. The black and white pictures were those of his parents. Some others were of both Leon and himself when they were little boys. The color photos were full of his children and their mother's, all in their own separate pictures.

Everyone, expect Millard, seemed so happy, somewhat content in their own way. Greg and Brett with their arms around the other's shoulders. Courtney's mother holding her as a baby; both were smiling graciously as if the sun were shining on them only.

Millard stole yet another toke of his beloved bottle before nonchalantly tossing the disturbing pictures to the side of the work bench in front of him. He lethargically watched as most of the photos teetered on the edge of the table before eventually falling down to the floor.

Before Millard could turn his uncaring head the other way, he spotted one of the fallen pictures glaring at him like a shiny piece of gold. With his bottle in his left hand, he knelt down and scooped up the photo. It was Courtney when she was a little girl. With her two front teeth missing and her tiny hands politely crossed while she sat in front of a painted mountain scene. On the bottom ledge of the photo it read, *Mrs. Tatum's Second Grade Class.*

Millard stared on at the picture for what seemed like forever before carefully placing it down onto his tool table and heading back up the steps, leaving not even a simple grunt behind him as a memento to the anguish that he was enduring.

CHAPTER 18

Ten past eleven in Sullinger, Mississippi. Sheriff Leon Collier made his usual rounds in his squad car that unbearably warm evening; only that night, unlike any other night, he brought along with him a shotgun that lay snug in his lap as he drove along the dark and lonely roads. He had put out a mandatory curfew for the townspeople, which didn't bode well with most residents, but it was a necessary inconvenience nonetheless.

As he tooled at a steady pace down the town's main strip he couldn't help but to stop right in front of the blackened market. He sat and smirked at the recollection of picking both Rayshawn and Keyshawn up for stealing potato chips out of the store. Leon remembered how much he wanted to yell their ears off for doing such a dastardly deed, and how hard of a worker their mother was, but no matter how mad he was at them, he just couldn't bring himself to say one harsh word to them.

Despite the carnage that it had wrought upon the six victims that it had destroyed, Leon still found it difficult to bring himself to believe that such an evil thing could even exist, and that the same abomination was in his town. Ever since he was a boy, he had become accustomed to strange happenings in Sullinger, he, much like all the other born residents had no choice.

He wanted a rational explanation to it all. Leon wanted to see an overgrown bear run out in front of him just so he could disprove the notion of a monster was prowling his town.

The day had overwhelmed the man to the point where he wanted to just pack both himself and his fiancée up and leave for brighter pastures. From meeting the two agents to wrapping his own kin in plastic bags and shipping them both off to his outhouse for cold storage, there really wasn't much else Leon wanted to do that evening but throw it all in and escape.

But there was still that one last ounce of valor left inside of him that wanted to see the entire ordeal over at last. It wasn't so much that he wanted to be the hero, or that he was out for revenge, Leon wanted finality. He wanted everything to end right then and there. No more murder, no more death. The man begged for peace in his long life, something that he had been seeking ever since he was a child. Seeing the creature captured and taken out of Sullinger, for him, would be the final piece of the jumbled puzzle.

As he carried on down one dark road after another, Leon suddenly and unexpectedly found himself right in front of Millard's house. He could see only the living room light on.

Leon wanted to go in and shout incessantly at the man for being such the stubborn bull that he was. For not caring enough to even say one word before seeing both his daughter and grandchild being carted off. But Leon was well aware that no matter how much a person screamed and beat on him, Millard Lang was stone, from head to toe. He realized that if the deaths of his own children couldn't crack the age old granite then nothing on earth possibly ever could.

In a way, he felt sorry for Millard. The man had nothing left in the world, and Leon believed that was the way he wanted it. He wanted to be all alone, to himself, no more aggravation. Leon longed for the same thing, and that alone scared him to death.

Without any further delay, Sheriff Leon grabbed the steering as tight as he could before veering away from the old man's homestead like a man on fire.

*   *   *

The television inside of Millard's home was on. The man could see shapes and sizes on the screen in front of him, but that was all they were. In his tanked state of mind, everything on the TV set were mere blurs.

The broken man laid on his stinking couch completely naked with empty beer cans strewn all around him and a half full bottle of Magnum dangling in his right hand. He was drooling all over himself while something that resembled a song came dragging out of his mouth.

He was hot, sweaty and as rank smelling as a farm animal. Half alive at that point, he wallowed about in his own filth on the couch until he managed to sit up and face the window in front of him.

He glared deeply out into the pitch black of the night as if he were detecting a presence from the yard. He stared on and on until his foggy eyes pointed straight at the sight of a tall figure lurching out of the barn and towards the shack.

Millard sat perfectly still on the couch with his mouth hanging wide open and his face drooping while urinating all over himself. The flies swooped and buzzed all around him as the window gathered more steam with every passing minute.

The man eventually gathered all of what was left of his

strength and stumbled outside with his bottle of whiskey in hand. The evening was hot and steamy, too hot even for nightfall, but for Millard, it was a simple warm and comfortable twilight.

The fireflies that swam to and fro appeared more like big city lights flashing off and on in his fuzzy eyes. He couldn't even feel the mud squish in between his bare feet as he staggered towards the slender figure ahead of him.

The two lumbered towards the other until both met face to face for the first time in their tumultuous relationship. Millard held his bottle of Magnum straightforward like he was offering it up to the thing as a peace offering.

He had to squeeze his eyes just to make out the form of the intruder, but after a few more uncoordinated steps he knew fully well what it was.

The figure stood tall and hushed over Millard, exhaling smoke out of its nostrils and into the man's wild hair. Millard looked up at the thing before placing his free hand on its rock solid chest; it felt like touching a cement wall covered in a slippery gel.

Still wobbling back and forth, the old man hiccupped, "Motherfucker…you killed my…kids."

The creature didn't budge an inch; it remained stationary over Millard while still breathing in and out like a raging bull after a violent rampage. Millard tried his best to at least catch a mere glimpse of its eyes that appeared beady, almost not there at all.

"Dammit…where in the fuck am I?" He stuttered as he teetered from side to side.

Just then, the brute took a slight step backwards, which in turn caused Millard to lose his footing to where he had to go down to one knee. From there, he vomited all over the ground.

Millard wiped his mouth before standing back up and once again placing his hands on the creature's hard face. "Why'd you kill them?" He whimpered into the thing's face. "I ain't got nothin' else 'round here."

The thing took Millard's hands from off its face, and with its own claws held them apart while gawking down at the old man. Millard appeared as though he were ready to break down and cry right there in front of the beast, but what looked like tears in his eyes was instead just the glassiness of both too much alcohol and not enough sleep.

Then, something began to cause Millard's ears to vibrate at that moment. His head spun around in every direction trying to find just where the noise he was hearing was coming from.

After nearly a whole minute of gawking wildly into the blackness of night, Millard's eyes opened wide to see something emerge from out of the dark, by way of the road.

Shivering as if he were freezing, Millard whispered, "Here it comes again, boy."

The frightened old man snatched his hands from out of the beast's hold and quickly hid behind it, cowering for his life.

Judging by the creature's calm demeanor, it seemed as though Millard and only Millard could hear and the see the horse that was galloping into his yard and closing in fast. His body shuddered and quaked with raw fear as the horse and its rider came to a full stop just a few feet away from where he and the creature were already standing. The rider sat on its jet black steed looking down at the old man.

The horseman then dismounted the animal and limped towards Millard. The closer the rider lurched the more the old man could hear the chains that were hooked around its ankles clink and clank across the ground. He could see its hideous face come into the view thanks in part to the bright full moon shining down from the starry sky.

The rider had the appearance of a scarecrow, complete with a tattered hat and strands of straw that protruded from just about every portion of its hulking body. Its legs were covered in a pair of ragged pants.

But it was the face that always seemed to grip the old man to the edge of fear and beyond. It had only a skull with a pair of yellow eyes and a thick, black stripe that struck down the middle of both. Its hands were that of a black man's that had broken, rusty cuffs on both, as well as bleeding blisters all over them like he had been toiling out in a field all day and night long.

The moment the rider reached out to Millard, the old man began to egg on the creature in front of him. "Go on, go and kill that motherfucker! Ya killed everyone else, go on and kill that damn thing!" he screamed hysterically while falling backwards to the ground.

The beast only turned back to Millard and watched as he crawled and wallowed about in the mud like a grazing swine. The horseman then retracted his scarred hands before turning and limping back to his waiting stallion.

From the ground, Millard could see his own naked self riding shotgun behind the rider. He had a pair of hollowed out, maggot ridden eyes and a shameful look on his sweaty face. The old man turned his face out of terror; he could only hear the horse gallop out of his yard.

Millard frantically tried to get to his feet, but it seemed that every attempt that he made was an abject failure, his hands and feet were entirely too slippery and the world around him was racing by way too fast.

Just then, Millard could feel something cold and hard grasp his body. Soon, he could see the ground leave him, as well as his yard that appeared to be passing him by at light speed.

Eventually, he found himself back inside his own house where his head softly hit the foot of the couch. Millard's vision was grainy at best; it was like he was looking through a dirty screen door from yards back.

He could see the beast stand in front of him just looking down with such an odd curiosity. The television in front blared on and on about only God knew what. At that point, both Millard's vision and hearing were becoming blurs. Suddenly, he could feel the calming sensation of unconsciousness begin to settle in as his muscles tensed up and his body began to shake and squirm.

Millard's lazy tongue went on endlessly about Shirley, hardheaded grandboys and yellow eyed scarecrows before the beast before him drew near to his face.

There was nothing more to hear.

Chapter 19

I t was both a cool and relaxing sensation, one that he didn't want to awaken from; a soothing feeling that Millard hadn't experienced in quite some time. From one end of his memories to the other raced Courtney, Rayshawn and other fond reminisces.

The warmth that he was basking in was such an orgasmic oasis that all he could do was smile. There really wasn't much else for him to do. Soon, something wet began to caress his rough face; the wetness was soon followed by a soft caress across his head. That was when the sudden shock settled in; it was so abrupt that his eyes didn't have any choice but to snap wide open.

"What the fuck?" he hollered as he wrestled about like a lunatic inside his own bathtub.

"Be still, it's just me!" Millard's lady urged from behind him, trying in earnest to restrain his arms. "Be still, Millard!"

It took a while before Millard could fully comprehend just what was taking place. In front of him was his fan that was blowing cool air from left to right as he and his friend both sat in the warm tub.

Once he realized that he was soaking inside his own bathtub the commotion that he was putting up soon ceased and a pacifying calm started to blanket his stiff body all over again.

His young friend continued to splash and rub Millard's smelly body down with the warm, soapy water as he fixated his eyes on the moldy, loose tile behind the fan.

Now that he was wide awake, the soothing relief that he had enjoyed while asleep had all but dissipated. The grim reality of conciseness brought only images of scarecrows and barnyard demons.

By then, Millard didn't know and really didn't care if what took place the night before was part of his drunken rampage or as real as the water he was lying in, all he cared about at that point was forgetting every aspect of death altogether. He wanted to forget everything that took place, from Shirley to Courtney and Rayshawn. He wanted his mind erased of it all permanently.

* * *

It was half past eleven that morning. As clean as he had been in days, Millard was clothed in only a pair of dirty brown overalls as he stood over the kitchen sink stirring a glass of Pepto Bismol and four ounces of Tequila. Neither he nor his lady could explain the physicality's of just how or why the potion worked so well on hangovers, but it was something that was never questioned, only relished like a flu vaccine.

Before he could even lift the glass to drink, a knock at the front door suddenly struck in.

Agitated, he slammed the glass onto the sink before storming into the living room to find mud tracks, both small and large, layered all over the floor. Immediately, he knelt down and rubbed out as much of the mess as possible.

From there he opened the door to the find the pastor of the church from across the field standing on the other end with a dismayed look on his portly face.

With a skittish stutter in voice, the man said, "Mr. Lang, I know that you and I haven't gotten along these past few years, but I just came by to give my regards to you and your family over the loss of your daughter and grandchild. The good Lord works in very strange ways, and—

"Nigga, shut the hell up and tell me somethin'." Millard blurted out. "You said the other day that my dog was over at your church. What was she doin' there?"

"Well, sir, she was scratchin' and clawin' at the front door. When my wife opened to see who it was, the dog just ran inside and hid up under the alter. It was almost like she was scared of somethin'."

Millard stood for a few moments and glanced at the aged floor boards of the porch while imagining his frightened best friend trying to escape from the beast. Then, with red eyes, the old man stared dead at the pastor and said in a gruff tone, "That's all I wanted to know. Now, get the hell outta here. And don't come back 'round here no more. Ya hear me? No more."

The pastor lowered his head before softly uttering, "Yes, Brotha Lang, I hear you."

Millard watched as the man sorrowfully turned and carried himself down the porch and out of sight completely.

The old man stood bitterly at the doorway for a few more moments before shutting the door and carrying himself to his bedroom to find his friend seated on the bed with a troubled appearance on her pale face. He could sense that all that had taken place was affecting her to the point where she could no longer tolerate it. Though he never questioned her, he was shocked to see her return after seeing two dead bodies in his barn.

He stood above her for a second or two before asking, "Are you hungry?"

At first, she acted as though she didn't hear him while she put on her sleeveless undershirt. Gradually, she lifted her head and replied, "No not really."

There was something inside of Millard that wanted to explode at her blasé response. Something that wanted to react with a nasty harshness, but he held on to himself, as tight as he could.

"Well…I dunno, maybe we can go up to Jackson and—

"Millard," the young woman all of the sudden jumped up from off the bed, "can't we just leave this place and never come back? Can't we just leave this whole town and go off somewhere together? I can't stand to be here anymore."

"After what happened yesterday?" he questioned like he was surprised.

Wiping tears from her eyes, she answered, "Not only that, but everything. Millard, this town is horrible. Nothing good ever happens here. Now…now Courtney and Rayshawn are dead. And that thing back at the creek. Millard, I can't sleep! I keep seeing that thing kill those boys!"

As he stood next to her, Millard could hardly even stand to look the woman in the eye. An awful sense of entrapment enveloped his entire body.

Clearing his throat, Millard said, "Okay…we'll go. Go ahead and get the rest of your clothes on. We gotta go and get somethin' to eat first."

Before he could even turn to walk away, the lady said, "Millard, don't you think we need to talk?"

"Talk about what?"

"About Courtney and Rayshawn," she carefully treaded.

Millard rolled his eyes and said in a loud voice, "I ain't got shit to talk about! Don't start in on me!"

"But they were your children. And what about Keyshawn?" she pleaded.

"Who," Millard frowned strangely.

"You're other grandson, Millard. What are you going to do about him?"

"Leon said that his granny would be down here soon, I guess. Hell, I don't know and damn sure don't give a rat's ass!"

Millard detached himself from his friend before going to the dresser drawer to retrieve an undershirt. Once he was through putting it on he spun around to find his lady still standing in the middle of the floor with a stone glare in her brown eyes. He realized that that same stare had been there ever since he mentioned Keyshawn's grandmother just a second earlier. The old man just twisted his lips as to say that he wasn't impressed before bolting out of the bedroom and into the kitchen to not only drink his liquid mixture, but to also retrieve a very valuable item from within the sink's cabinet.

He rooted and searched until his hand came in contact with a rusted coffee can. Without taking out the contents within the can, Millard shut the cabinet door, took off for the front door and headed straight for his truck.

He sat inside, and surprisingly, waited patiently for his lady to get dressed and come along. Outside it felt like one could just die from heat exhaustion, but the temperature was secondary to Millard. He couldn't keep his jittery eyes off the barn that sat in front of him. It was like he was waiting for it to come right out. But after so much anticipation, nothing but a lone field mouse snuck its way out of the dreaded structure.

Somewhat disappointed, Millard gripped his beloved can as tight as he could before finding the strength to turn away from the barn and start the truck's ignition.

The animal inside of him wanted to yell at his girlfriend to come along…but he chose to wait a little longer.

* * *

A person could always tell when the state capitol was drawing near simply by watching the spacious scenery improve with every passing mile. There had been absolute silence in the truck for well over an hour. Millard drove with his lips glued shut and his nappy hair flowing in the wind. The only thing that seemed to bother him physically was the leftovers of the binge drinking from the night before, besides that, he was a picture of dark isolation.

He could hear his lady's stomach growl and gurgle more and more. Every so often Millard would glance over at her. Her head was hanging out the window like a dog sucking in air. The more he stared at her the more the very sight of her upset his own gut.

The very instant the truck crossed the Jackson line Millard immediately spotted a Chevron station just a few yards up ahead. With a lead foot he pressed down on the gas as hard as he could and pulled right into the station.

Stopping right in front of the cashier's station Millard put the truck in park. He then unscrewed the top of his coffee can and pulled out a wad of bills.

"Take it," he grunted at the woman, handing her the money.

Completely floored and turning pale, the woman sat back in her seat and said, "Millard, those are hundred dollar bills. Gas is only $1.05."

"I know that, just take it and go!"

Trembling from head to toe, the woman stuttered, "Go… go where?"

"Go on and get the hell outta here!"

Millard watched as her facial features changed dramatically in seconds from worried to outright pain stricken. She leaned back away from the wad of bills that were being handed to her like it was poisonous. With tears in her eyes, her voice broke, "What...what are you talking about, Millard? Is there something in the gas station that you want me to get?"

"I want you to get your ass out of my damn truck and go on somewhere!"

The woman took the money and counted each and every bill. "Millard, this is six thousand dollars!" She said out loud as tears the size of raindrops fell on the seat. "But, Millard, I—

Aggravated and downright enraged, Millard hopped out of the truck, stomped over to the other side and roared, "Don't sit there and start all that fuckin' cryin'!"

With as much frenzy as he could collect, Millard flung open the door and yanked her by the arm out of the vehicle and onto the steaming hot pavement, allowing hundred dollars bills to fly everywhere.

"Get the fuck outta here!" Millard barked as he slammed the door shut and walked back to his side of the truck.

The old man didn't bother to look back in the rearview mirror at his lady; he felt that had he done so then he would have grown ever madder than he already was. Even as he tore out of the station and down the road he could still hear her shrill voice screaming and crying for him to come back.

* * *

Millard arrived back in Sullinger, in record time. All he wanted to do was go back home and close his stinging eyes for the rest of the day. Surprisingly to him, his lady friend's strident pleas were still ringing in his already thumping head. He thought that he would have shoved both her voice and image out of his mind by the time he got back in town, but no such luck, she was stuck in the back of his throat like a bad cough. Even the smell of her peach scented perfume still lingered, along with the tobacco aromas that hang around in his truck.

He whipped his tired old vehicle into the parking lot of Mikey's diner, left the engine running and got out. Without a single thought rambling through his head, Millard strolled into the half-filled establishment and made a direct bee-line for the kitchen.

"Millard, don't come in her startin' no trouble!" Mikey, the short, unshaven owner of the diner snapped as he dropped his spatula onto the hot stove and ran up behind Millard.

Millard stopped halfway between the kitchen's threshold and the stove. With his eyes only, he gawked around the dingy looking kitchen in search of something. The scent of ham and cheese sandwiches felt good to his aching stomach, but he ignored it the best he could.

The second he caught sight of what he came for he right away marched over to a wall and grabbed Courtney's grease stained white apron that was hanging from a hook.

Mikey looked as if he wanted to say or do something, instead, he remained still with a look of shame holding his small face.

Despite her father, Courtney was a well-liked person in town, which was why not one person that inhabited the diner uttered a single word as tight-lipped Millard, with apron in hand, walked out of the establishment and back to his truck.

* * *

Millard ripped down the dirt road at speeds well over 80mph before coming to a stop at lonely Claymore's Creek. He got out of the truck and wandered down the hill that led to the water.

There were still scant traces of blood patched in different areas of the embankment, and considering what took place two days earlier Millard didn't have to worry all too much about others interrupting him.

The old man stopped short of the part of the creek where he was strung up and dunked under. In all the madness of the event he somehow recalled seeing the beast swim towards him in the midst of his lynching. How it bypassed him and instead attacked his assailants. He also, unwittingly, remembered seeing Courtney and Rayshawn's dead bodies hanging from the rafters of his barn.

Millard was accustomed to gruesome visuals, no matter how ugly they appeared before his eyes. In the past the man had seen family members taken in more vile ways than he would have cared to recollect. Shirley was his best friend, but she was an animal, it was his daughter and grandson that caused his fleeting breath to escape him every now and then.

Millard held tight to Courtney's apron, he sniffed the aroma of bacon draped heavy all over the fabric. For a brief moment it reminded him of when she was a little girl. And just as quickly as the memory came, that was as fast as it eluded him.

All Millard could do at that point was grip the piece of raggedy cloth in his arthritic hands as the water from the creek splashed up against the sharp rocks beneath him.

Now, there was another mountain to conquer.

CHAPTER 20

Warm, heavy rain pounded Sullinger the following afternoon and didn't show any signs of letting up anytime soon. Folks in the town hoped that the torrential downpour would cool off the treacherous heat, but for the most part all the rain usually brought was more bloodthirsty mosquitos and stifling humidity.

Millard sat inside his truck listening to the rain beat up the already corroded metal. In front of him was a small, white chapel that sat pretty with its brand new coat of paint that people could see in the distance from the road.

He had been sulking in the parking lot for nearly fifteen minutes glancing back and forth from the chapel to the brown, 1986 Oldsmobile that was parked near the entrance. It was a vehicle that he had never laid eyes on before, but it wasn't difficult for him to figure out just who the driver was.

Feeling cramped and crunched inside his own truck, Millard heaved a huge sigh of discomfort before climbing out and defiantly walking towards the chapel with only his blue ball cap to cover his head in the pouring rain. He didn't even care if his blue jeans and Union Workers shirt got soaked along the way.

He pushed open the entrance doors and stepped inside

only to be greeted by an elderly white man that was dressed in an all-black suit and tie with his white hair slicked backwards.

"Sir, could I ask you to take off your hat while inside the church, please?" The kindhearted gentleman smiled.

"You can ask," Millard arrogantly replied before rolling his eyes and heading down the hallway to find a well lit room ahead of him.

In the room he could see a woman seated all alone clear down in the very front pew wearing a white flower hat and white dress. In front of her was a silver coffin with the lid wide open. Right away Millard could sense exactly what the new few moments had in store for him. He could feel his skittish stomach tighten, and what was once rain on his forehead had suddenly turned into sweat as he strolled down the aisle, splattering wetness all onto the white carpet beneath him. The overwhelming aroma of flowers inhabited the sanctuary to the point where Millard had to turn up his nose.

Without saying a single word, the man stopped and sat down next to the white woman in the front pew. She was a medium sized lady in her early fifties that had slight wrinkle lines that blessed her calm face and hands. She had curly brunette hair that smelled of a lemon scented perfume.

"I see the pallbearer wasn't able to get you to take off your hat." The woman said in her southern dialect while keeping her face clearly pointed at the casket in front of her.

"And I see that you've shaved your legs after all these years, too." Millard snidely remarked.

"And I smell that you haven't bathed since the seventies."

Uptight, Millard sat back in the pew, rested his left arm on the sidebar next to him and readied himself for combat.

"So, why is you up here in a white dress? Ain't this supposed to be a funeral?"

Sighing, the woman responded, "Most folks see funerals as a time of sadness. I, on the other hand, see it as a moment of cheer and happiness. My children have finally found peace. Therefore, I'm not here to mourn Courtney and Rayshawn, I'm here to celebrate them on their new path."

Twisting his lips as though she were speaking outright foolishness, Millard glanced back at the woman and said," I ain't seen you wear that old hat in years, gal."

"Gal," she giggled. "I see some things still ain't changed all too much." She then looked over at Millard and said, "Judging by your face it looks like you've been playing *Rocky* again. You still got that old outlaw in ya, huh?"

Millard rolled his eyes and turned the other cheek while trying to conjure a snappy comeback before the moment passed him by.

"It's funny that it should rain today, of all days. You should have been here earlier; the pallbearer said that this place hasn't been so packed in years."

Millard gawked around the chapel in search of something to say to the one person he had nothing in the world to say anything to.

"Where's the other boy at? What's his name?"

Groaning, the woman strongly emphasized, "Keyshawn, is with Courtney's best friend. I reckon I should have brought him along to the funeral as well, but I just didn't think it was right for him to see both his mother and brother laid up in some casket."

"It's better for youngens to see death now before they're grown." Millard assuredly remarked.

Laughing out loud, the woman said, "Uh oh, there goes the Millard Lang guide to life. Chapter eight, how to raise a child. What's the matter, too afraid to go up there and see your kids off one last time before they get buried?"

"I ain't got nothin' to see up there."

"Nothin' but your daughter and grandson," she snapped back.

"I've seen them before!"

"Dear God, man, I can see that not one shred of light has hit that dark, old heart of yours after all these years. You're like a record that just keeps on repeating itself."

Trying his best to keep the subject off of himself, Millard said, "So anyways, Courtney told me that you were down here some days ago."

Still watching the casket in front of her, the woman answered, "I came down to see how she and the boys were doin' after that storm. I must have gotten down on my hands and knees at least ten times beggin' and pleadin' with that child to come up to Ohio to live. She could get a decent job for a change; stop sweatin' away in someone's old kitchen. There's good schoolin' for the boys. She could finally get away from that good for nothin' Tyrone, once and for all." 'No, mama, I'm gonna make it on my own, no matter what.' "She always said."

Millard turned slightly to face the woman. For a few seconds he could actually hear Courtney right through her mother.

"That child was as stubborn as a stump mule. She must've gotten that from her father." The woman sarcastically grinned at Millard.

Millard only turned his sour face back to the coffin in front, not wanting to even look at the woman next to him any longer at that point.

"It was like she had something to prove to somebody. I just wish I would've begged a little more." She began to weep in a demure and shuttered fashion as to not allow anyone to see her tears.

Millard heard her sobs, but consoling others in their time of need and despair was not written anywhere in so called instruction manual. Tears, much like rain, would soon dry up and vanish.

"Now…now Keyshawn doesn't have a brother or mother anymore." The lady sniffed. "He keeps asking, 'Where's Rayshawn, grandma?' "And all I can say is that he and your mama had to go away for a while, honey."

Settling more into his pew, Millard exhaled, "Well, I can say this, she was a good girl, that Courtney."

Rolling her eyes, the woman scornfully remarked, "Millard, please, you barely even knew her."

"You wouldn't let me know her!" Millard all of the sudden erupted. "Every time a nigga tried to see the gal you just pushed me away!"

"God forgive me for wanting to keep my only child away from a boozing, pot smoking, woman beating bumb!"

"So now all of the sudden she's your child? Whenever you needed money she was our daughter, but whenever you got into one of your moods then she's yours!"

"Old man, the last thing I came down here for is to have it out with you!"

"Then don't start none and there sure as hell won't be none!"

At least three minutes passed before the woman crossed her thin legs and turned to Millard saying, "I'm having their bodies shipped back to Ohio after the funeral. I don't want either of them to be buried in this wicked town."

Twisting and squirming about in the warm pew like it was burning up, Millard turned to the woman and nonchalantly said, "Go on and do what you want to, Virginia. You always did anyways."

The two sat in their pew for another long pause before

Millard, having journeyed far beyond his threshold of agitation for one day, decided to get up from his seat and head for the door.

Virginia, too, stood up and followed in behind him straight outside into the hammering rain. "Millard, do you know why Rayshawn's face looks the way it does?" she shouted.

Millard continued on his way to his truck, not even taking the time to stop and answer her question.

"The funeral is at four! That's two and a half hours from now, just in case you're interested in joining us down at Perry's Corner!"

Through his rearview mirror Millard could see Virginia still standing in the saturating rain, helplessly watching him tear down the road. Even with their sizable distance apart he could still see her dreadful, insipid face as if she were inside the truck along with him.

His entire body burned with anger and confusion. He was mad as hell at Virginia and her loose lips, and he was confused on whether or not to attend the funeral. The last interment he appeared at was his father's back in 1978.

It wasn't fear that caused him to second guess, it was knowing that Virginia was right. He barely knew his own daughter, and as far as the boys went, he knew more about the lineage of a family of grizzly bears than he did his own grandsons' names.

He wanted so badly to ball up his fist and drive it straight into Virginia's face back at the chapel. It would have made him feel better, for the time being at least.

CHAPTER 21

The rain had let up to a steady sprinkle that afternoon, so it wasn't all too hard for Millard to see just what was taking place about two hundred yards ahead of him at the cemetery next to Perry's Corner.

Even though Virginia mentioned that the bodies would be buried in Ohio, she figured that a civil ceremony for all the friends and well-wishers would be a descent sendoff, being that the tiny chapel wouldn't have been able to accommodate the entire town.

With a glob full of chaw wrestling about in his mouth Millard looked on as Virginia, with Leon standing behind her, wiped her eyes and nose with a tissue while others stood and wept over the coffin. It was all for one woman and her child.

Millard, however, sat in his truck, moving only his tobacco chewing jaws from side to side. Just being two hundred yards away from the scene was mind numbing enough, and the last thing he wanted was to see a multitude of crying faces, that wasn't the way he wanted to remember his kin.

The old man looked on as five men lifted then lowered the flower laden casket into the ground. That was it for him. A mess of *Red Man* was spat out onto the ground, and the truck roared away.

Smoking weed and having sex were the various images that Millard tried to flood his brain with as he tooled down the rain slicked road while a bolt of lightning struck behind him in the firmament.

Their lifeless faces right before Leon and his deputy carried them both away kept running back into his head. The little boy's entire face had melted like it was placed in a bowl of hot wax. For a few transitory moments Millard tried to figure out just how it might have felt to be swallowed whole. The very jarring thought caused him to momentarily lose control of the steering wheel.

He felt claustrophobic, as if the world around him was closing in and waiting to devour him. He and God hadn't been the best of friends in years, but even the old man knew when he was being chased down. It wasn't the first time Millard had ever experienced such a vexing sensation, but for the first time in his life he could see that he was running out of road to run upon.

He was only ten minutes away from his house and he needed alcohol, in extreme doses nonetheless. To him, ten minutes was just another obstacle to stomp on.

As he pressed harder down on the gas, an unexpected whiff of cold air stiffened the man's bones. The bitter chill was soon followed by a strong stench that made Millard hold his nose before wisps of smoke began to fill the truck. Immediately, he pulled to the side of the road next to the woods and stopped.

From front to back and up and down he frantically searched until what looked like a face in the backseat started to take form. Soon, the rest of the body took shape until a large figure could be seen staring Millard face to face.

With sober, wide awake eyes, Millard Lang could at last see his unwanted visitor. It's wet face had the amalgamated, innocent appearance of an individual with Down Syndrome and a feline. Its light green, naked, emaciated body was slick with a translucent-like slime from its head to its clawed toes. It sat in the back seat just staring at Millard with a child-like sort of grin while snorting smoke from out of its nostrils.

Millard couldn't recount how many times he had ever been afraid in his life, or even recently for that matter. But at that instant, a moment in life when everything slowed to a steady crawl, he could feel fear not only creep up, but grab him from behind and shake him violently.

As scared as he was at that second, neither his face nor body showed it. The man was a picture of complete and absolute composure. With the cold in the truck not one trickle of sweat even bothered to bubble up.

Ever so gradually, he reached over to the passenger seat and grabbed his rifle before getting out of the truck and steadily carrying himself into the nearby forest. The creature followed in suit, climbing out of the vehicle and walking in behind the old man. With firm eyes locked ahead of him, Millard went along as the serene rain danced all over his head and face. He could hear the thing's heavy footsteps trail in behind him.

Millard stalked deeper into the forest until he came face to face with a tall oak tree. He then turned around to see the slender creature standing nearly thirty feet apart from him, just staring on endlessly, looking as though it were puzzled at what the old man was going to do next.

He didn't want to spend time gawking at it to try and figure out what it was. He wasn't by any means fascinated with its appearance or design. Millard only had but one thing in mind, and that was to eradicate the beast.

The man cocked his loaded weapon, raised it and fired at the thing point blank. But rather than it collapsing to the ground, the beast only backed away from the force of the slug like it was being shoved.

Millard once again shot at the thing, the loud sound of his rifle being fired echoed throughout the forest like a cannon. Like before, the thing only took several steps back. Millard fired over and over until his ammo was depleted. He noticed that every time a bullet hit the beast it sounded akin to something striking metal. Every so often it would make a growl; some of them were faint while others were loud and furious, like a raging lion roaring through a megaphone. They were ferocious enough to make the forest animals flee in terror.

"C'mon, c'mon and get me!" Millard dared. "Ya got everyone else, now come and get me, ya motherfucker!"

The beast let out a raspier grunt that seemed to even shake the old man for a brief glimpse. It then went down on all fours while continuing to stare at Millard like it were ready to attack.

"C'mon, ya bastard!" He continued on. "Sweet Mary keep callin' me home, callin' me home, callin' me home," the old man all of the sudden began singing as he readied himself for whatever assault was coming his way.

For years, Millard was always ready to die at a moment's notice. He had overheard people in town whisper quotes like, 'Why do all the good people in this town die and Lang keeps on living'? Or, 'Out of all the niggers the Klan has killed through the years, Millard is one that they keep missing'.

They were questions that the old man asked even himself many times over, and yet, God always seemed to keep him around for another day. Another day always turned into another month, and a month into years. Out of all the things that Millard hated about God, waking up each day was something he could never forgive.

The beast kept its stance focused solely on Millard. It then opened its mouth and started to grunt before standing back up and slowly back away.

"Come and get me! I've been waitin' for your stinkin' ass!" Millard angrily persisted until the mournful howls of bloodhounds in the distance behind him caused the man to cease his rant.

Both Millard and the creature turned westwards to where the commotion was emanating. The old man knew full well what was on the way, which was why he wasted no time in hobbling past the brute on his way back to his truck by the side of the road.

He was well aware that the posse that was hunting the creature also didn't care too much for him, either; and being that he didn't have any shells left in his gun, he wasn't about to go down without a fair fight.

The very instant he sped down the road Millard could hear a series of gunshots, as well as the painful screams of men and the roars of the beast ring out into the summer air. It became so visceral to hear that Millard had to roll up his window and cut on the radio just to shower it all out.

As much as he loathed Sullinger's "*Good old boys*", he didn't want to go back and view the waste. Just as long as the thing did the hunters worse than Courtney and Rayshawn, then he was well satisfied.

CHAPTER 22

In a blinding effort, Millard tried to return home as fast as he could without being seen by anyone along the way. His eerie, one on one encounter with his visitor, coupled with the grisly demise of the hunters were rapidly becoming faded pictures in his head.

Millard was a drained, blown out mess, both mentally and physically. His nerves of steel had eroded into nothing more than liquid, and his throbbing head only made him want to put a much needed bullet into his own brain. It was by no means the first time he felt so wiped out, but Millard could never recall feeling so buried underneath. The suffocating consciousness of all that had taken place ever since the storm was catching up with him while he was running at the speed of light just to get away.

Hour by hour the hammering rain was wilting away to a soft sprinkle which meant that Millard didn't have to use his windshield wipers so much. As he rounded the bend that led to his property, a startling sight seized him. Sitting on his porch was none other than his lady friend.

The old man could have wrecked his truck on the side of the road at that instant. He was shocked to see her back at his homestead considering all that had transpired recently. He wanted to get mad, but his confusion with her very presence kept his fury at bay.

Millard stopped the truck right in front of the house, got out and pranced his way over to the young lady who had her arms folded while getting soaked in the rain.

Before he could even reach the porch, Millard spotted the hundred dollar bills that he gave her the day before scattered all over the floorboards.

With smoking eyes, the old man grunted, "What the hell is you doin' back here?"

The young woman said absolutely nothing at first, instead, she kept her fiery eyes locked on Millard as if her blush red face were about to explode with wrathful vengeance.

"I asked you a damn question, gal!"

Scooping up the bills one by one, the woman stood to her feet and screamed into Millard's face, "I'm a grown woman, and you don't tell me when to leave! You don't have any right!"

Snatching the money out of her wet hands and stuffing them into his pants pockets, Millard began to advance towards the woman in an aggressive fashion. Pointing his finger, he snapped back, "Don't you go gettin' smart on me! I told you to get, and that's what I meant!"

The woman just turned her ever so defiant head in the opposite direction as if Millard weren't even there to begin with. Much like any man, Millard was never any good at telling what was on a woman's mind, and all the same, he couldn't have cared any less; her uncanny and stubborn behavior was just another part of the current madness that he wanted nothing to do with.

Staring bloody daggers into her eyes, Millard said, "Listen, I just got back from seeing that damn thing, and—

But before he could finish his sentence, the young lady

simply turned and strolled off inside the house through the front door. Usually in past cases with his friend, Millard would have had no problem showing her just who was in charge, but it was eating away at him as to why she bothered to come back at all, especially after he handed her six thousand dollars in cash to start a brand new life.

Enraged, Millard put his hands on his hips while allowing the sputtering rain to drench his face. As he started for the door, the sound of a vehicle pulling into his yard gave him reason to stop his every action. He looked back to see Virginia's Oldsmobile pulling right next to his truck. There was very little at that instant that could keep his breakfast from coming up right then.

The old man shuffled over to the car as Virginia, along with Keyshawn, climbed out. All three met each other halfway in the middle of the yard.

"What the hell is this?" Millard huffed.

Holding down her white hat, Virginia said, "I just figured you'd like to see your grandson one more time before we head back up to Ohio."

Without even looking down at the boy, Millard hastily replied, "I've seen him before. Now, get on your way. I got things goin' on right now"

Overlooking the old man, Virginia's eyes drowned at the sight of the shack before her. "My God, Millard, it looks like this house of yours never made it out of the nineteenth century. That is if you can still call it a house."

"Then turn around and get away as fast as you can if it offends you that much."

Sidestepping Millard's rude comment, Virginia gazed around the yard in search of something. "Leon said that they were murdered in your barn. C'mon, Keyshawn," Virginia said as she dragged the child along to the barn house.

"Where the hell is you goin to?" Millard yelled, hysterically running in behind the two. "Come back here, now!"

Virginia didn't stop until she made her way short of the barn's threshold, that was when Millard jumped in front of them both and immediately halted their further progression.

"You ain't gettin' in there and that's all there is to it!"

"I just wanna get a quick look at where they were found." Virginia urged as she desperately bobbed her head left to right and up and down, trying to see past Millard's tall frame.

"What the hell do you wanna see that for?"

"I think I have a right to see, Millard!"

"With the boy here?" he pointed.

Virginia looked Millard dead in the eye before saying, "It's just like you said, youngens have to learn early."

"You all get goin'!" Millard obstinately growled.

"Well, aren't you at least gonna invite the two of us in for a quick drink on such a hot day before we go?"

Millard happened to look down at Keyshawn. He, much like his late brother, was a chunky sight. Courtney was never any good at keeping her boys' hair well kept, so it didn't surprise the old man to see the child's nappy hair hidden up under a red ball cap. The more he peered down at the boy's startled eyes that was all the more he could see Rayshawn screaming for his life before the creature snatched it away from him. He wanted to see both him and his grandmother leave and leave forever.

"They got water down at Mikey's place!" Millard barked. "Go get some there!"

Virginia stood boldly in front of Millard with an offhanded grin on her wet face. "I think your water will do just fine, Mr. Lang."

Millard watched as Virginia heaved Keyshawn back to his shack. He knew Virginia inside and out. He was well aware as to why she wanted to go inside, and it had nothing to do with quenching her thirst.

He closed his eyes and clinched his fists as tight as he could before taking off behind them. Once he made it inside he saw his lady emptying overflowing buckets of water from the leaking roof.

"I wasn't aware that you had company." Virginia blushed at the sight of the young lady.

The young woman, who had a red bucket in both hands, stopped midway to the kitchen to turn back to eye grandmother and grandson as though she were looking at two intruders.

Looking back at Millard, Virginia quaintly smirked, "Well, Mr. Lang, aren't you gonna introduce us to your friend?"

Shrugging his shoulders, Millard shut the door and replied, "I hadn't planned on it."

Without uttering a mumbling word the young woman resumed her trek into the kitchen. The splashing of water along with the boorish ruckus of slamming buckets sounded as if she were redoing the entire kitchen itself.

"Cute girl," Virginia remarked with a nonchalant quirk in her tone. She then began to stroll about the dank living room, gawking around in absolute amazement. "God, Millard," she gasped, "I can't believe you still live in this…pit. You know you can do better than this, old man. This is below human standards, even for the likes of you."

"It works for me." Millard callously rebutted. "If you don't like it then get your asses out."

"Before we go, I was just wondering if you still had that one picture of Courtney when she was in the second grade. I have all of her pictures from every school year but that one."

Scratching his unkempt beard, he responded, "I dunno, it's probably 'round here somewhere. I don't feel like lookin' for it now." As soon as he through answering to Virginia, Millard's attention sailed down to Keyshawn. "Ain't you got nothin' to say, boy?" he raised his voice.

Keyshawn stood at full attention the very second his grandfather spoke to him. The alarmed look on the child's face suggested that Millard's voice scared him to no end.

"I'm talkin' to you, boy!" Millard yelled. "Why'd your mama let you and your brother get so fat, anyways?"

That's enough," Virginia stepped in front of the boy. "That's probably the very first thing you've ever said to him in all his life. Act like you've got some sense for a change." Virginia then took a hold of Keyshawn's hand and headed for the door before pausing and saying, "I guess I'll have to come back and get that picture before we leave."

"Do whatever you want, I don't give a damn." Millard's lazy tongue responded.

Just then, the young lady rambled back into the living room and stood next to her man with a disgusted glare on her face.

"So, where is ya'll stayin' at? Millard asked as he gladly opened the door.

"Surely not in this town," Virginia said as she stopped at the door. "I've got a room at the Motel Six up in Jackson."

"When are you leaving?" The young lady cantankerously spoke out loud.

For a few seconds a forced smile came across Virginia's face before she replied, "I still have a few loose ends that need tyin' up, but we should be gone by the day after tomorrow."

Millard stood by and watched as his lady and Virginia stared each other down as though they were two rams ready lock horns. He could spot the green-eyed monster in his woman's eyes from a mile away. In any other case the old man would have been delighted in seeing such a scene play out before him, but there was nothing even remotely humorous about what was taking place, he felt nauseous just being alive.

With the same crafty smile that she had been wearing ever since she first arrived, Virginia said to the young woman, "Honey, you don't have to look at me like that, what this man and I had twenty-four years ago lasted exactly three minutes." Virginia then turned around to face Millard and cunningly smirk, "I counted, Mr. Lang."

Millard only frowned before turning his blushing face in the other direction. He couldn't explain for the life of him what was holding him back from wrapping his hands around her tenacious neck.

"And please don't forget to find that picture, Millard." Virginia implored as she and Keyshawn headed for the door. "I know you still have it."

Both Millard and his lady watched as grandmother and grandson walked back to their car and drove away. Millard then turned up his nose and slammed the door shut behind him before starting for the couch.

"So, what did she mean by that?" The lady asked as she stood in front of Millard with her arms folded.

Rolling his eyes, the old man griped, "What the hell is you talkin' about now?"

"That comment she made about she counted."

"What the hell do you think she meant?" He screamed. "I'm sick and tired, and I ain't in no mood for no more bullshit!"

"What bullshit are you talking about, Millard?"

"You know damn good and well what I'm talkin' about!"

"I just asked a simple question, that's all!"

Jumping up from off the couch, Millard stood before his

woman and yelled, "Let me ask you a question! What is you doin' pickin' up buckets around here for?"

"I'm just trying to clean up a bit." She shuddered.

Advancing closer towards her, Millard gritted his teeth and said, "Look here, gal, I don't need—

Millard was yet again interrupted; at that instant the door was practically being knocked down by four loud thuds. Infuriated, the old man stomped over and flung open the door to see none other than Leon dressed in a black suit and tie, and a short, fat, black woman standing by his side.

"What is it, boy?" Millard hollered straight into Leon's face.

Momentarily stunned, Leon stuttered, "Well…we just stopped by to see how you was doin'. Me and Cornelia were just comin' from the cemetery."

As though he were exhausted, Millard exhaled and stood aside to allow his unwanted guests to step inside. He then shut the door and sat himself down on the wooden chair that was placed adjacent from the couch.

Although Leon was more than used to his cousin's accommodations, Cornelia on the other hand appeared as if she had stepped into a whole new universe. Her scrounged face politely tried not to take in all of the foul looking and smelling décor of the house, but it was virtually impossible to resist. She pulled up the bottom of her black dress and sat down next to Leon on the smelly couch. She then straightened her black church hat, crossed her thick legs and coughed a nervous cough, seemingly anything to distract from her current unspeakable experience.

Glancing behind him, Leon said, "Oh, I almost didn't see you back there, young missy. This here is my fiancée, Cornelia. Cornelia, this is"

Picking at his fingers, Millard sternly commanded, "Go on back in the kitchen and do what you was doin' earlier."

Without parting her lips, the woman did as she was ordered. Leon and Cornelia oddly glanced over at each other before simultaneously clearing their throats.

"Well, Millard, I know that you two haven't been on good terms over the years, but... did you know that your mama passed away?" Leon asked with a painful grunt in his tone. "I went over there to see if she wanted to go to the funeral, and well...it looked like she had turned off her own oxygen tank."

Millard sat and picked away at his peeling fingernails. He realized that Leon was awaiting some kind of response, perhaps even emotion, but the old man never even batted an eyelash. His cousin's words were like a raindrop falling into the sea.

"Millard, did you hear what I just said, man? I found your mama dead in—

"I heard ya, boy." Millard sighed. "I may be goin' blind, but I ain't deaf. It's just as well; the woman was ninety-five years old. It's better this way, she's outta her misery."

Allowing endless seconds of shocked pause to pass before speaking another word, Leon opened his mouth and said, "Well, me and Corey took her body down to the morgue. I can give her a proper burial next to uncle Switch, that's what aunt Elma always wanted. As far as her house is concerned, I was figurein' that—

"What else have you heard about this thing that's runnin' around town?" Millard intervened.

"Well, not much, besides what you and your girlfriend told me the other day, we ain't got much to go on right now."

"Hmm," the old man groaned as he slouched down into his chair.

"Boy, that sure was one fine funeral." Leon babbled on. "Pastor Jackson sure put his all into it today. And Keisha, Margaret Sheldon's youngen, she sang her little tail off. As pregnant as she is, she sure can sing. How old is she again, darlin'?"

"I think she must be fourteen or fifteen."

"Speakin' of, we passed Virginia leavin' outta here as we were pullin' in."

"Yeah," Millard awoke, "she just dropped by to see if she could stir up some more bullshit."

"I don't think she wanted to stop by for that, Millard." Leon pleaded.

"Whaddya mean, boy? She's always been that way. All women are like that."

"I'm sorry, but to what way are you stating, Mr. Lang?" Cornelia all of the sudden asked.

"You know how you gals get sometimes."

"We gals," Cornelia sat back and questioned.

"What Cornelia means is that she's just never met Virginia face to face before today, that's all." Leon nervously jumped in.

"You're husband to be says that you're a school teacher. Is that right?"

"Yes it is, Mr. Lang."

"I see." The old man rubbed his chin. You sound educated."

"Yes, Mr. Lang, I'll be starting at the school this coming school year." Cornelia proudly proclaimed. "Tell me something, I know that it may not be any of my business, but I was just wondering why you never bothered to show up at your daughter and grandson's funeral."

Without even looking in her direction, Millard simply stated, "You're right, it ain't none of your business."

Cornelia sat back with a staggered expression on her chunky face like she was told to go straight to hell. Leon on the other hand just cracked a shit-eating smile, looking as though he were trying to think of some way to quell the brewing storm that was looming over their collective heads.

"Ya know, Millard, I was tellin' Cornelia how we would play in the old barnyard when we was youngens." Leon fretfully chuckled. "How uncle Switch would get after us for bein' up in that loft."

Ignoring his cousin, Millard looked past Leon and said to Cornelia, "You don't sound like you're from around here, woman. Where the hell is you from anyways?"

Right then, the radio in Leon's squad car crackled to life with the vibrant sounds of a young man screaming at the top of his lungs.

"I think that's Corey goin' crazy." Leon said as he shot up from off the couch and stepped outside.

"I'll be right here, baby." Cornelia replied as she sat tall and stout on the couch ready to take on the single most challenging confrontation of her middle-aged life. "Well, Mr. Lang, if you really must know, I was born and raised in South Carolina. My father was an Army serviceman, so we were always moving from state to state."

"I see," Millard murmured, sounding unimpressed. "So, you think you're one of them smart gals, huh, with your proper talk and all?"

"I have yet to make such a claim to knowing everything, Mr. Lang. I just—"

"One of my kids' mama's was fat like you." He interposed. "She thought she knew everything, but apparently she wasn't smart enough to go to the hospital and get her tits checked out before dyin' of cancer. Dumbass woman," he growled under his breath.

Looking at the floor and smirking, Cornelia sighed, "You don't seem to have a high regard for women, do you, Millard?'

"Well, it all depends on what they're worth. Back in my day, women stood proud. You didn't have to question a female back then. But today, ya'll get out there and give it up to every Jim, Bob and Leon that comes on through. Ya'll got no respect for yourselves no more. Ya'll whine and cry until you get your way, and God forbid you don't get you way, because then you'll be burnin' your bras and growin' underarm hair like ya did a decade ago."

"Stop right there," Cornelia persistently pointed. "I may be a Christian woman, but I know when to put a clamp on folks like yourself."

"Then go on and do it, gal!" Millard sniped back as he sat up in his seat and beamed his red veined eyes into Cornelia's forehead.

"I can understand that you're upset over the deaths of your children, but the last thing you want to do is take it out on me or anybody else!"

Grinning from ear to ear, the old man said, "There ya go, tryin' to analyze somebody again."

"Leon mentioned that you were a little on the impossible side."

"Look here—

"No, you look here; I've known plenty of people like yourself over the years. You're the same kind of person both my father and grandfather was! You have all this hurt and hell deep inside of you, and the only way you know how to deal with it is by taking it out on others!"

"Uh huh," Millard sat back. "And where'd you learn that from, the Donahue show?"

"I learned it from—

"Shut the fuck up, bitch!" Millard shot back like a rabid

dog. "Your problem is that you come down to Sullinger, of all places, fuck the sheriff a couple of times, and think you have it all together!"

Cornelia uncrossed her tight legs and balled up her fists while her dark face took on a more dim hue of red. "You did not just call me a bitch!" She slowly stated. "I know you didn't call me a bitch!"

"I know I did, you're the only bitch I see right now!"

Getting up from off the couch, Cornelia yelled, "I don't have to sit here and take this shit!"

"You're just like all the other bitches out there! No wonder ya'll can't keep a damn man!"

"You're damn right, I'm just all the other bitches out there! I'm sick and tired of good for nothing niggas like your sorry black ass!"

"Get your fat ass outta here before I kick it!"

"You can kiss my fat ass on my way out of this shithole you call a home!"

Leon all of the sudden came right back with an astonished look on his face. "What on God's green earth is going on in here?"

"I need to get up out of this stinkin' place before I suffocate and die!" Cornelia screamed at Leon before heading for the door. "That bastard needs to be put out of his misery!"

Leon watched as Cornelia stormed past him on her way out the door. He then turned to Millard who was still wearing his haughty signature grin like a trophy.

Sighing as though he was exhausted, Leon asked, "Millard, what happened now?"

Millard shrugged his shoulders and answered, "Don't ask me, boy, your woman was the one goin' crazy up in here."

Leon scratched his sweaty head before looking up at the failing celling. "Ya know, Millard, I've put up with a lot from you these past few years, but you just don't know when or where to draw the line."

Millard turned his head the other way, prepping himself to hear yet another scolding tirade from his cousin.

"I wanna tell ya somethin', I've been lonely for nine years ever since Paula passed. Now that I've finally found someone that can make me happy again, here this comes."

Right then, Millard found it within himself to turn back to face Leon. But rather than the usual admonishing he received whenever he found himself caught in a jam, the old man instead got something he never expected, something he wasn't prepared for.

With a jittering voice, Leon continued, "I just got a call from Corey; he said that the McConnell brothers are missing out in woods somewhere."

"Ain't that a bummer?" Millard callously remarked.

"Yeah, it is," Leon strongly answered back. "It is a bummer because something evil is happening in this town, Millard! Everything is fallin' apart all at once and I can't keep up no more! Personally, I think you know more than what you're tellin' me about this whole situation! You're takin' it all too good!"

"What else can I know?" Millard hollered. "The damn thing killed two of mine, boy!"

"Nigga, I am sixty-two years old!" Leon shouted furiously, shaking from head to toe. "I ain't been a boy in years! You would think that after all that you've been through in your life that something inside of you would just calm down, but instead, it's all just made you worse! You're slowly dyin' alone with this old house of yours and you don't even give a damn!"

Millard's eyes scaled up the ceiling before he wiped his head and noticed his lady in the kitchen pretending to clean up while catching brief glimpses of the battle in the living room. He then sized up his cousin with his livid eyes. At that juncture he didn't recognize the large man who was standing in front of him, even though he thought he knew him all his life.

With his hands on his hips and tears welling up in his eyes, Leon stood and gazed around the shack before looking back down at Millard saying, "He's on his way, Millard Lang. God's on his way for you."

Millard watched as Leon bolted out of the house before getting up and slamming the door shut behind him as hard as could, allowing dust and parts of the ceiling to fall to the floor.

Like he was trapped inside a cell, the old man paced the floor back and forth, mumbling incoherent words that became more translatable with every step he made. "Who the fuck do these motherfuckers think they is? They come up in my damn house and try to tell me somethin'! Fuckin' cocksuckers! That damn cunt trash Virginia! Fat ass Leon and his fuckin bitch! All these faggots need to get the fuck outta my face before I kill somebody up in here!" He ranted like a lunatic while swinging his fists in the air.

There was an active volcano inside, it had been there simmering and bubbling ever since Shirley was found dead. It was festering to a boiling point; the steam was the venom he was spewing as he paced.

He picked up and tossed the lamp onto the floor. From there he knocked his chair onto its side and kicked over the television set all while carrying on about how folks were trying to tell him his business. He had totally blacked out to the point where he couldn't even see where he was.

* * *

Outside, on the other side of the front door, crouched the ghastly intruder with its ear pressed up against the door. It could hear the old man's tantrum loud and clear as the once sprinkling rain had turned back into a soaking mess.

The thing rubbed its slick claws up and down the door in an uncanny, sensual manner as drops of blood dripped from its gaping mouth and onto the wooden porch floor beneath it.

The demon's frigid aura gave the house the much appreciated cool down from the muggy air outside. It could have lowered the temperature inside the dwelling to that of a freezer if it chose to do so, but somehow it knew when enough was enough.

Much like Shirley once did for many years before meeting her gruesome demise, the beast laid down on the floor and guarded both the house and its angry owner.

CHAPTER 23

Virginia could have very well been driving on railroad tracks because her attention was anywhere but on the road upon which she and Keyshawn were traveling.

There was an image inside of her head that early morning; a glorious sight for a grieving mother to behold. A perfect vision of Courtney coming downstairs in her all blue graduation gown. Virginia could see herself snapping one photo after another of her glowing child as she prepared for the next step in her young life. It was such a splendid recollection that it caused a blissful smile to come across the woman's face at that instant.

She missed Rayshawn with all her heart, but there was something different about Courtney. At times, there relationship went beyond the boundaries of mother, daughter; oft times it would border on sisterhood between them both.

It broke Virginia's heart when Courtney decided to stay in Mississippi and not come with her to live in Ohio. It almost angered her to where she wanted to slap the girl's face bloody. But at that point, one day removed from the funeral, Virginia wanted to break down and cry all over the steering wheel at just the very thought on wanting to inflict harm upon her one and only baby.

"Grandma, where is we goin'?" Keyshawn asked as green popsicle juice drizzled down his chubby cheeks.

Snapping back to the road, Virginia calmly answered, "Were goin' back to your granddad's house, darlin'."

"Does he like me, grandma?"

"Does who like you, son?"

"My granddad," he mumbled.

Giving a whimsical tummy giggle, Virginia asked, "What on earth would make you ask that?"

"He yelled at me yesterday."

"Your mama, God rest her poor soul, used to yell at you and Rayshawn all the time, but that surely didn't mean that she didn't like or love you boys."

"His house stinks."

"I know, but it's not nice for you to mention such things. You're supposed to be polite."

"Who was that woman that was with him? Was she his wife? Mama said that she was his hoe. We see her at the store sometimes buying candy and potato chips."

"I highly doubt that she's his wife, honey," Virginia sighed. "Your granddad would rather drown himself than to get married. I really don't know who that young lady was."

"When are we goin' to Columbus, grandma?"

"Tomorrow morning, son," Virginia deeply exhaled.

"Are we taking Rayshawn and mama with us?"

Virginia contemplated momentarily before saying, "I've thought about it long and hard, and I think I've changed my mind on that."

"What kind—

"Keyshawn, please, "Virginia screamed, pounding her right hand on the dashboard. Once she was able to regain her composure from the child's rapid fire inquiries she looked over at him and rubbed the top of his head. "I'm sorry I yelled at you, sweetheart, but you shouldn't think about such things. God is taking care of your mama and brother as we speak; he knows exactly what to do."

Keyshawn finished the remaining slivers of popsicle before pitifully muttering, "I'm sorry, grandma."

Turning down a wooded path, Virginia placed her hand on Keyshawn's and said with a warm smile, "I'm not mad at you, baby, your grandma just has others things on her mind right now."

As she drove down the shaded glen Virginia could feel Millard's house approaching; she all of the sudden got the same sinking feeling she got years earlier whenever she would bring Courtney over to see her dad when she was a little girl.

The Oldsmobile cleared the wooden path and took off down the old, rugged road before entering a slim lane. What Virginia wished had been minutes inched only to seconds as the lane turned into a driveway. Like a bad dream, she had returned to the legendary house and its mad dog owner.

It wasn't that she was afraid of Millard, it was the fact that all of the memories she had of the man from the past came funneling back into her head all at once. It belittled her to think that she had perhaps one or two fond remembrances of the man while all the rest were ugly memories of what was never supposed to happen to begin with. Before seeing him at the chapel she hadn't laid eyes on the Millard since 1981.

Virginia stopped the car in behind Millard's truck and cut off the ignition. She then looked over to the barn to her right; the more she gazed into the structure it became apparent that perhaps her fascination of seeing where her daughter and grandson were killed had lost its luster. A jarring fear shook her body, it was over; in her mind the entrance way to the barn was sealed shut.

"What is you lookin' at, grandma?"

Keyshawn's voice caused Virginia to stir out of her entranced mode. She glanced over at the boy and said, "Nothin', sweetheart. Now, you stay in here, I'm only gonna be a second." Ya hear?"

"Yes, ma'am," he gulped.

Virginia got out and boldly swaggered towards the house as though she were embarking on a fateful mission into the darkest realm of humanity. She knocked on the door and watched it swing open to reveal none other than Millard's lady standing with a broom in her hand.

"Oh, good morning," Virginia gasped, surprised. "I just stopped by to see Millard."

With a blushing frown on her sweaty face, the woman replied, "He left out earlier to get some more bullets in town."

Virginia peculiarly peeked over the young woman's shoulder before looking back into her eyes again. Millard's truck was parked outside, and she knew whenever the old man didn't want to face anyone he would easily hide away like a mole in the ground.

Agitated, the young lady sighed, "I told you he wasn't here."

"I heard you the first time, honey. I just wanted to come in and see something for a second."

The woman rolled her eyes before stepping aside to allow Virginia in. As if she needed to, Virginia took another glimpse of the baking hot hovel that she couldn't believe she was back inside once more.

"My, my, it looks like another storm swept through here." Virginia shook her head shamefully as she viewed the knocked over television on the floor.

Sweeping up glass from off the floor, the lady commented, "Millard had a very bad day yesterday."

"We all did, darlin'."

"Well, he got a little carried away and…this is what we have here. I just got done fixing up the bedroom."

"If there's one thing I know about that man is his carried away side."

"I think that's why he walked instead of driving his truck; I guess he just wanted to get some things off of his chest."

"I see," Virginia muttered, having little care in her for Millard's so called depression. "Well, I really came back for that picture I asked him for yesterday, but if he's gone then I guess I'll have to go back home without it. The last thing I want is to wear out my welcome."

The young lady knelt down and tried to lift up the television; Virginia followed in kind, taking hold of the other end of the set.

"Where is your home, anyways?" The young woman grunted.

"I live all the way up in Ohio." Virginia strained as the two carefully hoisted the heavy TV back onto its feet.

"What made you move from down here?"

Breathing heavy, Virginia said, "Honey, if there is one thing I know for sure, it's that no one in their right mind wants to live and die Sullinger, Mississippi. There was nothin' here for me anymore."

"I wanted to leave from here, too, but I want Millard to come with me."

Virginia squared her eyes at the young woman in a pitiable sort of manner like she was looking a sickly child. "What's your name anyways, darlin'?"

The woman paused, appearing as though someone had slapped her right across the face. "Essya," she muttered, sounding like she was ashamed to speak out loud.

"Essya, that's a pretty name." Virginia sympathetically smiled. "Essya, as one woman to another I'm tellin' you right here and now that if you're waiting for Millard to change, then—

At that same moment, Millard clomped his way through the front door with a brown paper bag in both hands and a vexed glare on his unshaven face, looking like he had somehow stumbled into the wrong house.

Exasperated, he asked, "What the hell is this shit?"

"I told you that I'd be back for that picture, Mr. Lang."

"And I told you that I don't know what the hell you're talkin' about!"

"Millard, don't you have some pictures downstairs in the—

"Gal, shut your mouth right now." Millard sternly commanded behind gritted teeth.

Virginia watched as Essya did as ordered before planting her little self down on the couch. Millard then began to advance towards the woman with a ravaged look on his face, but not before Virginia decided to cut in right at the nick of time.

"Uh, Mr. Lang, why don't you and I go and take a walk?" She forced herself to smile.

"Take a walk where, dammit?"

"Let's go down to the old pasture. I'd like to see a few things one last time before I leave tomorrow."

A harsh yet stunned appearance all of the sudden grew upon the old man's face at that moment. He stared down at Virginia as though she had lost what little sense she supposedly had left

"Hold on real quick." Virginia said as she bolted outside to the car.

As she retrieved Keyshawn who was sitting in the car sweating half to death, Virginia could hear Millard's loud, hard voice yell and scream at Essya like she were an unruly animal he was trying to put in its place.

Just listening to the severity of his voice brought back the worst, most unwanted remembrances imaginable. She herself almost came to tears right before her grandson.

Grabbing the child's arm, Virginia said, "C'mon, were goin' inside."

The second she and the boy made their way back into the house, Millard's hollering ceased immediately before he took a pause to gawk down at Keyshawn.

Breathing heavy, Virginia said, "Alright, I thought that while we were out that Keyshawn could stay behind and help Essya clean up a bit."

Millard gazed around his home before asking, "Clean up what?"

"This demolition derby you have the nerve to call a home." Virginia rolled her eyes. She then knelt down to Keyshawn's size and said, "Okay, I want you to stay here and help Essya, and do whatever she says. You hear me?"

"Yes, ma'am," the boy answered with a sullen drool.

Virginia then stood back up, opened the front door wide and said, "After you, Mr. Lang."

Without parting his pressed lips, Millard stormed out of the house before her like an angry child. Virginia looked back at Essya as the young woman got up from off the couch and wiped her teary face with her own t-shirt. There was an insatiable urging inside that wanted to go over and wrap her arms around the young lady and tell her that everything was going to be alright.

But there were other pressing issues that needed ironing out before anything else. Virginia blew a kiss to Keyshawn before closing the door behind her and stepping outside to find Millard already out of his yard and across the fence.

Like she was a nimble teenager, Virginia sprinted her way to Millard as quick as her tired legs could take her.

CHAPTER 24

The man wasn't in the mood for yet another round of annoyances and disturbances; he had had his fill of humankind years ago, but to have folks all up in his face at once with one aggravating nuisance after another was beyond his threshold of tolerance. The rage was always there; at that point all it would take was one person to tip the scale.

Millard glanced back to see Virginia running her best to catch up to him, trying not to tear her blue jeans in the process. He had an idea as to what she wanted with him, which was why he didn't put up much of a fuss to come along.

"Can you please wait up, Mr. Lang?" Virginia pleaded. "It's too hot to be runnin' like this!"

Millard reluctantly slowed his gangly legs to a crawl in the hopes that they could get the ordeal started and over with sooner than later.

"Stop callin' me that." He bitterly grunted.

"Stop callin' you what?" Virginia asked as she at last caught up with Millard.

"Stop callin' me Mr. Lang. You ain't never bothered to respect me before, so don't start now."

"Well, excuse me…Millard." Virginia tossed up her hands. "I wasn't aware that you and I were on less formal terms."

"What did you have to talk about?" Millard questioned as he resumed his previous pace across the dew burdened field.

"Not much, I just thought I'd get you out of that old, musty house for a while."

"So you brought me out here to torment me again, huh?"

"Actually, I just came back for that picture I've been asking nicely for."

Smirking, the old man asked, "You ain't gonna stop until I give you that damn picture, is you?"

"I did ask politely."

"Fine, when we get back to the house you can have your damn picture! Are you happy, now?" He hollered.

"I surely appreciate it."

As the two strolled along, Virginia slid her hands down her back pockets and surveyed the wide open meadow; the bright morning sun glistened down on the grass, creating a shimmering effect of colorful light.

"If there's one thing I do miss about this old town, it has to be these beautiful mornings." She hummed. "Spacious, quiet, no boomin' and bangin' cars passing by; just sweet peace."

Millard listened to the woman ramble on and on about a place he was forced to wake up in every day.

"This poor old town, it's like the second a person sets foot here something strange happens."

"Whaddya mean?"

"You know exactly what I mean, Millard. This whole town in cursed."

Chuckling, the old man asked, "You still believe in all that bunk?"

"Don't stand there and play Skeptical Stanley with me. All two hundred and twenty-two of us saw Dusty Myers' ghost runnin' around that fiberglass plant one week after he was sawed in half while using the steam press there."

"Ain't no spooks ever bothered me." Millard shrugged his shoulders.

"Well, you may be able to stand tall in the face of death, but I on the other hand tend to stray away from stuff that I don't wanna understand."

Millard once again sidestepped her comments, choosing to cast them off like so much useless rubbish.

"So tell me, how long have you and Essya been together?"

"Who," Millard confusingly frowned.

"Your girlfriend, Millard," she sighed.

"Shit, I dunno, for some years, I reckon."

"Good thing you two ain't married, I'd hate to be around when your anniversary arrives."

"Who gives a shit how long we've been together? We don't keep up with stuff like that after so long."

"You're right, after so long dates and time itself seems irrelevant." Virginia huffed before stopping to view the grazing land ahead of her; the sun was by then fully in the sky and already beginning its daily duty of berating those beneath it. Millard stood and watched as she looked on as though she were suddenly transported to a different land altogether.

"What's the matter with you?"

Looking away, Virginia gave a whimsical giggle before saying, "I remember when Courtney was about eight, and she ran away from home because I wouldn't let her go down to Claymore's to play with all the other kids in the creek. It was a hot day, though; too hot for little folks to be rippin' and 'a runnin' around. Anyways, that child got so mad at me that she decided to run off."

Instinctively, Millard could right away tell where she was going with her beloved story; he could hear it in her shaky voice. He wanted ever so much to shut her out, but his ears kept him attentive against his own will.

"We scoured this town from top to bottom looking for that girl. I don't remember ever being so scared up till that point. Finally, something told me to go to your place, and sure enough, there she was, up in that loft, sleepin' away."

Millard stood and pondered for a few seconds before saying, "I don't remember that."

"I'm not surprised; you were passed out drunk in your basement all day long. Till this day it fascinates me as to why she chose to run over here of all places."

"Why would that fascinate you so much? I was her daddy." Millard contended.

"Is that right?" Virginia turned around.

"Don't stand there and start that bullshit with me, Virginia!"

"Start what bullshit with you, Millard?"

"I know that tone and it usually means that you're about to start some mess!"

"Why are you getting so damn defensive all of the sudden?"

"Because I've had to hear it from every other motherfucker out there and I don't wanna hear it from your ass again after all these years!" Millard roared as he turned and started back for the house.

"Don't you walk away from me, damn you! Come back here!" Virginia screamed as she grabbed Millard by the arm.

"Woman, you'd better let me go before I kick your ass from here all the back to Ohio!"

"What are you gonna do, Millard, beat me up? C'mon then and do it! Kick my ass and everyone else's if that'll satisfy you!"

"What the hell is wrong with you? Did you come all the

way down here to bury those kids or pick a fight with me all over again?"

"Those kids?" she retaliated ferociously. "Millard, you were never there for Courtney when she was little, and don't you dare say that I didn't give you a chance to be because you'll be a bold faced liar! You weren't there when she graduated, you weren't there when her boys were born, and you didn't even show up at their fucking funeral!"

"You don't know what the hell you're talkin' about!"

"Oh yeah, I guess I should give you a medal for standing up when that sorry Tyrone would come down and torture her! Oh yes, Mr. Lang, she told me all about those times! I guess you call yourself making up for lost time by beating up her children's father!"

"What the hell do you want from me?" Millard screamed as loud as he could into Virginia's face. "Whaddya want, motherfucker?"

"I want you to at least pretend that you have some sort of feeling or sorrow inside of you for a change! Millard, our daughter and grandson were both murdered inside your barn! You didn't even come to their funeral; you didn't even see them off one last time! You just blew it off like you do everything else in your worthless life!"

Millard wanted to let loose; he wanted to yell, spit and fight, and unfortunately for Virginia, she was the closest thing that was within arm's reach.

"And as far as Leon goes, Lord knows I love the man like a brother, but there's something he's not telling me about their murders! Everything about this smells bad! I don't buy that alligator story one damn bit!"

"Whaddya want me to do, shave my head bald like Kojak, dig the two of 'em up and try to solve the case on my own?"

Without so much as a battle cry, Virginia reared back and smacked Millard across the face with such a force that it caused the man to stumble backwards. Millard then grabbed Virginia by the arms; from there the two struggled and fought, back and forth. Virginia kicked, yelled and cursed while Millard did his best to force the woman to her knees. Both were high on adrenaline and blind fury but neither could seem to break the other down.

It eventually reached the point to where the two eventually gave up and ceased their violent rampage upon each other.

Virginia dropped to the wet ground crying and panting while Millard stood over her huffing and puffing as if he had just wrestled a bear. He looked down and watched as Virginia wailed to the sky above with her fists balled up.

Trying to catch her breath, Virginia wept, "I was at the grocery store, in the cereal aisle, when all of the sudden, the strangest thing struck me. Like someone had hit me in the chest with a hammer. I fell against my shopping cart just to keep my balance. One of the clerks there had to escort me to my car like some old woman. When I got home… that's when I got the call from Leon. He said that Courtney and Rayshawn were dead. Something had eaten them alive. I don't know if I can go on anymore. Our kids are dead, Millard. They're gone." Virginia then looked back up at the sky and howled out with a blood curdling wrath, "Dear God, tell me this is a fucking dream!"

Emotion was something Millard refused to deal with, especially when the sentiment was coming from a woman, but as degrading to him as it appeared he knew where Virginia's raw passion was stemming from. He hated it, but it was his last resort.

Millard inhaled the burning wood aroma that always

smelled like fresh bacon from a mile west before kneeling down and gently taking a hold of Virginia's wrist, only to have his hand slapped away.

"Don't you dare do that!" Virginia lashed out with an evil face.

Unfazed by her retaliation, Millard stood back up and observed his beauteous surroundings on that hot, summer morn. He was fully aware of just where he was, but it just so happened that it was the first time since he was a young man that he actually appreciated it.

"I don't know why you wanted Courtney to move back up to Ohio, they got storms up there, too." The old man sulked with a drooping face.

Virginia, with a beet red face soaked with tears, looked up at Millard and simply grunted, "True, but at least Ohio doesn't have you."

He couldn't explain why, but Millard's stomach sank at that instant, but the last thing he wanted was for Virginia to notice that he was taken aback by her spiteful remark.

Trying to keep his eyes away from her, Millard mumbled, "You'd better get up…this old field is full of ticks."

Slowly, Virginia rose to her feet and wiped her messy face clean. "Well…rather ticks than alligators and ghosts, I reckon." She jibed as she glanced over at Millard strangely. "We better get you back so you can get that fixed up."

"Get what fixed up?"

"Your face," Virginia pointed. "Essya will think that you and I were up to our old tricks if she sees that."

Millard took his hand and wiped a streak of blood from off the left side of his face. "Ain't nothin' but a little blood." He shrugged.

"Lord knows you and I both have seen our share of

blood over the years." Virginia sneered as she turned and silently started back for the house.

Millard dragged closely in behind her, making sure not to walk side by side. The chirping robins and sparrows gave a hushed melody for the march home, for the supposed cease fire.

CHAPTER 25

The walk back to the house seemed like it took forever, even if it was only a ten minute hike. Virginia and Millard both climbed their way back over the fence and into the yard. Their early morning tirade had taken the steam out of them both, and Millard realized that it wasn't going to be easy explaining how he got his scar or why Virginia's hair was ruffled and her jeans were all scuffed with wet and muddy patches covering the backside. What was even more mind-boggling for the old man was the fact that he couldn't believe that he actually cared what Essya thought to begin with.

They both glanced at one another with condensing eyes before stepping onto the porch; they knew that they had to wipe any kind of residual emotion from off their sweaty faces before entering the house.

Virginia brushed back her long hair while Millard kicked dirt clods from off of his overalls. One more quick and silent glance into each other's sulking eyes and it was time to head inside.

The very second Millard stepped through the threshold he found Essya and Keyshawn both sweeping the dusty living room floor.

"Well, that sure was a short walk." Essya commented as she wiped her damp brow before closely examining the two.

Millard could sense just by her shifty eyes that she could see something was wrong with the picture before her.

"Well, I sure hope Keyshawn has been a real good helper while we were out." Virginia pleasantly smiled as she walked over to the boy and rubbed his back.

"He's been a real good help." Essya blindly muttered while stepping towards Millard and inspecting his grizzled face up close. "Where did you get that scratch from? You didn't have it before you left."

"Don't start questionin' me, I ain't in no mood!"

"To be perfectly honest, Essya, I smacked the taste out of his mouth." Virginia boldly spoke out as she took the broom from out of Keyshawn's hand placed it up against the couch.

Essya stared back at Virginia before redirecting her eyes at Millard and touching the deep, red scar on the old man's face. Millard hastily pulled his head away and planted himself down onto the couch.

Virginia then stepped forward and wrapped her arms around Essya's shoulder like they had been friends for years. "Look, since we won't be leaving until tomorrow, how about you and I go into town and do some shopping. I don't think any of us have had any breakfast yet today. And while we ladies are out and about, Millard and Keyshawn can stay behind and finish cleaning up."

It was like someone had dropped a nuclear bomb on all three unsuspecting victims at once. All six stunned eyes glanced at the others as if everyone were a suspect in a horrible crime.

Millard leaped up from off the couch with the vigor of a teenager and chocked, "What the hell are you doin'?"

Virginia gave Millard her signature witty smile and replied, "Not a thing, Mr. Lang, I just figured that it would be nice for everyone to…step out for a spell."

Virginia wrestled around in her pockets in search of whatever before walking over and kissing a shivering Keyshawn on the forehead.

"I want you to listen to your grandfather and do everything…I mean, do what you can. Okay, honey?"

With tears starting to form in his eyes, the boy stuttered, "Yes, ma'am."

With a heavy burdened sigh, Virginia looked at Essya and asked, "Okay, shall we go?"

As he watched Virginia walk out the front door Millard couldn't help but to snap his head over to Essya who was wearing the most dumbfounded and frightened appearance on her small face.

"What is she doing, Millard?" She stammered.

Seemingly at a loss for words, Millard responded, "Beats the shit outta me. Just go on, she tends to get a little batty every so often. You should be alright."

Essya reluctantly turned, dropped her broom down to the floor and stormed out the front door, slamming it as hard as she could behind her.

Millard walked over and gawked out the window to watch as she headed for the Oldsmobile and got in. Seconds later, the car made a U-turn before pulling out of the driveway.

Once the smoke from the car had cleared the vicinity the old man slowly turned around to see none other than a scared little boy helplessly staring up at his grandfather like a cornered mouse.

"You're granny done gone and lost her damn mind, boy." Millard griped. "Has she been okay lately?"

Keyshawn didn't reply; he stood in the middle of the floor while his chunky, sweaty knees knocked together.

"I asked you a question, little nigga!"

"Uh, no, sir…she's just sad." The child jolted backwards.

"Well, she don't have to take out her sadness on me. You stay here. Ya hear me, boy?"

"Yes, sir," Keyshawn said under his tongue.

Millard brushed by Keyshawn on his way to the basement where he retrieved his rifle from off the shelf. He was more than aware that the boy was scared to death of him, and in a warped sense of mentality, Millard reveled in that power, just as he did when his own three were small.

Millard climbed back upstairs to find Keyshawn still standing in the same place he was before he left the room. The boy hadn't budged and inch from his spot; he just remained statuesque while sweat drooled down his forehead.

"C'mon here, boy," Millard ordered under a muffled tongue as he took the box of shells that he purchased earlier and began loading his weapon.

Once he was through loading, Millard opened the front door and waited for the child to unlock himself from his current position.

Millard rolled his eyes as Keyshawn stumbled his way out the door and onto the porch. The last thing in the world he wanted was to repeat the day before, and his restraint level was at an all-time low. There were many things that came to mind whenever Millard thought of Virginia, but leaving Keyshawn with him for however long was something not even he expected to happen. It caused concern for not only himself but also for her as well.

The old man carried on down the porch and back to the fence where he ascended the barrier with little or no trouble, however, Keyshawn was a different story altogether. The boy began to climb the first of the three railings of the wooden fence, but it seemed that every time he made a resourceful attempt that was all the more the fence fought back, causing the child to slip and slide off onto the ground.

Millard threw his gun down and stomped back to retrieve the boy. "Get your fat ass from off the ground and c'mon!" He hollered as he pulled Keyshawn up by his left arm and yanked him over to the other side of the fence. "And don't you dare start cryin', or I'll take off my damn belt! C'mon here," he hollered.

The two marched out into the pasture glen, all alone.

CHAPTER 26

Essya sat and watched as the same angelic, courteous smile that Virginia brought with her all the way from the state of Ohio strolled out of the market and back to the car. The woman put the two bags that she had in her hands in the backseat and pulled onto the road.

Essya honestly didn't know what was happening or why. There were numerous premonitions that had crossed her mind over the past twenty minutes or so, one being that Virginia might want to take her out to the woods and leave her for dead, other than that, the woman had no clue as to why she was inside the car.

Every so often Essya would quietly glance over at Virginia who herself was as fidgety in her seat as a five year old on a long car ride. She could tell by the direction that they were headed that they weren't going back to Millard's house. Essya anxiously held tight to the door handle and braced herself for a possible jump and run.

"Honey, you don't have to worry, I'm not gonna hurt you." Virginia calmly reassured as the car's speed began to creep down to 20 mph.

"You're not gonna slap me like you did Millard, are you?" Essya fretfully muttered.

"Like you've never fantasized about doing it yourself?" Virginia smirked.

Essya pondered on it for a second before asking, "Why did you hit him, anyways?"

"Darlin', if you have to ask that question then there may not be any hope for you at all."

"Then where are you taking me?"

It took at least ten seconds before Virginia opened her mouth and said, "I wanna talk to you, woman to woman. I don't want for you to sit here and think that I'm hot for Millard after all these years. I'd rather have a disease that have that man back in my life again. And I especially don't want you to think that I'm trying to butt into you two's business."

"Then why are you then?"

"Essya, I just have to know one thing, honey. What in God's green earth do you see in that…man?"

Essya eyed Virginia with the kind of malice that would have one believing that she was two seconds away from ringing the woman's neck.

"I really don't think that's any of your business." Essya coldly replied.

"No, child, I think it is my business, because for over twenty years, I, Gregory and Brett's mothers have all had to cope with that despicable man. So I'm curious to know just what kind of magical spell you've put him under to make this relationship of yours work so well."

Confused and scared, Essya blurted out, "I don't have any spell over him; we just love each other, that's all!"

Virginia laughed out loud before saying, "You may love him will all your heart, but are you sure he loves you back? I heard him yellin' at you earlier like a dog."

"What does any of this have to do with you?" Essya hysterically screamed. "You don't love him anymore!"

There came a moment of uptight silence inside the car as it bounced and jerked up and down the dirt piled road. Essya sniffed while wiping her teary eyes dry. She wanted so bad to just leap out and run, run away from everything and everyone, including Millard once and for all, she couldn't bear another day of madness. Coming back to Sullinger was becoming more of a foolish action than she could ever imagine.

All of the sudden, Virginia pulled the car to the side of the road, across from the still vacant Claymore's Creek, and cut off the engine. Just as Essya was about to push open the door and bolt, Virginia gently placed her hands on her shoulders and smiled. It was such an abrupt, out of nowhere act after their altercation moments earlier that it shocked Essya even more.

"What are you doing?" Essya beseeched.

"Honey, I didn't mean to make you cry. You have to believe me when I say that I'm not here to make you feel bad or to hurt you. I guess when I look at you I'm reminded of Courtney a little bit, young and pretty. When I look at you, I think of all the times that damn Tyrone would come all the way down here from Detroit to do absolutely nothing but hurt my children."

Essya sat and watched as Virginia's face began to swell apple red at that unexpected second. Once more, she was caught completely off guard by the woman's off color moods, but at least she wasn't as afraid as she was a while ago.

"I think of all the times she would call me crying her eyes out, and how I wasn't there to protect my babies." Virginia began to cry as she held tight to Essya's hand. "So, when I look at you and the way Millard treats you, it only burns me up inside because I see yet another young lady whose life is being turned upside down by some sorry man…just like mine was."

At the snap of a finger, something inside of Essya started to stir out of control. It began deep within her stomach and eventually made its way up to her throat. She turned her head and whimpered loudly, "But…he's all I have!"

"You're a pretty girl; you could have any guy you wanted. Where are your parents? Don't you have any siblings?"

"My brothers and sisters all live in Tijuana, and I haven't seen my father since I was six. I see my mama every now and then, usually when I come across some money."

Essya watched as a compassionate glare came across Virginia's face the more she went on about her life story. Soon, the ravenous fear that she was wrapped in ever since leaving the house began to loosen.

"Please don't tell anyone else this, but…I used to be a ho. Out of all the men that I've been with…Millard was the only one that bothered to keep me around."

Virginia pulled Essya into her arms and hugged her as tight as she could; the both cried in each other's bosoms like they had never wept before.

"Oh my God, sweetheart…this can't be your life." Virginia said as she pulled herself away from Essya and wiped her blushed, wet face clean with a tissue that she took from out of her shirt pocket. "I think I've spent almost a hundred dollars on Kleenex since Leon called me the other day." She smirked before handing Essya a tissue. "There's more to your life than this. There's a whole wide world beyond the evil grip of Sullinger. Do you wanna take a walk?"

Essya shook her head yes before opening the door and getting out. The second she closed the door she spotted the red sign across the way at the top of the creek that read, *"No Trespassing."*

"Is that where those boys were killed?" Virginia asked as she stepped out of the car and stuffed her keys into her pants pocket.

"Yeah," Essya quaked. "It feels like it was just yesterday when it happened."

Essya watched as Virginia carried herself over to her side of the car before placing her hands on her arms and staring pensively into her eyes. "Essya, I'm going to ask you a very serious question, and I need for you to be as honest with me as you can. Was it really an alligator that killed them and my babies?"

Essya didn't have an answer within her that would make any plausible sense. Ever since the incident at the creek days earlier she had tried her best to shove the horror to the very back of her mind, making sure not to even mention the word *kill* if she could help it.

"No…I don't know what it was." She squirmed.

"What do you mean you don't know, honey?"

"After it killed the boys it stood in front of me and Millard. It was invisible."

Virginia stood back and covered her mouth in angst at what she just heard. "My Lord," she gasped, "are you saying that it was one of these damn ghosts that did it?"

"That's what I told the sheriff, but he doesn't think too much of me as it is. Do you believe in ghosts?"

"Darlin', if I had a quarter for every lost soul that I've seen wander this town then I'd be richer than the Queen of England herself."

"You mean that there are really ghosts here?"

"Something happens the very moment a person enters this jerkwater town, you're never the same again. A person can't even rest in peace here. To the outside world, Sullinger, Mississippi doesn't even exist."

Essya stepped out onto the empty dirt road and glared at the creek ahead. Words could not even come out of her startled mouth. Her mind was like computer circuitry all ripped and torn to shreds. She could still hear Kenny and his friends scream for their lives as they were being slaughtered one by one by the demon that had invaded Sullinger.

"This damn town ain't never done me or anyone else any good." Virginia carried on. "Even ole' Claymore's Creek has drowned a couple of folks way back when."

Essya slowly turned back to face Virginia who was leaning up against the car with her arms folded.

"Tell me somethin', have you ever been to Phillips tool shed?"

"I've never even heard of it." Essya rolled her eyes upwards in a pondering fashion.

"It's a little shed in these woods where me and my sister would go every time our daddy would beat on us when we were kids. C'mon, I'll show you."

Essya followed Virginia into the quiet woods where shimmering colors and light shot through green leaves and any other edifice that the sunbeams could penetrate. Birds, squirrels and the ever so present raccoons were all engaged in whatever affairs they were enjoying while the two ladies rambled on ever so freely along a tiny stream.

"I sure hope that I can still find it after all these years, not unless someone tore the old place down." Virginia commented as she brushed aside a crooked old branch.

"Virginia, can I ask you a question?"

"You sure can, darlin'."

"How did you and Millard...you know?"

"You mean how did me and Millard get involved?"

"Yeah," Essya winced.

"I knew that question had to come up sooner or later. Well, we used to work down at the old fiberglass plant together. I had just broken up with my fiancé of two years after finding out he cheated on me. Sure enough, here comes Millard to cheer me up. He was a real ladies man down there."

Essya all of the sudden stopped dead in her tracks. There had been many shocks and surprises over the past few days, but none as jolting as what she was privy to hear at that moment in time.

Quaking, Essya asked, "You mean…he wasn't always like he is now?"

Virginia stopped walking, turned around and waved her hand saying, "Lord no. Don't get me wrong, he wasn't no Prince Charming, but he wasn't always the barbarian we know him to be either. He was actually a pretty decent person at one time."

Essya didn't know what to think or how to feel just then. Processing so much at one time seemed to throw her off. She didn't even have any comprehension as to what day it was.

"We went out a few times, dinner, dancing and—

"Millard danced?" Essya's eyes bulged out.

"Yes, girl, big feet and all," Virginia laughed out loud as she resumed her walk.

Essya carried on beside her, anxious as ever to to hear what she had always wanted to know about the man she called her one and only love.

"So anyways, it was the annual Fourth of July town picnic. It was one of those hot July nights, the kind that makes ya feel like you're about to melt inside your own clothes. Millard and I got so piss drunk that we ended up leaving the crowd and stumbling back to his truck. Nine months later, here comes Courtney."

"So how did you get him to love you?"

"Love me?" Virginia stared strangely at Essya.

"Yeah, I mean, what did you do to make him treat you nice?"

"Essya, I knew that Millard had other babies mama's out there, and just like you I thought I was going to be the one who would be able to crack that man's icy ass and show the world the real Millard Lang, but I was sadly mistaken."

"So what happened?"

"A slap across the face happened, and then another, and another after that. Even a dog knows when it's been beaten enough. That's when I finally woke up and realized that a woman can't waste her life tryin' to change a man, especially when that man can't be changed. That's exactly what you've been tryin' to do all these years, ain't it, change that old goat?"

Essya bit down on her bottom lip, feeling absolutely hopeless. "I do sometimes."

"He's hit you, too, hasn't he?"

"Essya just shook her head yes before uttering, "I thought perhaps a baby would make him change his ways. He got me pregnant once."

"What happened?" Virginia panted as she and Essya stopped in the middle of the forest.

"He gave me this long speech about how he had enough of kids, and how he didn't have time to be a daddy again. He made me go up to Jackson and…get rid of it. I'm numb to it all by now."

Virginia stood and stared thoughtfully at Essya before saying, "You know the sad thing about Millard, the one thing that I actually feel sorry for about the man? Him and God are gonna have a serious face to face meeting when it's all said and done, and I have a feeling that our beloved Mr. Lang won't like what the Almighty has to say to him in the end."

"He always said that he was going to hell when he died."

"If he believes it…then perhaps he will."

"He did try to make it up to me one time, though."

"Oh really," Virginia squared her eyes. "How so?"

With a twinkle in her eye, Essya gladly replied, "He said that one day he would take me to the Gulf of Mexico for a vacation."

Essya watched as Virginia beamed her brown eyes at her, looking as though the woman were staring at a naïve young girl. Virginia then resumed her path, casually commenting, "It sure is beautiful out here, especially in the summertime."

Following Virginia, Essya asked, "So, how much further is this tool shed?"

"Well, judging by those two maple tress just up ahead, I'd say were not too far now. I used to bring Courtney out here all the time she was little."

Blushing, Essya said, "I don't think Courtney ever really liked me. She'd always roll her eyes at me every time we saw each other."

"Well, honey, you were sleeping with her father. I'm guessing that's where a lot of the animosity came from. Add to the fact that Millard seemed to give you more attention than he ever gave her could be another possibility."

Essya mused on Virginia's words momentarily before coming to the conclusion that she was one hundred percent right; it was the brutal truth that Essya tried with all her might to evade all those years. She did everything within her power to avoid Courtney in their small town. She was smart enough to realize that her relationship with Millard aggravated Courtney, and just seeing her blazing eyes the other day in the barn as she was leaving sent evil electricity up and down her spine.

"I wonder what the sheriff is gonna do about all these murders, if he cares."

"Me and Keyshawn were at the hotel up in Jackson. I flipped through every channel searching for something on my babies. Come to find out that no one had heard about what happened. It's like Sullinger, in a way, is like Las Vegas, what happens here, stays here. Ah, there it is." Virginia exhaled as she spotted a small, crooked shed up ahead in the distance.

The ladies hiked their way onward towards the ram shackled structure and stopped short of the entrance.

With her nose turned up, Essya commented, "This is where you and your sister came to play? It almost looks like Millard's house, but don't tell 'em I said that."

With her hands on her hips, Virginia answered, "Don't worry, honey, he'd probably agree with you on that. "Yep, our daddy was a notorious drunk, and whenever the whiskey told him to, he would wail on us and our mama. This was the only place on God's green earth Vikki and I felt safe."

Virginia continued on, and without much effort she pushed the creaky, wooden door open only to allow a moldy cloud of dust to escape from the paltry looking shed and out into the wilderness.

"Whew," Virginia covered her mouth, "I sure don't miss this God awful stench."

Essya fretfully followed in behind while trying to fend off cobwebs and scampering chipmunks along the way.

The shed was no bigger than two outhouses put together. There were two closed, grime stained windows on both sides of the wall as well as a dusty old table that sat in the middle of the floor. Virginia stood by one of the windows and gawked about her childhood fondness.

Trying not to inhale too much dust, "Essya gulped, "This place looks like something from out of a scary movie. You know the kind where the killer always takes people then chops them up?"

"Thank the good Lord we didn't have those kinds of sick and perverted movies back when I was a girl or else my sister and I would have never come here to begin with." Virginia said as she brushed cobwebs off of her legs. "I can't believe this place is still standing after all these years. I wonder if anyone else knows about it."

Virginia then wandered over to a corner and noticed a dirty green tarp all crumpled up and covering something big. She took the large tarp from off the bundle to reveal a collection of doll babies and board games.

Holding her mouth in amazement, Virginia said, "My heavens…I can't believe they're still here."

"Are those Barbie dolls?"

"They sure are. Barbie dolls, our Monopoly set and Scrabble." Virginia replied as she knelt down and began rummaging through the discoveries. "My sister and I would play with these all day long until the sun went down. Sometimes we'd skip school just to come here."

"Are you gonna take them with you?"

Virginia said nothing at first; it was like she was stuck for words. A moment or two passed before she coughed and said, "No…I think I'll just leave 'em here…for the next little girl who needs to stop by."

Essya chose to stand back and watch in subdued wonder at the grown woman before her fiddle with baby dolls and games like she had morphed back into a child all over again.

She couldn't remember seeing another human being be at such peace as Virginia seemed at that instant in time. Essya realized that she had not only come to Sullinger to put her daughter and grandson to rest, but also her own long-suffering soul. It was the same kind of contentment that she wanted ever so much for herself; just to belong to one person, just to have her love returned in kind, and if she couldn't have that much, then loneliness would be her companion, as long as her soul was happy with the result.

Wiping tears from her eyes, Virginia stood up and sighed, "Well, I don't know about you, my dear, but I am hungrier than Doc Willis' billy goat. Millard will think that we've done gone and ran off somewhere without 'em."

"Virginia…come out here!" A deep, thundering voice sounded from the other side of the shed's door.

Both women stopped what they were doing and froze while staring directly at the door in front of them. Neither said a single word. Virginia's mouth was a closed tight tomb while Essya's eyes were as wide open as an owl's.

To Essya, the voice outside was completely foreign, the tone hardly even sounded human, it resembled that of a grown man grunting, trying to speak for the first time.

Shaking, Essya took a hold of Virginia's hand and asked, "Do…do you know who that—

"God help me, please." Virginia stammered. "Just stay still and try not to talk."

Both women shivered with stomach churning fear. It was already beyond a hundred degrees inside the shed, but the fear made it feel like one hundred and forty. The sweat that streamed down Essya's face seared into her eyes causing them to sting.

Essya could hear who or whatever was outside rustle about in the bush like it were circling the shed. Like a lighting quick cat, Virginia yanked Essya over to where the green tarp was lying on the floor and hurriedly tossed the musty canvas on top of them.

Just as the very last inch of tarp was being laid to conceal Essya's tennis shoes the door swung open with such a velocity that the shed itself wobbled.

There was a small gap in the tarp that allowed Essya to see only the intruder's claw-like feet as it skulked about the tiny shed. She wanted to scream or at least cry at the sight she was forced to see before her. All she could conjure in her head was the fateful day back at the creek; right then, inside the old shed, the devil was revealing himself more and more.

"Virginia…it's time to come home now." The thing spoke in the same deep, dark pitch.

Essya could feel Virginia's hand squeeze her's with such force that it was hurting. She glanced over at the woman and noticed her shedding tears of absolute fear.

Virginia's sweaty hand was becoming harder to hold on to due to the fact that the woman was shaking uncontrollably.

Essya looked up to see the beast turn and begin for the back of the shed, where she and Virginia were hidden underneath the tarp no less. Essya squeezed Virginia's hand right back as its heavy feet clomped towards and eventually past them to inspect the board games that were lying next to the tarp. She listened as it snorted in and out. Its blinding body odor was enough to make her want to sneeze.

It then sniffed closer and closer downwards as if it knew just where its prey was already hidden. All of the sudden, just as Essya felt that the beast was about to seize both her and Virginia, Virginia did something that was totally unexpected; she yanked herself and Essya from under the tarp and tore out the front door into the forest.

Hanging on for dear life to Virginia's hand, Essya couldn't help but to look back to see a dark, slim figure closing in fast on their heels. Ahead was nothing but an endless menagerie of trees, not one sign of a road or clearing was anywhere in sight.

As she was being pulled along, Essya turned back again only to see nothing but forest behind her, but she could still hear the heavy footsteps gain closer than she could before.

"Hurry, honey…I think I can see the end!" Virginia wailed as she let loose of Essya's hand.

Essya was free to pump her own two arms and break loose of the woods. Just as her feet were able to gain a strong enough hold on the ground something sharp and cold grabbed her t-shirt and ripped it from off of her body.

"Help me!" She hysterically yelled as she jerked her body backwards and watched her own shirt dangle in the air like something invisible was holding it up.

"C'mon', girl," Virginia squealed as she snatched Essya's hand once again and pulled her along to the light ahead that was the clearing.

The instant they escaped the forest, both women jumped into the Oldsmobile. Essya watched with petrified eyes as her newfound friend fumbled her car keys about in her sweaty hands.

"What's the matter?" Essya hollered like a mad woman.

"I can't find the car key!" Virginia screamed back, spinning her head from the collage of keys to the forest.

Essya held her half naked self while watching the forest in dreaded anticipation for the creature to come racing out at a moment's notice. "Hurry, please!" She slobbered.

Once the right key was found, Virginia jammed it into the ignition and tore off down the road without even looking back.

"Are you okay?" Virginia asked.

Shaking out of control while holding her body, Essya answered, "Yes…I think so! Where are we going?"

"We gotta get back to Millard's, I gotta get my baby!"

"We gotta go to the sheriff, too, maybe he can kill it!"

"Knowing Leon, he's probably asleep somewhere in his squad car!" Virginia remarked as she wiped sweat from out of her eyes. "We'll catch up to him later; right now, Keyshawn is all that matters to me! I got a real ugly feelin' that we ain't dealin' with some ghost, young lady!"

Just as Virginia was about to make a sharp turn down a dirt road, something jumped on the car's roof, something that was heavy enough to create a sinking dent into the vehicle. The women screamed out loud before Virginia swerved from one side of the road to the other.

Soon, right through the metal roof ripped a claw that tore into Virginia's neck causing the frantic woman to lose control of the car. Right away, Essya grabbed a hold of the steering wheel and pressed down as hard as she could on the brake.

The car stopped with such a force that it caused the beast to fly off the roof of the vehicle and land on the ground in front. Essya wasted no time in looking to see the creature; blindly she shoved Virginia's lifeless body aside so she could climb in the driver's seat. Once she was able to get her bearings in order, she turned the car around and recklessly sped off in the opposite direction.

"Please don't hit me no more, daddy!" Virginia moaned in and out of consciousness while bleeding from the neck.

"Hold on, Virginia, were going back home!" Essya cried as she drove on the seemingly endless road, hoping and praying to God that her precious Tequila would be right where she needed him to be.

"I'm sorry, Millard…I won't do it again!" Virginia rambled on in her semi-comatose state.

Essya would every so often glance over at the wounded woman. She felt such a chasm of both sorrow and pity for her, the hell had come back into Virginia's life, and now, Essya herself, was trapped.

"Please, Millard," Essya's jaws trembled, "please help us!"

CHAPTER 27

Millard held his Winchester as close as he could to his face. His eyes were transfixed on his selected target in the far off distance. The object bobbed in and out of the river's shallow stream. Millard's eyesight, though poor, was able to spot almost every angle of the object. His vision was proficient enough for his liking because in mere seconds his prey would be dead forever.

He ever so carefully tickled the trigger with his index finger as a flock of sparrows chirped and whistled back and forth just mere feet in front of him. After days of backwards happenings that led to countless loss, Millard's mind was a clear aura of serenity. His ears could pick up the deafening sounds of crickets buzzing all around him in a synchronous chorus.

One more gracious leap from out of the sparkling stream and the old man pulled the trigger, releasing the dynamite blast of a shell that nearly decapitated the brown rabbit.

"Got ya, motherfucker," Millard gleefully shouted as he got up from off the grass that he and Keyshawn were hiding in and rushed into the two foot high creek water to grab the kill.

Like a child, Millard splashed about in the creek searching for the hare. His hands rooted under until they were able to retrieve the victim.

"Open the bag, boy!" Millard shouted as he pulled the dead and bleeding rabbit from out of the rolling stream.

Keyshawn opened the brown cloth bag that was already stuffed with three dead garter snakes. "Put that fucker in there." The old man ordered as he came prancing out of the water and onto dry land. "Go on, boy, and hurry up!" He yelled, shoving the rabbit into Keyshawn's face.

With his hands shaking, Keyshawn took the rabbit by its floppy ears before accidentally dropping the thing to the ground. Millard only rolled eyes in disgust and snatched the little boy's hands. "Is you retarded? Pick that damn thing up and put 'em in the bag!"

Keyshawn once again attempted to pick up the animal, and eventually was able to stuff it securely into the bag he was forced to hold.

"Damn, boy, is you turnin' faggot like your uncle?" Millard cracked a smart smile. "That boy couldn't even pick up a damn mouse if his life depended on it. C'mon, we got our lunch for the day." Millard said as he took the bag from the child and started back down the pasture.

Keyshawn followed in behind Millard as he had been doing for the past hour or so. They trampled across the steamy field at a steady pace. The old man had absolutely nothing to say to the boy; there really wasn't really anything to say or talk about out loud.

He was mad at Virginia for leaving Keyshawn with him. He hated it whenever she would pull one of her so called "stunts." And as open of a mind as he tried to keep when it came to her state of mourning, he just couldn't bring himself to forgive her for her sanctimonious way of getting her point across.

Every so often he would glance back at the chubby little man just to make sure that he was keeping up pace wise.

Not surprising to him, Millard found that every time he would turn that was all the more he was reminded of Greg at Keyshawn's age, round and timorous.

All of the sudden, there came a hankering for a bit of pleasure. The old man snickered to himself before asking, "Boy, when was the last time you ran?"

"Huh," Keyshawn wheezed while keeping his eyes stuck to the grass like he was enthralled with watching his own two feet.

"What, do ya got shit in your ears? I said when was the last time you ran somewhere?"

"I run when I play football with Rayshawn."

"Well, run up here and keep up with me." Millard looked back as the child pumped his stocky legs forward until he was by his side. "Didn't your mama ever teach you and your brother how to stop eatin'?"

"My mama let us eat popsicles and pizza."

"I can see you've done eaten a lot of pizzas, boy." Millard smirked.

"Mr. Grandpa, did you know my mama?"

Taken off guard by the question at first, Millard shrugged his shoulders and arrogantly replied, "What are you, dumb or somethin'? Your mama was my daughter."

"You knew her when she was a little girl?"

"I said that she was my child. I knew your mama when she was a tiny baby!"

"My grandma said that the devil killed my mama and Rayshawn."

Glancing down at the boy with a curious eye, Millard asked, "Is that what she said?"

"Yeah, she said that the devil lives here."

"Lives where?"

"Here, in our town."

Twisting his lips, Millard said, "Your granny is 'bout as crazy as a coon."

"You mean a raccoon? Me and Rayshawn ran after a raccoon back at our old house before he got himself killed."

"She's crazy alright."

"Mr. Grandpa, why did you shoot my daddy?"

"Because your daddy is a no good bastard, that's why!"

"Is you gonna kill 'em when he comes back again and beats up my mama?"

Holding up his weapon of choice, Millard boldly replied, "I'm gonna use this here rifle and blow his fuckin' balls off, and you can believe that much!"

"My mama said that she hopes you kill 'em next time so he won't bother us again."

Millard looked down at the boy with a somewhat confused grimace. "What else did your mama say about me, boy?"

"She said that one day the devil is gonna come and get you, and that she hopes you die, too. And she hopes that you and my daddy burn in hell together, too." He nonchalantly commented.

Coming directly from the lips of an eight year old, Keyshawn's response sounded so innocent and oblivious, but to Millard, they were the usual words that he had become accustomed to from other townspeople on a daily basis, other people but Courtney. It caused him to slow a few steps in his rapid pace back to the shack.

"Mr. Grandpa, why did the devil kill my mama and Rayshawn? My grandma said that the devil only comes for bad folks."

"Boy, I don't know." Millard answered in an annoyed tone."

"Mr. Grandpa, do you like fat people?"

"What, boy," Millard questioned with a growl as he once again glanced down at the child with a bowled over expression on his worn face.

"The boys and girls at my school don't like me and Rayshawn because we're fat. They call us fat boy and fat fucker." Keyshawn breathlessly explained. "Mr. Grandpa, is a fag a person who likes a man?"

"A fag is a man or a woman who…aww, boy, you ain't gotta worry 'bout that! Don't you know how to kick people's asses? You're a big boy, those big ole' hands of yours should be able to knock anybody out."

"My mama doesn't like for me and Rayshawn to be fightin', she said if we fight in school then she was gonna whoop us."

"Well, your mama ain't here no more, so next time some little bastards calls you a name then you can kick their damn asses!"

"Hey, Mr. Grandpa, when will the devil bring my mama and Rayshawn back home? We still gotta go to the store and buy some ice cream."

At that very instant, Millard irately threw his rifle to the ground and grabbed Keyshawn by the shirt collar before kneeling and yelling into the child's face, "See here, your mama and brother ain't comin' back! They're dead! I don't know what your grandma has been tellin' you, but it's all bullshit! They're dead and they ain't never comin' back! Ya hear me?"

Keyshawn began to break down and cry the tighter Millard gripped his collar. But all the boy's incessant sobbing did was make the old man not only angrier, but it also made him feel claustrophobic.

"You shut up that damn cryin'!" He barked as he stood up and popped the child on his ample backside. "Pick up that damn bag and c'mon, Greg!"

Back at the same angry place he was in just a day earlier, Millard took off his hat and wiped his sweaty forehead. He wanted to snatch Keyshawn by the throat and do so much more damage than before, but there was something keeping him in place.

The longer he stood in the middle of the quiet, grazing pasture, the more he could hear the playful sounds of children in the far off distance. Millard looked off to the east to see two little boys racing across the grass like roadrunners.

"Come on, Greg!" A skinny little black boy delightedly shouted out at the chunky black boy that was haplessly chasing in behind him.

"Wait up, Brett, or I'll tell daddy! You know I can't run fast like you!"

Millard watched as the careless boys took off down the field until they could no longer be seen by the naked eye. Replacing their image was a tall, old windmill that could be heard slowly creaking in its common circular fashion as a light breeze whistled through the valley on that hot, late morning.

Behind him, Millard could hear Keyshawn sniff and cough. He looked back to see the boy pick up the bag of dead animals.

Millard's mind always had an insatiable habit of repeating his own words back to him, no matter how vulgar and hurtful they sounded. He couldn't shake Courtney out of his head. To hear that she wanted him dead should have not even caused him to perspire, but there was something about hearing Keyshawn replay his mother's rant against him that seemed to give him chills all over his aching body.

He wanted so very much to get rid of everyone, once and for all, especially Keyshawn. He had absolutely nothing more to say to the boy. Millard's lowly shack was only a few yards ahead.

Millard's hearing wasn't any better than his eyesight, but the screeching of tires coming onto his property wasn't all too far from earshot. Before he and Keyshawn could even climb the fence, Millard saw Virginia's Oldsmobile careen into the driveway, swerving in all directions before crashing into the broadside of the barn.

Millard, with a confounded stare on his face, climbed over the fence and watched as Essya tried in earnest to drag a lifeless Virginia from out of the car.

"Millard, help, it's after us!" She desperately screamed before accidentally dropping Virginia to the ground.

Millard right away cocked his rifle and hobbled over to assist the young woman with Virginia. He looked at Essya's bare chest wondering just what in the world was happening.

"What the hell is you two doin'?" He asked as he hoisted Virginia up into his arms.

"It's that thing, it's still chasing us!" Essya cried out as she grabbed Keyshawn by the hand and ran towards the house. "C'mon, Millard, and hurry," she screamed.

Millard turned towards the shack before spinning back around to see the intruder running towards his direction from off the road.

"C'mon, Millard, it's coming!" Essya hollered from behind the door.

With all his might, Millard ran to the house, up the porch steps and clamored inside before nearly having his own backside cut off by Essya slamming the door behind him. He could hear the creature pound its way onto the porch. For a moment he thought it would crash right through the door.

Millard carried Virginia into the bedroom and laid her limp body down on the unmade bed. He then took his rifle and started back for the living room.

"Grandma's bleeding!" Keyshawn hollered as he stood over Virginia and held her hands.

"Shut that damn boy up!" Millard snapped as he prepared for his long overdue battle with his uninvited guest.

Quickly putting on a t-shirt, Essya, sounding amazed, yelled, "Where are you going?"

"I'm gonna go outside!"

"Are you crazy?" She griped. "Don't go back out there!"

"Just shut the hell up and stay right there, I'm gonna—

But before Millard could continue, Virginia's entire body began to shake violently before it fell right off the bed and onto the floor. Millard immediately dropped his rifle and ran back over.

"What's wrong with her?" Keyshawn screamed.

Holding her head up, Millard gritted his teeth, "I forgot she had epilepsy. Get that towel off the dresser real quick."

A stunned Essya did as ordered and handed Millard a white towel. From there, Millard stuffed it into Virginia's foaming mouth.

"Come on now…just hold on." Millard whispered into Virginia's face as he held her in his arms. "What the fuck happened?" He asked Essya.

"We were out in the woods, and then it just came after us! It jumped on the car! It tried to tear out Virginia's throat! It followed us all the way back here!"

Millard, Essya and Keyshawn all paused to listen as the beast climbed its way up onto the roof and stepped about as if it were pacing back and forth. To Millard its scratchy footsteps resembled the sound of thunder rumbling by.

Essya and Keyshawn sat down on the floor next to Virginia and Millard as Virginia's epileptic onslaught continued. Millard looked upwards at the ceiling. He was well aware that with all the weight on top of the roof that it wouldn't be too long before it all came crashing down in on all four of them.

Millard, Essya and Keyshawn all sat on the floor and listened attentively at the creature that was growling and grunting, sounding like it was mad.

Millard had no words, not even a mere thought crossed his mind at that painstaking event. He just sat and looked on at the wall in front of him as he stiffened his body to the point where no fear could enter.

CHAPTER 28

Jim pulled down the rusty, metal lever that slowly raised a torn and twisted cage from out of the murky pond that it had been resting in.

Steven and Leon both looked on at the wreck as it dangled in mid-air by only its strong, steel cord.

With his mouth hanging wide open, Leon gasped, "This is what ya'll kept it in?"

"That's right," Steven stepped forward. "For eight years this was its home away from home."

Rubbing his hands up and down the sturdy, moss layered cage bars, Leon frowned, "What is this…iron?"

Lighting a cigarette, Steven replied, "Not exactly, Sheriff. You see, those bars are a rare type of alloy called omnium. Our people discovered it in some mountains over in the Iraq desert. It's virtually unbreakable, or so we thought until a few nights ago."

"You got that right," Leon chuckled. "Look how it's been bent in half, man."

"The storm sure did a number on the old cage." Jim remarked while coming down from a series of metal stairs.

Leon stood back from the pond's edge and inspected his surroundings. It was a wooded area encircled by nothing but green flourishing weeping willows and brush. Just a few feet away from the pond sat a small, tin shack.

"Is that where ya'll stay at over yonder?" Leon pointed.

"Yep, those are our living quarters." Steven answered. "Wanna take a look inside?"

Scratching his chin, the sheriff skittishly replied, "Well, I might as well while I'm here."

Steven and Jim led Sheriff Leon towards the shack. Steven then used a key to unlock the steel door. Once the door was pushed wide open Steven stepped aside to allow Leon to get a full view.

Timid at first, Leon gradually walked inside to find himself suddenly transported from his rural, backwoods town to a spacious, military-like hideout that resembled a bomb shelter.

Two already made cots were placed side by side in a nearby corner. A refrigerator sat clear on the other end of the room while two Apple computers were positioned in the middle of the floor.

The place smelled of tough cologne and oatmeal cream pies. There were steel cabinets above the refrigerator that shined from just about every angle a person's neck could turn.

With astonishment in his speech, Leon asked, "This is where ya'll been livin' for all these years?"

"Well, I have, Jim came aboard some time later. I had a partner, but one night while he was attending to the subject, it ended up escaping its last containment unit and killing him. After that incident we used the omnium to fortify the cage. It hasn't escaped since then, or until now, that is."

Steven stepped aside and watched as the sheriff continued his tour of he and Jim's living quarters. Just by the subtle amazement that Leon was putting up, Steven could very well tell that the man felt like he was in another time or place. All the computers and monitors that kept a watchful eye on the entire town must have belittled the man to the point where he felt insignificant and small.

Just for that one sliver of a moment Steven felt sorry for both the sheriff and his town. Everything and everyone in the tiny berg was so out of touch with the rest of the world that it felt like Sullinger was the land that time didn't even care about.

Exhaling, Leon said, "Well, I'm awfully sorry to hear about your last partner, but I got one question. Jim mentioned the other day that the thing was invincible. How were you able to bring it down that night your partner was killed?"

Steven went over to one of the steel cabinets, opened it and pulled out a solid silver-like gun. "This right here, my good Sheriff, is quite possibly the single most powerful firearm known in the free world today. We call it the "Brain Buster."

With ogling eyes, Leon studied just about every portion of the weapon like it was something from outer space.

Steven then held up a small capsule which contained a lime green substance inside before saying, "These tranquillizer darts are filled with a chemical called X-49. It's a lethal combination of mercury, cyanide, and our personal favorite, liquid nitrogen. Just one of these babies can kill a full grown African elephant within seconds. However, they only put our friend to sleep for up to ten hours."

Steven handed the weapon to a wide-eyed Leon who slobbered all over the gun's sleek, metallic alloy. "It must weigh at least five pounds."

"Yep, the elements inside the darts may be simple at best, but once our scientists figured out just how to take it down, we spared no expense. The nitrogen freezes the heart and lungs while the mercury and cyanide flush the body with poison in about eight point two seconds. Had we used it on another subject, after the eight seconds, the subject's insides would have literally exploded."

Chuckling nervously, Leon said, "Good Lord, I'd hate to see what it does to a human being."

"I hope I'm never around to see that." Jim grinned.

"So you mean to say that the thing is strong enough to survive all that's inside that capsule? What about just regular old bullets?"

"Regular bullets are like bee-bee gun shots to it." Jim said. "It's body stays perpetually saturated in a gelatinous-like substance. The darts have only five seconds to be effective, or else."

Leon handed the strange weapon back to Steve and proceeded to wander about the facility once again while fanning himself with his straw hat. "This is a real nice set up ya'll got here." Leon sighed. "I can't imagine how me and Corey missed this place all this time. Heck, I don't even remember that pond out there, and I've lived in Sullinger all my life."

Leon meandered towards the row of TV monitors in the middle of the floor and began to inspect each individual screen. There were all filled with live images of the town, from the main square, to Claymore's Creek, all the way to the police station.

Scratching his face, the sheriff said, "I don't know about all this spyin' stuff. But, as long as you fella's find what you're lookin' for. Speakin' of such, where do ya'll think our friend is now?"

"There's a good chance that it's still over your cousin's house as we speak." Jim said.

"What makes ya think that?"

"Just a curious hunch," Jim shrugged his shoulders. "For some reason or another, it's seemed to latch onto your cousin."

"Yeah, we still can't explain it ourselves," Steven added.

Leon stuffed his hands into his pockets and looked away saying in a sullen voice, "Maybe this thing has found something as evil as it is. A kindred spirit, I reckon. And Millard is an evil man. It took me years to admit that fact out loud, but…it's a fact, nonetheless."

"He must be evil if he's willing to shoot at both me and Steven."

"And that's another thing," Leon spun around, "he ain't got no right to be shootin' at somebody that ain't never once hurt him. I should've brought his ass in that day, but, with all that's been goin' on, it slipped my mind. But we do need to hurry up and get this thing quick. It's destroyed enough as it is. Hell, no one has still heard from the McConnell brothers since yesterday, and I know good and damn well they went huntin' for the thing."

"Sheriff, we really need to evacuate this town at all costs." Steven remarked. "It's the only way we can safeguard the residents' lives."

"There's no need for that." Leon held up his hands. "If Jim says that it's at Millard's then that's where we'll go, whether Millard likes it or not. That reminds me, why don't you boys come by the house tonight for a home cooked meal? Cornelia's fixin' up some lasagna and some of that garlic toast or garlic bread, whatever it's called. After that, we can go over to Millard's and get that devil. At night is better, nobody will be in our way."

Suffering from an abrupt case of the jitters, Steven blurted out, "Well, Sheriff, I don't think that would be—

"That sounds great." Jim all of the sudden chimed in. "We haven't had good food like that for a long time."

Steven stood behind Jim while handing the young man the ugliest eye he possibly could, like Jim had done something so unspeakable.

"Good, we'll be waitin' on you two."

"You know, Leon, I think it'll be safer if just Jim and I handle this on our own." Steven forced himself to smirk. "The last thing we want is for the whole town to know about this."

"They already do," Leon laughed. "Heck, you got some folks who haven't left their houses in days because of it."

Right there, Steven's heart dropped to his feet. He couldn't believe what he was hearing from the sheriff's nonchalant mouth, as though having a killer creature in town were a regular occurrence. Steven's entire mouth at that instant went bone dry.

"Maybe that's a good thing, Leon," Jim said. "It seems that people here are always afraid of something. Me and Steve keep hearing these stories about ghosts running around town. What's that about?" He giggled.

At first, Leon kept his lips pressed together like he was too shy to speak, but after a while, the man took his hands out of his pockets, sat down on the table next to one of the monitors and groaned as if something heavy were troubling him.

"Well…Sullinger's ghost story isn't exactly something most of us tend to discuss with outsiders, but…since it's just the three of us. You see, way back when Mr. Lincoln emancipated all the slaves, ole' Jason Sullinger's slaves revolted. A lot of folks said that Jason Sullinger was the meanest slave owner in all of Mississippi, and his slaves were gonna take out their revenge before running away to freedom."

Steven stood against the wall and listened with half-hearted ears as Leon rambled on about a story that the man could have honestly cared less about. Nonetheless, he kept his eyes locked on the sheriff, wanting to give the appearance that he was interested.

"The slaves killed all seven of Jason's daughters, as well as his wife. Before they got to Jason, however, the slaves heard him inside his bedroom chanting some kind of spell. You see, Jason and his wife were into all that witchcraft silliness. Once he was done chanting, they went in and took Jason down. From there, they hung Jason, his wife and all the girls outside on the same weeping willow tree that Jason used on the slaves in years past before burning down the Sullinger mansion. Well, around the spring of 1902, folks said they saw all seven of the Sullinger girls runnin' around the town square, playin' as though they were still alive."

Glancing over at Steven, Jim cracked a grin and asked, "So, wait a minute, you mean to say that these little girls are haunting this town?"

"Not exactly, you see, the spell that Jason was chanting that night ended up putting a curse on Sullinger. It goes, whoever dies here, doesn't matter how they die, their souls stay right here in town. They don't go to heaven. They don't go to hell. They stay put right here…forever."

Steven, with a rusty scowl soaking on his face, pulled his body from off the wall and walked towards the sheriff. "I guess I can't convince you to evacuate, can I?" He humbly questioned.

With a cordial smile, Leon said, "Steve, my friend, there's no need to do that. We'll take care of everything this evening. I've gotta go make my rounds. I'll see you two this evening."

With his two surly eyes, Steven stood still and watched as the sheriff walked out the door. A scolding heat then wrapped itself around the man's stiff body at that moment. The heat poked and stung him like a horde of enraged hornets.

All he could do was replay Leon's words of how everyone in town knew about the beast. He couldn't get Leon's pudgy, carefree face out of his head. The man really looked as though he didn't have a single worry in the world, and that alone caused Steven's knees to buckle all the more.

"Do you believe that story of his?" Jim asked from behind.

Steven could hear something, a series of sounds, but in his blurry head they all rushed by at the speed of light.

"Did his story disturb you that much, Steve?"

As though someone had splashed water into face, Steven suddenly came back to life. He began to stumble over to the table where he was sitting before, staring endlessly at one of the monitors that overlooked Mikey's Diner.

Grunting out a blasé snigger, Steven answered, "We've been guarding a monster. Who am I to doubt?"

"Then what is it?"

Hesitating to answer, or just searching for whatever proper words to utter, Steven slowly replied, "Nothing… nothing at all. Why don't you go down to that hardware store and get us some wine for dinner tonight."

"Sure," Jim said before stepping out the door.

Steven listened to the door shut behind Jim before saying in a drifting mumble, "They all know…everyone knows."

CHAPTER 29

Millard and Essya stood over the sink cleaning the newly gutted rabbit and snakes that were killed earlier in the day. Thanks to the creature, the temperature inside the shack was dropping dramatically by the hour, and it wouldn't be too long before everyone inside would be forced to bundle up in something warm.

Millard quietly pulled out the remains of the rabbit's insides before tossing them into a steel bucket beside him on the floor. He could very well hear the beast stomp and trample about above him on the unstable roof, but as unsettling as it was to know that there was something beyond comprehension just a few feet above his head, Millard had absolutely nothing on his mind but eating.

Every so often he would catch Essya glancing over at him. He watched as her shaking hands fumbled the sharp knife she was holding. He honestly couldn't tell if she were trembling from the cold, fright or both.

Millard twisted his lips as he watched the young lady nervously fidget with one of the dead snakes before eventually and accidentally dropping it out of her bloody hands.

Sighing, the old man whined, "What the hell are you doin', gal?"

"Millard…what are we gonna do?" She impatiently whispered.

"Do about what," he shrugged.

"About that up there," Essya pointed. "Can't you hear it?"

"What do you want me to do, girl, go up there and shoot the damn thing down?"

"Yes," she squealed.

Without muttering a word, Millard callously looked over at Essya before brushing right by her and sashaying into the living room. He waited for the woman to join him before he sat down on the chair that was placed beside the couch. Then, picking at his blood stained fingers, Millard sank his rugged body down into the seat.

"Why don't you do just that?" Essya tossed up her hands. "Why don't you go and kill it? You kill everything else you see."

Millard only cracked a nonchalant grin before casually murmuring, "Bullets don't work on the damn thing."

"Why not," Virginia slurred as she came stumbling into the living room from the bedroom.

Racing to her aid, Essya desperately asked, "Are you okay?"

"I'm fine, honey; I just got one helluva migraine right about now." Virginia muttered before sitting her weak body down on the couch. Virginia's forehead was wrapped with a wet cloth while her neck was secured with a bundle of paper towels. "God, I feel like I just got hit by a car. What time is it?"

"Ten after two." Essya answered. "Do you want something to eat or drink?"

"No thank you, darlin'…I don't even have the stomach for food right now."

Millard stared hard-heartedly for a moment or two at the ragged woman before resuming his finger picking detail.

"What was this I heard about bullets don't work on it? Do you mean to tell me that it actually followed us all the way here?"

"After it attacked you, I drove. It kept up with us all the way."

Shaking her head, Virginia moaned, "God, have mercy. Well, Mr. Lang, what's the battle plan?"

"Battle plan?"

"Yes. Don't you have a way for us to get outta here without getting us all killed?"

"Woman, didn't you just hear me say that bullets don't work?"

"How do you know that for sure?"

"Because…I tried to kill it yesterday in the woods," Millard said.

"You saw it?" Virginia choked. "So what happened?"

"Nothin', the fucker just stood there and screamed at me."

"Then we have to call Leon so he can come over and do soemthin'".

"Gal, I ain't got no phone."

Looking totally confused, Virignia asked, "Millard, how can you not have a phone? You have a TV, for God's sake!"

"Who am I gonna call, your ass?"

"We have to do something or else that thing that's on the fuckin' roof is gonna come down here and eat us all up!" Virginia ranted. "You saw it, Millard, that ain't no alligator, and it sure as hell ain't no ghost! That thing on the roof is something that I've never seen before in my life!"

It seemed the louder Virginia's voice grew that was the angrier the beast became as its incessant roaring intensified. All three persons looked up as pieces of wood came falling to the floor due to the creature's constant stomping.

"Millard, what is that up there?" Virginia screamed.

There was only one explanation that the old man had inside his head at that second, one that he hoped would keep everyone at bay for the time being.

Without taking his eyes off of his fingers, he carefully explained, "The night of the storm, some damn bastard tried to break into my house. When I chased the sum bitch out into the barn I felt somethin' hit me from behind. Somethin' damn hard. Nearly broke my back. I just figured it was the other fella's buddy. I felt its cold hand that night knock me upside my head. The next day, Shirley started actin' strange. The fucker was hidin' up in the loft. Shirley knew it, but I couldn't see the thing."

Turning around to Essya, Virginia questioned, "That's what you meant when you said that it was a ghost, didn't you?"

"Yeah," Essya shook. "It touched me, but I couldn't see it. I knew it was there. I watched it kill Kenny and his friends… every last one of them."

"The fucker scared poor Shirley to death, even had her runnin' to the church across the way there. Next day, it killed her."

"Shirley, the dog, is dead?" Virginia looked on amazed.

"'Fraid so," Millard flippantly replied.

Appearing befuddled, Virginia said, "Wait a minute, so far this thing has killed my babies, some boys down at the creek, and your mangy dog, but it's somehow found it in its heart to spare you?"

"I ain't no smart man, never claimed to be."

"You're damn right about that!" Virginia snapped back. "How can you sit there so calmly on your smug ass as if nothing is happening or hasn't happened? You're telling me that this bastard from hell was just blown here in some storm and found a home on your property?"

"I can't explain it; all I know is that my ass is still here!"

"Now were all stuck here while it paces back and forth on that roof! Oh, and let's not forget that since Mr. Lang here chooses not to invest in a phone, we have absolutely no way of reaching the outside world! So forget about calling Leon or anyone else for that matter! We're all gonna be eaten alive because Millard has a brand new friend who protects him!"

"The two men that were here the day Courtney and Rayshawn were killed could have stopped it." Essya brazenly added.

Snapping her sore neck around, Virginia urgently asked, "What two men?"

"They were these two men; they knew what the monster was. All they wanted was to ask Millard some questions, but Millard shot at them and told them to go away."

"You shut your damn mouth up, gal!" Millard shouted.

"No, I won't shut up!" Essya defiantly fired back.

With tears forming in her eyes, Virginia raised herself up from off the couch and stood over Millard in an intimidating manner. "These men could have done something! They could've stopped the thing from killing my babies, and you acted like some old asshole!" She screamed with all her angry might.

Just then, as Virginia's painful rant increased, the beast above seemed to become more irritated, sounding as though it were ready to tear right through the ceiling after her.

Looking up, Virginia yelled, "What's wrong, am I hurting your best friend's feelings? Why does it wanna kill me, because I won't kiss your stinkin' ass?" Virginia then turned to Essya and cried, "Why does it wanna kill you, because you wouldn't clean the shit stains out of his dirty shorts?"

With every outburst, the demon's rampage persisted to where large shards of wood even fell onto Millard's lap and head.

"C'mon and kill me then, hell, I ain't go nothin' else to fuckin' live for!"

"Grandma, no," Keyshawn came wailing into the living room.

"What the hell do you want from me?" Millard pounded his chest.

Virginia advanced towards Millard, flailing her arms at the man and hollering, "I fuckin' hate you! I hate you so much!"

Essya did her best to restrain the enraged woman as Millard jumped up from out of the chair to defend himself.

The old man stood back and watched Virginia carry both herself and Keyshawn back into the bedroom, crying an aching river of tears along the way.

Essya stood there before her man, staring him up and down. The look of disgust on her blushing face caused Millard to step back; he had never seen such a glare in her eyes before, such a shameful expression.

He stood and watched as she retreated to the bedroom along with her two newfound friends before dragging himself back to the kitchen.

CHAPTER 30

I t was well past four p.m. that afternoon as Millard sat at the kitchen table grudgingly eating away at his baked rabbit that no one else in the house had the nerve to feast on.

It had been quiet ever since the spat earlier, even the beast seemed to be more relaxed to a certain extent; its persistent pacing on the roof had slowed to that of nothing more than crawling and scraping rather than full-bore rampaging.

Once he had finished swallowing the last scrap of meat from off his plate, Millard got up, went over and took out a bottle of Bartles & Jaymes before rambling his way into the living room. He was well aware that Virginia, Essya and Keyshawn were all huddled up inside the bedroom. He was cold, but venturing into the room to retrieve his long john shirt was a mission that he did not wish to undertake; just knowing that they were all confined inside his house together made him sick to his stomach.

Just as he was about to sit down on the couch and watch television, his cold ears caught the sound of something scratching down below him. Millard wanted to go and get his gun, but it too was inside the bedroom. Instead, he emptied the remaining contents of his wine bottle onto the floor before carrying both it and himself down the basement steps.

After all that had and was still taking place, the man was prepared for just about any and everything at that point.

Surprising to him, his body broke out into a violent sweat with every step he took downwards. The closer he reached the floor the more Millard could hear the scratching and rummaging that sounded like a large rodent were taking up roost in his homestead.

With his empty wine bottle clutched tightly in his hand, the old man rounded a corner to find none other than Virginia checking through various drawers inside Millard's tool cabinet.

Although her presence had been menacing to him ever since he met her at the funeral home the day before, just knowing that it was her and not something else caused the sweat to evaporate.

With a tired grunt, Millard asked, "What the hell are you doin' down here?"

Startled enough to drop the papers she had in her hands to the floor, Virginia whirled around and gasped, "I was hoping to find what I had been practically begging for all this time."

Millard walked past Virginia who was busy picking up the papers from off the floor. There sat between two large cabinets a rusty, steel locker with no door attached to it. Millard simply sat himself down inside the darkness of the locker to where only his rugged face could be seen.

He waited until she sat herself down on a stool right next to the tool table before reaching into his hip pocket and handing to her what she had most desired.

Without a moment's hesitation, Virginia's eyes began to water at the sight of the face she was staring at in the photo.

Trying her best to conceal the tears, with a stiff upper lip Virginia muttered, "Thank you… Mr. Lang."

Millard only turned his head to the cracked floor, wishing that he hadn't poured out his liquor after all.

"What…did you two talk about before she died?" Virginia sniffed.

"She just came by to see how I was doin' after those little bastards tried to drown me."

With a quivering bottom lip, Virginia questioned, "What did she look like? What did she smell like?"

"I don't remember all that." Millard griped.

"You don't remember what your own daughter looked like before she died? Before she was taken away from you?"

"Why in the world would I want to remember all of that?"

"Oh, I don't know, maybe because she's your child?"

"Do you want for me to be ballin' and cryin' like a little baby? Would that make you feel better?"

"No, I honestly don't believe you'd mean it." Virginia replied as she stuffed the photo into her pants pocket and gazed around the musty old basement. "It's sure been a long time since I was last down here."

With a crude grin, Millard asked, "You remember what happened the last time you was down here, doncha?"

"That was a long time ago, Mr. Lang." She sighed. "Why is it so damn cold in this house all of the sudden? It's like a hundred and twenty degrees outside. And what's with that God-awful smell?"

"It's that thing; every time it's around everything just starts gettin' cold all of the sudden."

"I wonder what it could be." Virginia vigorously rubbed her arms.

Millard turned his head to the floor once again before looking back up to find Virginia staring at him with a hard study attached to her face, like she was trying to figure something out.

"What's the matter with you?" He frowned.

It took at least an entire minute for her to reply. "I'm still stunned that I'm here…with you, of all people."

"You're the one that chose to take walks in the forest and drive here and there with the gal upstairs."

"It's not that, I just never imagined that I'd be here, sitting face to face with you after all these years. You used to be my best friend, Millard. I always wondered what I did to make you turn on me."

"Here we go." Millard groaned as if he were aching.

"I wonder what Brett's mama would think of you now if she were still alive today."

"I really don't care all that much." The old man pouted.

"That's just it, Millard, you don't care. Did you care about Brett when he went to jail for the first time at the age of ten? Did you care about Greg when you found out what he and Terrence were doin' down at the creek? Nope, you just beat poor Greg senseless."

"He was suckin' another boy's dick!" Millard defensively responded.

"But he was still your child. He needed his father, not an executioner."

Millard rolled his eyes and sank deeper into the shadow that he was already sulking in. He could feel the headache creep up on him all over again.

"After Brett's mama died, what did you do? You told him to get out of your face with all that crying. Now, after all of that, did you honestly think I wanted you around Courtney?"

"It didn't matter what I thought, you were gonna do what you wanted no matter what."

"She always told me how you would show up to defend her and the boys from Tyrone. I was going to commend you for doing that, but I won't. You didn't do it for them; you did it for yourself because you felt guilty. Every time Millard got that self-pity bug up his ass. That's when you'd show up to save the day. Deep down, all of your kids just wanted their father around."

Millard's face slowly emerged from the shadows, and with a crusty grunt he said, "I ain't apologizin' for nothin'."

"Nobody's askin' you to apologize, Millard. Nobody ever asked you for one thing. Hell, I never even asked you for child support."

"Good, because you wouldn't have gotten a single dime from my ass," the old man bluntly retaliated.

Virginia sat back, looking like she was overwhelmed. Her eyes then blundered about the dimly lit basement as if she were suddenly lost in the space. "You're wondering why it hasn't bothered to kill you yet. Why it hasn't burst into this house and torn you into a million tiny pieces like it did everyone else? This is the devil, Mr. Lang."

Millard hopelessly dropped his exhausted head to the floor, wondering just what he was doing at all anymore in his wretched life.

"The devil has other plans for you. You see, while everyone you once loved and cared about are being wiped out before your eyes, I believe that it's saving the best for last. And just like the devil, he'll tear through everyone, young and old, just to get to the one person he wants the most."

Millard's entire body materialized from out of the locker the second Virginia was through making her speech. He then sat his wine bottle down onto the floor and clapped his hands in a mocking manner. "You done, or should I get ready for the next act?"

A crafty smile stretched across Virginia's face right then before she cut her eyes away and said, "I yelled at Keyshawn this morning on the way over here. My mind was still on his brother and mother. Bless his little heart, he asks so many questions."

"You damn right he does, I had to put a whoopin' to his hide this mornin' just to shut 'em up."

"Old man, if you ever put a hand on my child again, you won't have to wait on the devil to come and kill you."

It was as though Millard were knocked back by a bullet to the chest. Never before had he seen such fire in Virginia's eyes. Never had such a simple facial gesture put so much trepidation in his sour soul.

Millard just used his customary swagger to brush off the fatal warning before reaching into his back pocket to pull out his pack of Red Man.

"Essya lets you chew that filth?"

"I ain't ten years old." The old man reacted defiantly. "I don't need nobody tryin' to save me"

"I stopped trying to save you years ago. I just put your sorry behind in God's hands and let him deal with you."

"Then let 'em deal with me, dammit!" Millard lashed out as he ripped open the patch, snatched out a stalk of chaw and stuffed it into his mouth.

Appearing unfazed by his brutal rebuttal, Virginia said in a down tone, "I always wonder what Rayshawn's last thoughts were before he…that's just not supposed to happen to a child."

Millard, however, ignored her subtle ramblings and chewed harder on his tobacco before catching Virginia gawking past him.

"What the hell are you lookin' at?"

"Tell me something, Mr. Lang, do you still have that stash lying around here?"

Snickering, Millard said, "Wouldn't you like to know?"

"I'm just curious, that's all. After all, you're the one that's been to the Gulf, not me."

"You said you never went there before!" Essya screamed from the top of the basement steps, startling both Millard and Virginia half to death.

Shocked and embarrassed, Millard jumped up from out of the safe confines of his locker. Before he could even strike up the stairs, he happened to glance back at Virginia who was smirking while taking a bottle of vodka from out of a cabinet. There wasn't a single fiber in his body that didn't want to turn around and whip the woman from one corner of the basement to the other, but his vengeance would hold for the time being.

He climbed up the stairs to find Keyshawn seated on the living room couch watching cartoons on the television. Millard then turned to the kitchen; there was only one more place to search. He went straight for the bedroom. The second he opened the door he found Essya sitting on the bed writing something on a piece of paper. He shut the door behind him before standing tall in front of her.

"What the hell are you doin, gal?"

"I'm leaving, and this time I'm leaving for good." She faintly answered, sounding as though she were speaking in slow motion.

"Leaving for what? What the hell is the matter with you? You know that thing is out there."

Essya stopped writing long enough to look up at Millard and ask, "You didn't think I knew, did you?"

"Knew what?"

"About Keisha," Essya sniffed.

"Keisha who," the old man shrugged his shoulders as his eyelids blinked in a rapid succession.

"Don't do that, Millard."

"Do what, dammit," he yelled.

"Look at me like I'm stupid! I'm not stupid!"

"Who the hell said that you was stupid!" he hollered back.

"Shut up!"

Stunned to hear such ire come out of her mouth, Millard at first was at a loss for words. "Who you tellin' to shut up," he yelled as he advanced towards her.

"Are you gonna hit me? Well go ahead then." Essya boldly remarked. "You didn't think I knew about that girl. You didn't think I knew about her? And you have the nerve to just stand there like you don't know what I'm talking about? Are you serious?"

Millard stood back and scratched his head while bashfully glaring down at the floor beneath him.

"Is that how you lure us women in? By promising a free trip to the Gulf if we sleep with you?"

Millard's entire body went numb. His knees felt limp and rubbery, which was exactly why he dropped himself down on the foot of the bed.

As soon as he sat down Essya got up from off the bed, took off the shirt that she was wearing and began to examine the cuts and scars on her back from where the creature attacked her earlier.

"You see these?" She pointed. "This is where it began, and this is where it will end." Essya said as she put the shirt back on and stared for the door. With a sullen face, she then uttered, "I figure I'll just go outside and let it eat me up."

The beast above snarled and snorted; by then, everyone in the shack had become accustomed to its ceaseless motions. But to Millard, it was doing precisely what he himself wanted to do, lash out at the world.

"It's funny; the only friends I got are the ones that I met just yesterday."

"Why do you wanna go out there?"

"Why wouldn't I want to? To you I'm nothing more than a quick blowjob. You can go back to Jackson and get another one of those for ten dollars."

"I kept you around this long, haven't I?"

Essya folded her livid arms and said, "Me and Virginia were talking this morning before we got chased back here, and—

"What the hell has she been fillin' your head with?"

"Only things that she's been through with you," Essya replied. "She told me how much of a charmer you once were."

"Shit," the old man grumbled, "that dumb heifer will say anything to make me look bad. What I used to be? Hell, I ain't never changed!"

Essya's tone of speech grew listless as she uttered, "Ever since you first told me that you were taking me to the Coast years ago, I always imagined you and me sitting on some beach, watching the wave's crash onto the shore. You'd be smiling for a change."

Millard sulked on the bed, rolling his eyes while recalling the first time he and Essya met. He remembered a feisty, independent woman that was eventually torn down and broken into countless pieces, pieces that he had been stepping on for years ever since. He despised a woman that could stand her own ground; to him, it wasn't a fair playing field.

"I don't know," he forced himself to mumble, "maybe after all this shit is over, me and you can…maybe we can go down there and—

"Don't do that," she interjected. "I can tell that saying nice words kills you. Don't go out of your way for me…Mr. Lang. I don't wanna go to hell with you."

Without breaking a sweat or shedding a single tear, Essya turned and softly walked out of the bedroom, shutting the door behind her.

Staggered into silence, Millard slowly got up from off the bed and began to go after the young lady. As he reached for the doorknob, his eyes became distracted by the piece of notebook paper that she had unknowingly dropped to the floor. He knelt down and picked it up.

Dear Millard, I love you so much, but I can't take anymore. Love Essya.

Millard crumpled up the paper and stood in the middle of the floor while his stone reflection stared soberly back at him in the cracked mirror that sat on his dresser. He knew Essya wasn't going outside.

She was right; it did kill him to say nice words.

CHAPTER 31

Evening: Around Eight P.M.

T he shining crystal chandelier above reflected inch-wide grades of colorful light that shimmered dazzlingly around the dinner table beneath it.

Steven, Jim, Leon and Cornelia were all seated at the brightly lit table inside the sheriff's one floor, two room house. Plates that were once layered with fresh baked lasagna and aromatic garlic bread were completely wiped clean, with only a few scant traces of sauce lining each of the dishes rims. Cornelia picked up the half full bottle of Chardonnay and circled the table, generously reloading scarcely filled wine glasses.

"No more for me." Steven kindly refused, patting his bloated belly. "One more sip and I won't be worth a damn later on tonight."

Jim exhaled, "That was one incredible dinner, Ms. Rutner."

"It sure has been a long time since we've last had a home cooked meal, ma'am. We surely appreciate it." Steven added.

"You two have been callin' me ma'am and Ms. Rutner all evening long. Cornelia will do just fine from here on out." Cornelia humbly smiled as she sat herself back down at the table next to Leon. "I'm sure being all alone in that shack, or whatever you call it, can be pretty lonely at times. No matter how far away from home you are, a home cooked meal always brings us back to reality."

"Well, being lonely is the last thing either of us has to worry about, Cornelia." Jim remarked. "So, when do you two love birds plan on tying the knot?"

A delightful beam came across Cornelia's face at that moment. "I always dreamt of a summer wedding. That pasture out near the cemetery is where we're going to have it."

"You sure you wanna have it in the middle of summer, with all the bugs and heat?"

"It's beautiful down here year round, but the real reason we want it in the summer is so that it can be done before school starts back up again." Cornelia explained. "Everyone in town already knows that Leon and I are shacking up. It wouldn't look right if we got hitched in the middle of fall. It tends to set an even worse example, if you catch my drift."

"Steve was once engaged." Jim pointed as he wiped his mouth with his napkin.

Steven just happened to glace over at his young partner while trying to conceal his blushing face.

"Oh really," Leon asked, finishing up his last ounces of wine. "What happened?"

Completely caught off guard, Steven modestly laughed from his belly, "That was a long time ago. I got engaged to my high school sweetheart, Wendy Trumann. I proposed to her on our prom night, right in the middle of the dance floor. Then came the call from Uncle Sam. Poor Wendy, she begged and pleaded with me for us to run off to Canada or Mexico, but, call it the crazy old solider in me, I just couldn't run away from a fight. She gave me my ring back, and I never saw her again. That's life, I guess." He shrugged.

"No, that's stupid male pride." Cornelia commented. "That girl loved you and you ran off to fight. Only a man," she humorously added. "What about you, Jim? Any love stories to tell?"

"Not me," Jim sounded off like a giddy child. "All my so called love stories begin and end with a phone number and a slap across the face. I think that's why I joined the Marines. I got tired of being rejected." He laughed. "So tell us, is this the first marriage for you two?"

"For me it is, but it'll be Leon's second." Cornelia pointed out.

"You were married before, Leon?" Jim asked.

Smiling meekly while leaning back in his seat, Leon sighed, "For twenty-two years. My wife passed on from cancer 'round nine years ago. We had two kids, a boy and a girl. Of course, they're not kids no more. My son is a policeman way out in San Diego, and my daughter teaches high school algebra in New Jersey. We're hopin' that they can make it down here for the wedding," Leon shook his head.

"What made them move so far away?" Jim questioned. "Besides what's been happening here the past few days, Sullinger is a pretty quiet town."

"That's the thing about some folks here, once they graduate, they tend to move on. Sometimes, they'll leave before they finish school. Ole' Sullinger doesn't offer much to the younger generations. I reckon they see this old town as a one way road to nowhere. It's dryin' up here. The fiberglass plant closin' years ago didn't help matters, either. Yep, they all up and leave like yesterday's wind, and never look back again."

"Well, after your story earlier today, I guess no one would want to stick around here too much." Jim sniggered.

"Oh Lord, did he tell you that ridiculous Jason Sullinger story?" Cornelia moaned.

"He sure did." Jim laughed.

"I swear, I've never heard anything as silly as that story in all my years. Ghosts," Cornelia huffed.

"The reason you can't see any of them is because you weren't born here." Leon remarked. "I saw my first ghost when I was only six years old. My first grade teacher, Mrs. Henderson, fell down the steps at her own home and broke her neck. About two weeks later, there she was, roamin' around down by the creek."

"Are you serious?" Jim glared on in astonishment.

"That's right. When you live here in Sullinger, you're bound to run across one just as easily as you would a dog or cat."

"Me, personally, I haven't seen a spook or specter yet, and the folks who have seen one don't like talkin' about it." Cornelia said.

"There are a lot of strange things that we've noticed about this town ever since we've been here." Jim explained. "For starters, every station in town plays nothing but oldies. Plus, there's no mayor here. But hey, were not ones to argue about strange things, considering what we've had to watch over all these years."

Steven awoke from his sullen stupor at that very second and again looked over at an exuberant Jim who seemed happier than usual for some unexplainable reason.

"Steve, you've been around this thing longer than anyone." Leon said. "What keeps you so close to it after all these years?"

Steven wanted to break away; anywhere but the dining room table would suffice, but being surrounded only caused him to remain pinned to his chair. Clearing his throat, he replied, "My main reason is that I've seen firsthand what it's capable of doing. This is no ordinary being, I can assure you of that much."

"Ever since this thing started killing people, I've been wondering if perhaps it may be something that mankind hasn't discovered yet. Something that we've overlooked all these ages," Cornelia curiously mentioned.

"Our scientists believe the same, but they're having difficulty discovering just how old it is, or, if it may be the next step in evolution. If you believe in evolution, that is." Jim stepped in.

"Is it carnivorous?" Cornelia inquired.

Steven gritted his teeth before answering, "All these years, it's never eaten a human...until the little boy the other day. It mostly feeds on small animals."

Shivering from head to toe, Cornelia said, "I hate talking about the Godforsaken thing. It reminds me of that no good Millard; If you wanna talk about Godforsaken things."

"Yeah, Steve and I found that out the hard way a few days back when he shot at our car."

"He shot at ya'll?" Cornelia gasped on in horror as she looked over at Leon. "Why didn't you arrest his sorry ass?"

Leon just shook his head and murmured, "I dunno, I reckon I had other things on my mind at the time."

Nodding her head shamefully, Cornelia moaned, "Lord forgive me, but that man, if you can call him a man, has to be one of the worst excuses for a human being I have ever seen. He didn't even bother to show up for his daughter and grandson's funeral!"

"You never did tell us why your cousin is the way he is, Leon." Jim queried. "I mean, there has to be some kind of motivation behind all that rage."

Steven, who was conspicuously sitting dead quiet and still in his chair, handed his inquisitive partner a freezing cold doom gaze, like he was telling the young man that he had only seconds left to live. He had no choice but dwell in the moment that had been handed to him.

He watched as Leon settled himself in his chair and rolled his eyes to the back of his head. The man held upon his face a stoic expression, like the story he was about to impart tortured him. Both Jim and Cornelia sat up in their individual seats and readied themselves for what they expected to be the telling of a lifetime.

"Ya know how when you go and buy a brand new light bulb? You screw it into a lamp, and that bulb lights up the whole room. Then, after so much time, that bulb starts to lose its power, until, it eventually burns out. That's Millard for you."

Much to his own surprise, however, Steven's ears, which for the entire evening had all but managed to keep out all other conversation, happened to perk up at Leon's story.

"Believe it or not, Millard was a good person at one time. He came from good parents. They took 'em to church every Sunday. He was captain of our high school basketball team. Yep, Ole' Millard had a lot of potential way back when. Then, now don't quote me on this, but, when he was about, I'd say in his late thirties, his father was beaten and killed for messin' around with some other man's wife."

Steven kept his eyes locked on Jim who appeared captivated by Leon's story. There was something stirring inside Steven during that evening, and he wanted his partner to feel the same anguish that he had been drowning in for the past ninety minutes.

"Uncle Switch loved his women. Well, his death kinda tore Millard up inside. He and his father were real close. Soon after that, somethin' began to change about him, and it wasn't an overnight change, either. It was more gradual, through the years. He'd stop hangin' out at the hardware store. He would cuss folks out over the littlest things. He even stopped talkin' to his own mama. It's like somethin' just…broke inside of him. And not even God himself could fix it. Yes, sir, Millard used to be the kind of man a person could come up onto his porch, have a beer or two, and sit and talk for hours. It be like talkin' to an old friend. It's a damn shame if ya ask me."

Steven, Jim and Cornelia all sat hushed at the table, huddled up together like sardines, while listening to a recollection of a person that was long dead.

"Well, Leon," Jim wearily exhaled, "if there's one thing I do love about you, it has to be your stories."

"Like I said, don't quote me on that. That's just my take on the poor old soul."

"That's sad about his father, but it's still no reason for him to be so mean to people." Cornelia sighed.

"But you still love him, don't you?" Jim asked.

With a drab and dry attitude, Leon replied, "Love ain't got nuttin' to do with it, son; we're just cousins."

"You sound a bit upset."

"Yesterday, Cornelia had it out with Millard. I should have seen it comin', but I figured maybe he would've been a bit more civil, considerin' that his own daughter and grandson had just been buried. But, I reckon I was wrong."

"He's got two other kids, doesn't he?" Cornelia yawned.

"Two boys," Leon answered. "The youngest one is Brett. That rascal has been in and out of trouble since he was ten years old. The Jackson police picked him up a few days ago for robbin' a liquor store for some beer. That was his last strike. That poor fella won't see the outside of a prison until he's at least sixty. Then there's Greg. He's the oldest of the kids. He's one of them homosexuals, so you can imagine how those reunions turn out. But I think out of all his youngens, Courtney was his favorite. He'd always be there when she and her boys were in trouble. The last time her boyfriend was down here, Millard ended up shooin' one of 'em. Now, not only does Millard have the Klan comin' after him, but he's also got a Detroit gang gunnin' for 'em, too."

"Oh my Lord," Cornelia fretted, "can you handle all of that?"

"I sure hope so," Leon groaned. "From what I've been hearin' around the grapevine, these folks should be on their way real soon. It's gonna make me and Corey's jobs a whole lot more difficult after tonight."

Steven sat up at full attention in his seat and beamed his jittery eyes at the wine glass that sat in front of him before stuttering nervously, "Uh…speaking of tonight, Leon. Do you really think you and your deputy can tackle this assignment? I mean, all Jim and I have to do is just plant one of the darts into it and it's over, just like that."

"There ain't nothin' you can do or say that'll change my mind on the matter," Leon assuredly smiled. "Corey may not know how to load a shotgun, but when it comes down to a good ole' fashioned scrap, the boy can handle his own pretty darn well. Plus, after were through here, I'm gonna get on the phone and call up some boys over in the next town to come and help us out tonight, too."

Steven sat back in his chair, completely bowled over by Leon's cool and relaxed approached. His own hands at that second began to tremor as though he had no control whatsoever over them. Suddenly, he couldn't hear a single soul at the dinner table; all he could see were mouths moving and laughing like the situation at hand were just another day at the office.

"Well, before you boys head out tonight, would ya'll like some fresh baked blueberry pie" Cornelia politely offered as she rose from behind the table.

"I sure would, Cornelia." Jim eagerly spoke up. "I've been smelling that pie all evening."

Once his hands ceased their constant quivering, Steven casually shoved aside his plate and said, "No thanks, but I would like…Oh God, Leon, what's that behind you?" He chocked, pointing at the window behind the sheriff.

Leon, with his plate in hand, spun around in his chair, gawked out the window and said, "I don't see—

But before Leon could even finish, Steven whipped his thirty-eight from out of his hip pocket, pointed it directly at the sheriff's forehead and pulled the trigger, burying three slugs into his brain.

"Sweet Jesus, "Cornelia screamed out as she frantically dropped the plates that were in her hands to the floor.

Much like a skilled marksman, Steven targeted the woman's face. He pulled the trigger and watched with a pair of blank eyes as the bullet shot straight through her face, knocking her back into the wall behind her.

Jim reared over and vomited on the floor while Steven placed his still smoking gun on the table and sat completely still in his seat. The smoke from the gun smelled like smoldering embers as a steady stream of vapor whispered into the air.

Rising up from off the floor, Jim yelled, "What the…fuck?"

Steven remained in his chair as his eyes studied the smear of blood on the wall from where Leon's brains went flying. Then, with an absolute clear mind, he got up from the table and began pacing the floor.

"Steve," Jim hollered, why? Why did you have to kill again?"

Steven stopped pacing long enough to stand and watch Leon's dead body convulse right there on the floor before him. He then turned to his partner and yelled, "You heard what he said! Some gang of thugs from Detroit and the Klan are on their way here! Plus, he's gonna call some of his hunting buddies over in the next town? This whole town will be a warzone by dawn!"

Steven started to pace the floor once more, trying ever so fervently to figure out what his next move should be.

"We should have had this wrapped up days ago! But oh no, we had to do it his way! We don't have the luxury of fumbling and fucking around! We have a job to do! And if I'm correct, I don't recall anyone telling us to be nice about it! And I sure don't give a fuck about some old bastard's sob story!"

Jim's whimpering eventually turned into uncontrollable sobbing as he pounded his fists on the dinner table. "You didn't have to fucking kill them!"

Enraged with his young partner's sniveling, Steven, with all his strength, lifted Jim to his feet. He then slapped him across the face as hard as he could before screaming, "You listen to me, soldier, you knew exactly just what you were signing up for when you joined this little expedition! Our people told us to protect that devil at all costs, no matter what! By any means necessary! You think this is brutal? You think this is sadistic? Two dead bodies lying around? This isn't shit compared to what that fucker can and has done!"

With tears flooding down his face, Jim woefully gazed down at Leon whose eyes remained wide open in a state of shock.

"Look at me!" Steven commanded as he forcefully turned the young man's head towards him. "They tell us that what we have here is the single most incredible discovery of this century. Personally, I couldn't care less. I just wanna find it, take it home and be on my fucking way. We can't let it all go down the toilet because a lawman and his slack-jawed deputy trip us up every step of the way. This ends tonight!"

Steven held his partner by the collar while watching him suck up his own mucus. In Jim's pain stricken eyes Steven could see a terrified little child, someone that wanted nothing to do with what was happening all of the sudden. Steven wanted to say something that would, for the time being, give his partner a moment's solace, anything that would hold him at bay while he finished up the assignment that he had been handed so long ago.

Steven kissed Jim on the forehead before whispering into his ear, "Now, go outside and get the ax in the trunk."

"What for," Jim stammered.

Looking dead into Jim's eyes, Steven, without pause or stutter replied, "I'm gonna cut them up. We can blame it on the creature."

"Holy God, Captain!" Jim crumbled. "Do you have to do that?"

"Jim, it'll give us more time and credibility if we chop them up and blame it on the specimen! Rushing into Lang's house will be all the more justified!"

"This doesn't make any since, Steve! You already shot them!"

"It's not like I planned all this from the get go. If Leon had evacuated the town like we suggested, then all of this could have been prevented. Now, go get the fucking ax!"

Jim shook his head and stormed out the front door. Steven waited until his associate exited the house before glancing down at the floor to catch Cornelia stretching her right arm outwards towards the dinner table.

The man crouched down and scrupulously rubbed his

chin while surveying the struggling woman slowly crawling as though there wasn't a bullet lodged in her face at all.

He stood back up and went into the living room. From there, he tore off a shred of cloth from the couch's lining before going back to Cornelia.

Standing over her, Steven wrapped the cloth around both fists and used the straightened middle section of the fabric to strangle the woman.

Cornelia fought with every remaining ounce of energy she had left inside her half dead body as spurts of blood spewed out of her severely damaged face.

As calm and passive as Steven appeared, it amazed even him that she was still fighting, let alone alive at all as her hands waved about in the air like she was trying to grab a hold of him. Steven only pulled back with all his might until the snap of her neck could be heard. At last, her hands collapsed to the floor.

At that same moment, Jim stepped back inside with the ax in hand. Steven got up and tossed the cloth to the side. He then looked back at Jim and asked, "What time is it?"

Jim looked down at his silver watch and despondently said, "Five after nine."

Steven ventured back to where Leon was lying and grabbed the phone from off the table that was above his dead body.

"Who are you gonna call?"

"Brooks. I'm gonna tell 'em to meet us here tomorrow. He can help us transport the thing out of state." Steven replied as he dialed the seven numbers and waited for the dial tone to pick up. "Great, I got his voice mail." He complained. "Brooks, this is Winemore. The mission has been compromised. I repeat, the mission has been compromised. We're gonna wrap this thing up tonight."

Steven stood and described every gruesome detail he had acted out over the course of the last few minutes, right down to Cornelia's last breath.

"Subject X–811 is held up at some old man's house about fifteen minutes from our current position. From where you are, you should be able to make it here to town a little before noon tomorrow. You can meet us at the sheriff's station. Once you get in town, you can ask around for directions. You shouldn't have to worry about getting lost, every road in this town leads to one place. Anyways, we'll be waiting, with subject in tow. Winemore out."

Steven hung up the phone and placed it down onto the dinner table. From the table he turned to Jim and commanded, "Hand me the ax."

Jim reluctantly gave Steven the ax. In a certain, hesitant way, he sort of wished Jim had continued to fight him on the matter. There was that inkling inside of Steven that had hoped for perhaps a little more arguing time before doing what he felt he had to do; anything that would possibly delay his current course of action.

With his ax, Steven went about his duty, chopping off heads, arms and legs in reckless abandon before scattering the various body parts from one end of the living room and dining room to the other. His technique appeared more strategic and well thought out than something that was supposedly drawn up on the fly.

Once the dismemberment was complete, Steven happened to glance over at Jim who was wearing the palest, most devastating expression on his petrified face that he had possibly ever seen in his life, or ever wanted to see. He could no longer even bear to look at the man.

From there, Steven began for the wall behind him where the light switch panel was located. Just as he was about to cut off the dining room lights, without even the slightest kind of warning, the dinner table violently flipped over onto the floor, all by itself, sending the dishes crashing to the carpet.

Both men looked on in absolute horror. Without turning off the lights, they both made a mad dash for the front door without looking back.

As they stepped outside, Jim closed the door behind him; Steven went back with an agitated look on his face.

"Leave the damn door open!" he barked.

"Why?"

"I told you, so we can blame it on the creature, you dumb fuck! Whaddya want me to do, write it all down for you?" Steven impatiently yelled as he yanked the young man aside and pushed him along to the car. "Get in before something comes after us!"

Without haste, both men scampered into the station wagon. Once inside, Steven reached into his pocket, hoping to find the car keys in time while glancing back and forth, from the dashboard to the supposedly haunted house behind him. His sweaty, trembling hands could hardly contain themselves.

The very second the keys were found, Steven started the car and pulled out of the driveway. Once they were on the road, Steven became a bit more settled, there was more road separating him from Leon and Cornelia's house.

He could hear Jim's teeth chatter so loud that he thought they would actually shatter inside the boy's mouth. "Jim." He said as he turned the car down a dark, wooded street. "Soldiers like us don't get medals or purple hearts. There aren't ticker-tape parades or pretty girls to fuck our brains out once we get back home. They don't make movies about soldiers like us. Soldiers like us...we do our duty, and by the grace of God, we get to come home in one piece. We don't even get a fucking thank you. We just go home."

Steven realized that it would be an eternity before his partner would ever forget what took place that steamy night in Sullinger, Mississippi. He felt so much agony for the young man, the same man that he had taken under his wing and nurtured; the same man that he called friend.

His own body feverishly squirmed as if his skin were crawling. Steven couldn't help but to look ahead at the long blackened road that would eventually lead to Millard Lang's house.

CHAPTER 32

Millard's inert body leaned up against the counter in the dark and frigid kitchen. He was drinking a half empty can of Coors while staring endlessly at the three persons that were huddled together on the couch in the living room watching television.

Much like his guests, he, too, was freezing, but he wasn't cold enough just yet to where he required extra clothes, instead, he chose to bear it for a while longer.

He stood and pondered endlessly on about life before the storm, every detail in his existence, from waking up, eating breakfast, to getting a blowjob from Essya, and getting drunk had out of nowhere seemed trivial to him. He helplessly watched as his miserable reality transformed dramatically in a matter of days, and there was absolutely nothing he could do about it.

In the living room sat three individuals, two women and a child. One woman was losing her love for him while the other wanted his blood scattered all over town, and all the boy longed for was his mother and brother back in his life again.

It just so happened that Courtney, Greg and Brett all raced across his mind as well, from their childhood to their adult years. He didn't need anyone to remind him that he had wronged each of them, in different ways. The old man realized that he was hard and boorish. To him, it was the way of the world.

The extreme temperatures inside only caused Millard to brace himself as hard as he could, while the ice layered walls in the kitchen felt as though they were about to collapse upon him at any second.

Out of numbing anxiety, he started to stumble back and forth, from the counter to the refrigerator, until he managed to stabilize himself on the edge of the stove. He found his eyes locked on the bloody butcher knife that he used earlier in the day lying in the sink. With his chapped hands, he picked up the cold utensil and held it as tight as he possibly could.

He looked down at its dull blade in an entranced manner, like he and the knife were one. The old man's brain had for the moment gone completely blank. Kids, women and monsters had all taken a leave of absence; all that was left was his weapon.

Much to his own surprise, Millard found himself pointed directly towards the dimly lit living room. The knife, too, was targeted in the same direction. His hands began to tremble at that second, as if he were having a spasm, until the blade that he was holding just dropped from his right hand and onto the floor.

Millard looked up to see Essya glancing back at him from the couch where she was sitting. Without saying a word he picked up the knife, placed it back in the sink and blundered into the blue tinted living room.

Millard wanted to be anywhere but at his own house. If hell was to be his next destination then so be it, and quickly; anything conquered his current location.

"Dear God, what does it want?" Virginia helplessly groaned at the crumbling ceiling that the beast was trampling upon. "What were you doin' in the kitchen, tryin' to think up a way for us get eaten quicker?" She eyeballed the old man.

Too cold and bitter to snap back, Millard sat himself down next to Keyshawn, who was seated beside his grandmother with Essya next to her. All three were wrapped in one big, blue blanket.

Ever so gradually the old man snapped out of his dazed condition and fixed his eyes on the television. By then, the entire house was an icebox. The windows were all frosted and the pipes were frozen solid, which only meant that grabbing a drink of water was out of the question.

All four sat on the couch wheezing in and out while smoke billowed from out of their frustrated and terrified mouths.

"What the hell is this we watchin'?" Millard frowned.

"Do you have to curse every time you ask a question?" Virginia griped as she tried to massage some warmth into Keyshawn's plump arms.

"It's *Unsolved Mysteries*, Millard." Essya replied, wiping her runny nose. "They're trying to find this man who chopped up wife and kids with an ax, and then ran off to Mexico."

Millard only rolled his eyes and burrowed himself into the couch, believing that the deeper he sunk the more his temperature would hopefully rise.

From time to time his eyes would wander upwards at the creature's incessant stomping and roaring that only increased with every passing hour. Even he was amazed that with all of the rampant pacing back and forth that the roof hadn't collapsed altogether hours ago.

"God bless you, sweetie." Virginia said as she wiped Keyshawn's stuffy nose with the blanket. "I don't know how much more of this he can take, Millard. He's just now getting over a cold." She fussed.

"I've felt cold before, but this isn't any kind of regular cold. It feels strange." Essya shivered.

"She's right." Virginia said. "This cold makes my body

feel like it's gonna break apart or somethin'. What is it, Millard? What does it want from us?"

Millard kept his eyes on the TV and responded, "I wish I knew. All I can say is that with me being here, it won't hurt none of ya'll."

"How can you be sure of that? How do you know it won't tear you apart along with us?"

"Please, you two, don't fight anymore!" Essya pleaded. "I think it only makes it even madder."

After a few moments of quiet, Virginia looked over and said, "She's right, I've noticed it, too."

Millard listened as Keyshawn's stomach bubbled and gurgled like a clogged sink. He thought at first it was him that was making such a racket.

"Lord, boy, what on earth is the matter with you tummy," Virginia asked.

"My supper made me sick." The boy whimpered.

"What's wrong, boy?" Millard looked down at the child. "You don't like snake?"

"Some folks prefer civilized food over serpents and rodents." Virginia answered.

The more Millard gazed upon the suffering child, the more he began to realize that it didn't take a doctor to see that he was in unbearable pain. He did the first thing that came to mind at that instant.

"Hey, boy…look here." He motioned with his hands.

Keyshawn's lazy, watery eyes looked up at his grandfather and waited for the old fellow to state his business.

"Ya didn't know that I once had a brother, too, did ya?"

Keyshawn just shook his head no while endlessly gawking at Millard like he was an unusual oddity.

"Yep," Millard sighed. "His name was Miles. He was my little brother; about five years younger than me."

"Where is he?" Keyshawn asked.

"He's dead." Millard replied in a snippy tone, sounding as if the boy should have already known. "That man is far from here."

"Did the devil take him?"

"Keyshawn, baby, don't say that." Virginia patiently chastised.

"Don't know for sure. You see, Miles loved his women. He loved 'em a whole helluva lot. So one night, he goes over to some whore house in Biloxi and—

"Alright, Millard, that'll do for now." Virginia quickly stepped in.

"Is he gonna come back to life like my mama and Rayshawn?"

"Keyshawn, baby, we talked about this the other day. Remember when I said that you're mama and brother won't be comin' back again? That's what death means."

"They're gone…forever." Millard slurred under his breath.

Just then, both Millard and Virginia locked eyes on each other in what seemed like a calm inducing manner. It was so jarring that it caught them both by surprise.

"Is that the devil on top of the house, grandma? He smells like dookie."

"Son, I don't know what that thing is."

"What if it comes in and gets us like it did mama and Rayshawn? Are you gonna shoot it like you did the bunny rabbit, Mr. Lang?"

Millard waited before muttering, "Were gonna have to wait and see, boy."

All four bodies shivered and solemnly watched television while the blue glow shined on their somber faces, as well as the rest of the hideous looking living room. Someone wanted to say something, anything that would distract from the noises on the roof, but at that point, words just seemed so ill-tempered and useless.

"Yep, that's ole' Sullinger for ya." Millard recalled. "We call it home, but home is what's gonna kill us in the end. Ya hear that, boy? Don't ever come back down here no more. This town ain't fit for nobody but the dead."

Millard's mouth was moving, but not even he himself knew exactly what was coming out. He chose to babble on as though it was expected of him to do so.

"I think that's why I shrugged off all the murders. It's a part of Sullinger. I remember when Clementine Scruggs was strangled by a spook. That gal was only twenty-two. Ole' Sheriff Anderson said she just died in her sleep, but we all knew better. And then there was little Paul Reynolds. He was found in the woods with his head twisted to the back. That boy was only six. Yes, sir, you die in Sullinger, you better believe that you ain't restin' in peace no time soon."

"I can't believe you're over there talking about ghosts killing people!" Essya yelled. "Is that all you know, death?"

"I agree," Virginia said. "Enough of this dead people talk. Ya know, son, your grandfather used to be able to sing when he was younger."

"Don't bring that up." Millard grumbled.

"Yep," she continued as though Millard hadn't said a word. "Everybody in town knew that he could sing. He could sure blow the pipes off of some of the folks they got out singin' today. He even cut a record, too. What was that song you always sang?"

"Sweet Mary keep callin' me home." Essya spoke in a dull tone. "I heard him sing it in his…sleep."

Keyshawn's brooding eyes began to brighten as he and his grandfather stared each other down. The gesture was by no means sentimental or endearing. The longer they peered into each other's eyes, the more Millard could see himself as a little boy all over again.

"Listen," Essya abruptly whispered, looking up to the ceiling. "It's stopped moving."

Robert Stack's serious voice on the TV was the only sound that could be heard inside the house. Beyond his mysterious tone, nothing else was audible. Every set of eyes gazed up. They all held their breaths, waiting for another growl or the sound of footsteps, but after five whole minutes everyone seemed to gain the impression that possibly the beast had mercifully moved on.

"Hold on here," Millard said as he got up from off the couch and walked over to the front window. He wiped the frost from off the glass and gawked outside into the silent darkness. "I don't see nothin'", he mumbled.

"Remember, Millard, it can turn invisible." Essya cautioned as she, Virginia and Keyshawn all sat up on the couch while slipping out from underneath the blanket.

"That damn thing sure did a number on your car, Virginia." Millard noticed.

Making her way to window beside Millard, Virginia said, "Well, at least we can get outta here in your truck and get to Leon."

"I got an idea." Essya eagerly announced. "Maybe if we all walk behind Millard while we're going to the truck, then hopefully it won't hurt us. Remember back at the creek, Millard? Maybe it didn't kill me because you were there."

Without removing his face from the window, Millard replied, "I ain't takin' that chance. At least let me pull the truck to the front of the house so you all can make a quick getaway. Go get my keys in the bedroom…Essya."

For at least three seconds, every breath inside the shack

stood perfectly motionless, like something or someone had stopped time altogether.

"Millard, it called my name while me and Essya were in the woods." Virginia said as she nervously looked out the window. "It sounded just like my father."

With a somewhat dumbfounded appearance on his face, Millard glanced over at Virginia and said, "It spoke?"

"Yes. Don't tell me you didn't know that."

He said nothing. Instead, the old man turned back to the window. "What the hell was ya'll doin' out in the forest to begin with?"

"I was lookin' for me and my sister's old hideout. Millard, we saw its feet. It had these animal's feet. Please tell me you know what this thing is. Tell me that you're just too afraid to say it out loud." She begged.

"Woman, I'm gonna say it for the last time. I ain't got a clue what it is. All I know is that ya'll better get the hell outta this town before it kills every livin' person. That's why I tried to get Courtney and the boys out before it was too late. I can't imagine why that girl came back here after we fought!" Millard furiously yelled.

"Well, you can suffer for that later. Right now, all that matters is that little boy and Essya. Whatever happens to you and I happens. But we need to get them outta here and now. Do you agree, Millard?"

Millard nodded his head yes while continuously gazing out the foggy window, hoping that he wouldn't see his unwanted friend anywhere in sight.

"Good. If this demon wants to be with you, then let it. Perhaps you can somehow…persuade the thing in another direction while they escape in your truck."

"You're gettin' outta here, too, woman."

"Whatever. You just do what you have to in order to get

everyone to safety, and maybe, just maybe, God will find it in his heart to reserve a cool spot for you down in perdition."

"God can kiss my black ass." Millard protested. "I just can't wait to get ya'll outta here."

"I found them!" Essya joyfully proclaimed as she ran back into the living room with the truck keys.

Millard turned and took the keys before stuffing them into his pocket and saying, "Hold on, ya'll stand back. I'm gonna look outside for a second."

As Millard grabbed the doorknob, he right away noticed how hard and stiff it was. He then tried to twist the knob.

"What the hell?" he growled.

"What is it?" Virginia restlessly asked.

Struggling with all his might, he responded, "The damn door is frozen shut!"

"Then let's kick it open! Whatever it takes to get outta here," Virginia said.

Both Millard and Virginia relentlessly kicked at the ice covered door. With every kick, pieces of both ice and wood chipped away onto the floor.

"I think we almost got it!" Virginia cried out.

"Wait a sec," Millard paused. "Stand back, I'm gonna rush it."

He stood back about three feet and readied himself for the charge. The door was over fifty years old; busting it down wouldn't have been that big of a mountain to climb.

"No!" Essya suddenly shrieked at the top of her lungs as one of the creature's legs broke through the ceiling.

Millard looked up to see the beast trying to make its way inside. All it had to do was shimmy the rest of its stringy body through.

Millard banged and pounded against the door, but to no avail, the door just wouldn't budge far enough for a person to squeeze through.

The old man feverishly watched as the creature's other leg slipped through the collapsing roof. There was only one thing he could think of doing at that critical stage.

"Ya'll get downstairs to the cellar now, motherfuckers!" He hollered before swiping his rifle that was leaning up against the wall and hurrying in behind the others.

All four bodies raced down to the basement as fast as they possibly could. Millard slammed the door shut behind him. He then cocked his gun and pointed it directly at the door. Behind him, Essya, Virginia and Keyshawn were all locked together in each other's arms, tight and secure.

They could hear the beast break through into the living room; its thud sounded as if a boulder had crashed on top of the house as dust particles sprinkled from the cellar's walls and ceiling.

Its footsteps could be heard stomping from one room to the other. Millard could tell just which rooms it was visiting. It started in the living room, from there, it ventured into the kitchen, from the kitchen to the bathroom, and then the bedroom, which in the end, left only one more area on the tour.

It thumped its way down the steps. Keyshawn began to weep so loud that his grandmother had to muffle his mouth with her hand in order to keep him quiet.

The second it approached the door, it started its relentless snorting and growling rant. The thing's claws scraped against the door's wood up and down like it knew that it was torturing those on the other end.

Essya, Virginia and Keyshawn stood in place, crying and shaking while Millard, still in battle mode, stood stalwart. There was no quivering. Not one bead of sweat dared to form on his forehead. He listened intently as Virginia whispered a desperate prayer to God.

If the bullets from his rifle didn't work the day before, then he was beyond determined to make them work at that instant, of all times.

Millard was aware that it could have simply barged its way through the door at any second; instead, it chose to linger outside, biding its time. For the time being, the old man figured that he was the only thing that was keeping it from annihilating those he was actually trying to protect.

"I hear a car!" Essya shouted with sheer elation.

"I hear it, too! Is it the Sheriff, grandma?"

"I sure hope to God, honey!"

Everyone listened as a vehicle pulled into the yard and stopped. Then, the sound of doors being slammed shut echoed into every set of ears. That was when the beast decided to run back up the stairs.

"Millard, what if it's Leon and Corey?" Virginia breathlessly said. "Someone has to warn them!"

Millard momentarily looked back and then lowered his weapon. "Leon," he hollered. "Leon, we're down here in the basement! That fucker is in the damn house!"

Millard stood still and listened to the front door being kicked in. Soon, the noises of running feet began to ricochet across the floor and towards their vicinity.

"Thank you, God almighty!" Virginia cheerfully sobbed as she hugged Keyshawn to death. "Thank you, Jesus!"

Millard unlocked the basement door and opened it only to see Steven and Jim standing on the other end.

"What the," he gasped, sounding stunned. "Where's Leon at?"

"He's dead, you old fuck!" Steven answered back before punching Millard square in the nose, causing him to fall backwards onto the tool table.

The two agents, with their tranquilizer guns in hand,

forced their way inside and stopped midway between the door and the tool table.

"What are you doing?" Essya yelled, running over to attend to Millard whose bloody nose was gushing all over the floor.

"We're here to retrieve our property, little lady." Steven replied. "Get her, Jim."

Jim rushed over and yanked Essya away from Millard. He then tossed her body up against the cabinet door that was behind Virginia and Keyshawn.

"Get the fuck outta here!" Millard screamed as he tried to get to his feet.

Picking up Millard's rifle from off the floor and pointing it at his right leg, Steve said, "You just stay down there."

Virginia, Essya and Keyshawn all shouted out in horror as Steven shot Millard in his lower leg. Their screams, however, were nothing compared to that of Millard's howls, as another bullet exploded through the same joint, nearly separating his knee.

Essya once more tried to run to his aid, but she was instead pushed back into the cabinet behind her. Millard laid there on the floor, writhing in unspeakable pain and cursing a blue streak of obscenities. He could no longer feel any sensation in his right leg as blood oozed from out of the wounds.

"That's for shooting at us the other day, you sorry old bastard!" Steven barked.

"What are you two doin'?" Virginia screamed. "Don't you know that there's somethin' up there?"

"We didn't see anything upstairs." Steven said. "But since Lang and our specimen seem to be such close friends, perhaps he could tell us just where it is." He then proceeded to step on Millard's injured leg and sneer, "C'mon, Lang, where is it?"

"Kiss my fuckin' ass, you jack rabbit faggot!" The old man spat. "Get the fuck off of me!"

"There's no need for that kind of language, old fella." Steven devilishly smirked.

"It's invisible, that's why you didn't see it!" Essya urgently explained.

"We know it can vanish at will, ma'am." Jim said.

"What are you two doin' here?" Virginia asked. "Where's the Sheriff at?"

"I told you he's dead. Are you hard of hearing?" Steven pointed the rifle at Virginia. "Now, we don't have time to explain our life stories, so we're gonna make this short and sweet. That thing is property of the United States Government. It escaped us during the storm and ended up here, in this old man's place."

"What is it?" Virginia asked.

"That's classified information, ma'am." Jim, with a stone face said.

"You hateful bastards," Virginia hollered as she ran towards Jim and began pummeling him with slaps across the body and face. "You all probably let it loose just to see what it could do!"

Steven let up off of Millard and backhanded Virginia, sending her crumbling to the floor. "C'mon, son, you gotta know how to deal with people." He scolded his partner. "Now, this is how it's gonna go down." Steven turned back to Millard and the others. "We're gonna kill all four of you, then we're gonna capture our property and be on our way. No if's, and's or but's." He calmly explained.

"Oh, God, please no!" Virginia pleaded, crawling along the floor and pulling Keyshawn to her side. "Please, don't kill my baby!"

Steven knelt down to face Virginia. "We're sorry, little

sister, but we can't leave any witnesses behind. This thing is top secret. Not even the President knows about it. Now, I'll shoot the boy in the back of the head. He won't feel a thing, I promise."

"Please, don't do that!" Virginia desperately pleaded as she cradled her crying grandson in her arms.

Millard tried to reach over and grab Jim's leg, only to get a boot to the face for his trouble. Jim then snatched Essya from off the floor. She fought for all she was worth until one of her flailing arms accidentally shoved aside a series of coffee cans that ended up falling to the floor. What spilled out of the old canisters was something that everyone, except Millard and Virginia, was completely shocked by.

Shiny gold coins splattered all over the basement floor in reckless abandon. The others gazed on in utter disbelief. The coins sparkled and glowed; not one of them seemed to have a spot of rust or grime on them.

Steven, with Millard's rifle tucked underneath his right arm, scooped up one coin after another. His eyes marveled at the ancient texture of the beloved treasure.

"You gotta be… kidding me." He said in a stutter. "This can't be real. Spanish doubloons! You old fuck!" He looked down at Millard. "How long have you had these in here? All this has to be worth millions."

As much pain as he was in, Millard right there saw his entire life's worth slip away like water through his fingers. He cherished his treasure, but there was something deeper and more meaningful that was nagging at him as he listened to Essya, Keyshawn and Virginia weep and cower with guns pointed at their faces.

"The Delgallia," Steven articulated. "If my history is correct, that ship sunk back in the seventeenth century off the Gulf Coast somewhere. Where the hell did you get all of this? You could single handedly make this crap town into a metropolis. And you keep it all to yourself? You son of a bitch," Steven irately ranted as he stepped over and kicked Millard across the face.

Essya, sensing the perfect opportunity to strike, crawled over and bit Jim on the leg. Jim used the butt of his gun to hit the young lady in the face, causing blood to spew from her mouth.

With blood beginning to well up in his eyes, Millard looked over at his girlfriend in a manner that he had never bothered to view before. He lowered his head, as to not see her anymore.

"C'mon, grab all the coins and bring these three upstairs. We'll take care of Lang later, he's not going anywhere." Steven ordered as he knelt down and ravenously started to pick up every coin that he could possibly gather into his pockets. When he noticed that Jim wasn't joining him in his looting detail, Steven glanced up and said, "C'mon, kid, get you some!" He salivated, grabbing up whatever looked shiny on the floor like a mutt after scraps.

"Steve, what are you doing?" Jim questioned with an apprehensive expression on his face.

Steven was far too busy snatching up coins to respond to his partner's ardent plea. Nothing or no one at that point could pull him away.

As he excitedly leapt up from off the floor with the vigor of a five year old, Steven took sharp notice of Jim and the four hostages all staring him down.

"What the fuck is this?" Steven's eyes widened. "You all have the fucking nerve to look down on me? I served my country for thirty-three years! And how did my country choose to repay me? By sending me down to some hole-in-the-wall town that not even God himself could find, just so

I can babysit some slobbering animal! I think my country owes me a helluva lot more than that!" He lashed out before stepping towards Jim with a throng of coins dropping from out of his right hand. "You can finally quit the service and open that business you've been dreaming of. I can go home and retire. This is our ticket, kid!"

Shaking, Jim leaned back away from Steven like he was carrying an infectious disease. Such an action, however, only seemed to incite a rage inside the already intoxicated man.

"Don't you fuckin' look at me like that, you little bastard!" Steven screamed as he slapped Jim across the face. "C'mon, let's get this shit over with!" As he shoved the others up the steps, Steven looked back down at Millard and contemptuously uttered, "I'll be back for you later, old timer. I wanna see you beg me for your life."

"Fuck you!" Millard yelled as he tried to reach for Steven's leg.

Steven again pointed Millard's own rifle at his leg and planted yet another bullet into his already destroyed appendage.

"No one talks to me like that. I've survived suicidal gooks in the middle of the jungle. You're just a civilian that got in the way. Right now, I don't care why the specimen hasn't killed you after all this time. It doesn't even matter anymore."

Millard looked on in insufferable agony as Steven crept up the stairs. He could hear Essya, Virginia and Keyshawn all crying and screaming.

At that point, his entire leg had been reduced to that of a dead piece of flesh that was loosely hanging on to the bone.

With every last ounce of power he had left, the old man crawled his way over to the first step. Both saliva and blood spat out from his mouth. His eyes were bleeding to the point where his vision was growing dim.

The second he was able to get a hold of the first step, he grabbed onto the wooden railing and propelled himself to his feet, with only his healthy left leg aiding him. Before the old man could even set his right leg down, it immediately gave way.

The bone in the leg cracked in half like a withered branch, sending Millard reeling backwards onto the cement floor wailing in wicked pain. He could actually hear the bone snap and pop.

Yes, the pain was brutal, it was downright demonic. Throughout his entire body it felt as though he were being electrocuted.

But he was also finding that with all the screams that he was hearing upstairs, the pain in his leg seemed to subside. It was still there, but his brain was not allowing him to feel so much of it. There crept upon him a numbing sensation.

Millard opened his eyes and stopped yelling long enough for him stretch his body across the cold floor and climb his way up the steps one by one. The closer he reached the top of the stairwell the clearer he could hear Steven go and on in his belligerent, so called, "duty filled" rant.

"Now, I want you to listen to me, because it's going to be the last thing you will ever hear again." Steven steadily clarified. "I'm going to shoot all three of you with one of these darts. Death will be instantaneous. That means you probably won't even feel anything after a few seconds."

"No, please, don't kill my baby!" Virginia screamed. "I swear, we won't say anything about that monster!"

"It's too late, darling, you've already seen it."

"Keyshawn hasn't!" She anxiously pleaded. "He hasn't seen it!"

"It doesn't matter! This is going to happen!" Steven sternly yelled back. "Just tell us where in this shithole our property is, and everything will be over before you know it!"

"We don't know where it went to!" Essya said.

"Would you rather die quick and easy, or slow and painful? Because I promise you that our friend doesn't know the meaning of the word mercy, litter sister."

"You oughta be ashamed of yourselves!" Virginia blasted back. "You call yourselves soldiers! You two are no better than that demon! You're just like it!"

"Grandma," Keyshawn hollered.

"Get up, Butterball! You're gonna be first!"

With every working muscle in his old body, Millard continued to propel himself out of the basement and up into the first floor.

Every grunt and groan he belted out was not only out of pain, but from seething fury. He was determined to kill someone that night, even if it meant that his own broken body would be destroyed in the process.

"Motherfucker," Millard ferociously wailed as he scraped across the floor towards the living room.

"Mother," the beast suddenly growled from somewhere inside the shack.

Unexpectedly, the commotion from within the living room ceased. Not one cry or scream echoed out. It almost sounded as if everyone had just up and left the house altogether.

"I'm gonna...getcha!" Millard raged on. "I'm 'a comin'!"

"I'm...coming," the creature repeated, sounding just as angry as its human counterpart.

"Comin' to getcha!" The old man snarled.

"I...come...to...get!"

As Millard rounded the corner that led to the living room, he saw everyone standing around in a huddle, all staring off into the kitchen as though they knew exactly where the beast was located. Their collective jaws hung wide open at what they were hearing. Not one of them seemed to notice that Millard was rapidly approaching.

"I'm…coming…to…kill you!" The creature continued.

Before Millard could even look back, the beast sprinted out of the kitchen and into the living room right past him like the wind. It stopped right in front of a petrified Jim, who couldn't even move. With only its right claw, the beast grabbed Jim by the neck, and like the crack of a light switch, twisted his neck, leaving the young man's head dangling to the side like a rag dolls.

Jim didn't even get a chance to let out a single scream or yelp. He was dead before his body could even collapse to the floor like a sack of rocks.

Virginia, Essya and Keyshawn all screamed out in total fright before the creature stepped over Jim's lifeless carcass.

Using only his one good leg, Millard lifted himself up and leaned against the wall. Like a scared little child, Steven dropped Millard's rifle and began to shuffle back and forth in a confused manner, away from the creature.

"Come here, old man!" He hollered as he ran over to Millard and used him as a human shield.

The two men scraped and struggled, trying their hardest to take the other down. The beast approached them both. It didn't even have to take a second look at Millard before it pushed him to the side and attempted to grab Steven by the neck. But the man proved to be too slippery, as he managed to back away in time, only to drop his dart gun to the floor.

"Keep 'em away from me, Lang!" Steven hysterically yelled as he tried to run for cover.

The specimen must have seen the weapon being used in times past, perhaps on itself, just seconds before the dart's poison pulled it into unconsciousness. Whatever the case, it seemed well versed in knowing just how to point a gun, and how to pull the trigger, just as its captors were so accustomed to doing.

With little or no hope in his eyes, Captain Winemore watched as the barrel of the weapon was pointed directly at his face.

With one pull of a pointy finger, a dart was released from the gun, which went hurtling at top speed into Steven's forehead.

The man fell backwards onto the floor. At first, there was no movement from Steven, then, after the passing of the eight seconds, the violent convulsions set in. His entire face, which was rapidly filling up with poisonous fluid, ballooned to twice its original size. His eyes, nose and mouth all stretched out, until his own head quietly exploded wide open. The sound of flesh splitting apart was reminiscent to that of a hot dog frying and wheezing on a stove.

"Don't look, baby." Virginia said to Keyshawn, trying to shutter the boy's face from the gruesome sight. "Don't look at 'em."

Essya immediately ran over to Millard's side and helped him to stand. "C'mon, try and walk!" She beseeched.

"All ya'll get outta here before—

Without warning, the beast dropped the gun to the floor and shoved Essya backwards, sending her body tumbling over the couch.

Up above in the ceiling where the creature fell through, the half-moon shined inside like a bright fog lamp, revealing the unspeakable horror that was the barnyard invader. Its beady, half-witted eyes beamed down on Virginia and Keyshawn the closer it slithered towards them.

"Go away," Virginia helplessly squealed while putting herself in the front of Keyshawn.

"Get the fuck outta here, damn you!" Millard hollered

as he hopped over to pick up his rifle that was lying on the floor.

The very second he was able to retrieve the weapon, he cocked the barrel and fired at the thing, only to have the loud buckshot bounce right off of its iron frame. He fired again and again until the gun's chamber was completely empty.

The brute, with its boney arms outstretched, went straight for Millard. Millard stood on his one foot, tall and ready with his weapon in hand to give a giant swing. But before he could even swipe at the thing, it snatched the rifle from out of his hand and hurled it clear into the kitchen. From there, it pushed the old man to the side like he was a mere annoyance.

"Keyshawn, run and get out here, baby!" Virginia urged.

The boy did as his grandmother ordered and tried to make a mad dash for the already opened front door, but he just wasn't fast enough; the beast leapt over the couch like a nimble cat and snatched up both him and Essya into its slimy arms.

Virginia jumped on the creature's back and began to pound on its rock hard body. Her frail hands bled incessantly with every hit until the thing managed to spin around and fling the woman from off its back and into the television, causing the box to turn over and spark out of control.

Virginia's body jolted with every flash and flicker that the damaged television could hand her before the beast, with its screaming prey in tow, started for the front door.

"Come back here!" Millard howled while hopping on his left leg over to the thing.

Standing face to face with his unwanted visitor, Millard grabbed both Keyshawn and Essya from out of its tight grip and tucked them securely to his own bosom.

The beast's shining eyes stared down at Millard in a

bewildered manner. Both it and the old man stood in the middle of the floor. The old man fought to maintain his balance on one foot while Essya and Keyshawn cried and held on to Millard's overalls as if they were holding on for dear life. Millard couldn't take his eyes off of the creature for fear that it would strike at a moment's notice.

He didn't have a clue as to what it possibly could have been thinking, and deep down, his own thoughts were as invisible as the thick air he was breathing inside the house. But above all else, one thing was as clear as day, he was determined as ever not to let Keyshawn and Essya out of his sight until either it went away or he himself was dead at last.

The beast snorted its hot smoke from its deformed nostrils right into Millard's hair before raising its right claw and slashing the man across the face. The force of the blow made Millard fall backwards to the floor. The old man tried in earnest not to allow his own blood to blind him on the way down.

Out of what could be identified as burning rage, the beast raked its claws across Millard's chest, exposing parts of flesh that had no business being revealed in the first place. Essya and Keyshawn screamed for mercy, even though neither of them was being touched in the grueling process.

Millard turned over onto his stomach. The thing tore into the old man's back, clawing and digging while exhaling smoke. Millard himself bawled out in pain. He felt the blood drizzle and splatter all over his body as the unrelenting torture persisted. He was fighting to spit up blood that he was relentlessly chocking on.

With his eyesight nearly gone, all he had left were his undesired memories. Unwarranted spankings, babies mothers who only wanted to be loved, and a lone grandson who needed someone to talk to.

Millard recalled the day he discovered Greg down at the creek having sex with another boy, and the numerous slaps that he had laid across his own son's face that cool afternoon.

Brett, as he reached out for his father at his mother's funeral; the cold and harsh manner in which he just brushed him aside, as though he were some homeless person at side of the road.

Courtney and all the years he defended her and her boys. Millard figured that he was doing the right thing all along, when in fact, he may have only been worsening the situation.

The demon's attack saw no relent. Millard's entire back was a checkerboard of exposed ribs and flesh.

Then, after what seemed like a thousand forevers, out of the blue, the specimen stopped what it was doing. It stood back, watched and listened to the three human beings on the floor cry as blood dripped from off of its claws. No growls, snarls or snorts, just absolute disorientation. All it could seemingly do was stand and observe. The hazy moonlight caused the abomination's entire body to glow with an angelic tone, until it eventually backed out of the heavy light, leaving only its hulking shadow in view.

It appeared as if it didn't know what to make of it all. It was accustomed to the weeping and yelling from humans before taking their lives away from them, but to witness such weakness emanate from the one being that it sought refuge from seemed only to throw it off balance.

There were no words for it utter, now that it was able to speak. And just as mysteriously as it arrived days earlier, its somber departure out the front door and into the darkness of night was equally puzzling.

Two dead bodies, and one in shock, all lay motionless on the floor, three others sobbed loud enough to be heard for up to a mile away. Had anyone been passing by, they possibly would have kept on moving out of fear.

Millard was in such unbearable agony that it caused him to bite down on his own tongue. The suffering came in both physical and emotional tones. It was strong enough to where grinding his teeth caused four of them to shatter into bits.

He had never before succumbed to such brutal pressure and grief in his entire life. Even breathing was becoming difficult and cumbersome.

Slowly, Virginia raised her head to see just what was taking place. She caught Essya and Keyshawn both weeping in the old man's arms, and then…she saw Millard.

In between blood curdling yells, coughs and screams, he managed to catch a single, lifesaving breath.

"Oh, God," he wept. "Oh, God, please help me! I'm so sorry!"

Chapter 33

The next day
11:37 a.m.

"**D**amn shit," Brooks grumbled as he wrestled with his oversized map of the state of Mississippi while trying to drive his mid-sized truck down a dirt ridden back road.

Despite having the air-conditioner roaring at full capacity, his dark, sweaty brow was still dripping with perspiration that he had to wipe away from his eyes as well as the map every ten seconds.

The road ahead of him was a seemingly endless stretch of nothingness that provided the man with little or no hope of ever reaching his desired destination. Out of frustration, Brooks tossed the map behind him into the back compartment that stored a variety of high powered rifles and a seven foot tall ominium enforced cage.

He kept his restless eyes locked to the side of the passing road for any sign or clue that would lead him to a familiar setting.

"Way to go, Captain." The young man groaned as he stroked his unshaven face. "Not only do they send you both to the ass crack of the south, but now, I can't even find the damn place." Brooks griped to himself before picking up his cell phone that was lying on the seat next to him and pressing the redial button. "C'mon, Steve, pick up. Don't leave me hangin' like this, for God's sake."

When the phone rang over ten times like it had been doing for the entire trip to Mississippi, Brooks gave up and clicked the off button before irritably tossing the phone back down onto the seat.

Ever so reluctantly he pushed forward, turning down a wooded path that led straight ahead to a small white house. The man was already a mess of nerves, fully aware of just what he was going to have to pick up once he made it to Sullinger. Sedated or not, just seeing the so called "prized specimen" wasn't exactly what he had signed up for when he joined the Corps four years earlier.

Believing that the house would be the last stop on the already deserted road, Brooks pulled the truck over and waited. He glanced over to see two old white men sitting in separate rocking chairs side by side, both peeling potatoes.

For Brooks, being black in the deep south was just one of the two reasons he never took on the assignment that his two partners volunteered for, the other reason was the malicious heat.

He strongly hesitated at first to get out of the truck. Perched upon a banner on the porch was a tattered rebel flag that looked as though it were about to fall to pieces within seconds.

Even though Brooks was already armed, it was his domineering suspicion that typically got the best of him, which would possibly explain why after four years of service to the United States Marine Corps the man held tight to his desk job like a fish to water.

The man breathed in the damp summer hotness and mumbled, "Just get out, walk slowly and try not to trip over your tongue, nigga."

Brooks cut off the ignition and climbed out of the truck. With his sweaty hands stuffed inside his pockets, he humbly dragged his feet across the road and to the shabby old house like he was a teenager on his first date.

"Good day, gentlemen!" He waived with a compulsory smile on his face. "I was just wondering if I could grab a moment of your time!"

Only one of the elderly men paused what he was doing to look up at Brooks. He was a portly, white haired man, clothed only in a pair of stained, blue overalls and muddy work boots.

The other fellow was a thinner build of a man who saw fit to only wear a stained, white tank top shirt that revealed the scaly liver spots that layered his boney arms. A pair of blue jeans, no shoes and a blue ball cap that read, *"Jackson Noodling Corps"*. He never bothered to tear his attention away from his peeling detail.

"Well, what can we do ya for, young fella?" The larger man cordially grinned, narrowing his eyes at Brooks who had finally managed to approach the porch.

"Well, sir, I seem to be a little lost." He meekly replied.

"Well, now, ain't none of us ever really lost. But, if ya can't find your way, then we sure hope to the good Lord that we can be of some service to you. The name's Andy. And this fine gentleman here to my right is Jack."

Feeling a sudden and surprising sense of security and ease, Brooks' body unclenched itself. "Good to meet you both. My name is Bradley Brooks, and I was hoping to get some directions."

"We'll sure try to help you the best we can, but we can't

promise much." Andy said without losing his million dollar smile. "You ain't from around here, is ya?" He questioned as he took off his glasses.

"No, sir, I was born and raised in Pittsburgh."

"Pittsburgh," Jack suddenly looked up. "Ain't that up yonder in Pennsylvania?"

"Yes, sir, it is."

"I once had a cousin who lived up there. Lots and lots of hills up there," Jack's eyes broadened.

Chuckling, Brooks said, "Besides the Steelers and Penguins, Pittsburgh is best known for its hills. It's not too fun when it snows, though."

"You'd be surprised at how many out-of-towners we get comin' through these here parts, askin' for directions, especially the ones from up north." Andy amusingly fussed while tossing a freshly peeled potato into a large wooden bucket. "They always sweat like pigs in a slaughter house. What can we help ya find today, my friend?"

"Well, uh, I was hoping you could point me in the direction of a town by the name of Sullinger."

Just like that, both Andy and Jack ceased their every movement before staring straight ahead at Brooks as though their very lives depended upon it.

Their red faces were completely blank and incoherent. Andy seemed the more shell-shocked of the two men. He was finding it difficult to hold on to the unpeeled potato that he had just grabbed from the bag behind him. Jack, on the other hand, straightened his Coke bottle eyeglasses and began to gently rub his sharp switchblade across his cheek, as if he were in deep meditation.

Brooks looked on with great unease as Andy placed both his bowie knife and potato in his lap before he slowly leaned forward in his rickety rocking chair and seriously asked,

"Now, son, just what in God's creation would you be wantin' over in ole' Sullinger?"

Being that his mission was top secret, Brooks hesitated to answer at first. Instead, he uttered the first thing that came to mind. "I'm supposed to be meeting up with a couple of... colleagues of mine." He stuttered.

The old men glared over at each other and sighed before rocking back and forth in their chairs in a simultaneous chorus.

"You say you got colleagues over there in Sullinger?" Jack squinted.

"That's right, sir. Is there some sort of problem?" Brooks cringed to ask.

Andy stopped rocking and said in a sort of dawdling stammer, sounding as though he didn't want to answer the question, "Son, I don't quite know how to break this to ya, but...there ain't nobody over in Sullinger no more."

"That's right," Jack jumped in. "It's been that way for about, I'd say, nineteen years, now."

As if someone had just knocked him out, Brooks held his breath and blinked, "I beg your pardon?"

"Well, about nineteen years ago, 'round this time of the year, I reckon, everybody in that devilish town just vanished into thin air. It seemed like it happened overnight." Andy pensively explained.

"Yep, everybody either up and left or just fell off the face of the earth. Darndest thing I've ever heard of. One day, everyone was there, then, the thing next thing ya know, everybody's done gone away." Jack said.

Catching his breath, Brooks sniggered, trying to buy some time in between thoughts, "Wait a minute, there has to be some kind of mistake. You see, I have friends over there. One of them left me a message just last night."

"And just what would these friends of yours be doin' in a dead town?" Andy inquired.

"They were conducting…business there."

"Well, if somebody is over there, then good luck to 'em. They're a lot braver then we are."

"Hold up, the last time I talked to one my colleagues, it sounded like the entire town was busy with activity!" Brooks adamantly implored.

Andy sat back in his seat while stroking the white stubble on his chin. Brooks could tell that just bringing up the name of the town was unsettling both men to no end, like he was uncovering a long, hidden, dark secret.

With a look of dismay on his face, Andy commented, "Like I said, you're friends are a lot braver than we are. But, there ain't nothin' stoppin' you from headin' over there. Sullinger is right down that road. I'd say about twenty or so miles."

"That old town was always kinda queer to me." Jack shook his head. "Ain't nothin' right ever happened over there."

Brooks turned to his direct right to see nothing but the same dust ridden path that he had been traveling on ever since arriving in the city of Jackson. He then began to slowly march away, back to his truck. "Okay, thank you, gentlemen, you've been very kind." He stammered in a grim tone.

"Young man," Andy steadily uttered, locking his blue, steady eyes on Brooks. "Now, I don't know how ya'll do things back up yonder north, but down here, well…we folks tend to take life a little more serious. When ya get there, get your friends, and ya'll get outta there. Don't go sightseein' or snoopin' around in folks' houses. Sullinger ain't no place for people no more. If ya ask us, we think somebody is pullin' a very nasty prank on you. But, that's just our opinion."

Brooks' blood suddenly ran cold and hard through his veins. He quietly shook his head and resumed his walk back to the truck. As he hopped in he couldn't help but to look as the two old men sat in their rockers, staring back at him, as still and solemn as if they were listening to a sad song playing in their heads.

Immediately, he cut on the ignition and pulled away as fast as he could, as not to look at the gentlemen a second longer.

*   *   *

Brooks dragged down the deserted road while repeatedly pressing the redial button on his phone and listening to Steven's message over and over again.

Thanks to cruising at a minimal speed, getting to Sullinger took well over an hour. Even with the A/C blasting right in his face, he was still a sweat drenched pool of mush; it was the intense fear that had him dripping from almost every pore. The dreadful words of Andy and Jack kept blaring back in his head like a cathedral's bells.

They were old men, possibly in their mid to late eighties, and with the beastly summer sun bearing down on them all day, every day, that alone possibly meant that their minds were wearing thin, Brooks contemplated.

To think that an entire town's population, no matter how small it was, could just up and vanish into thin air was both preposterous and outright flippant, he kept telling himself.

Perhaps there was another storm on the horizon that led the people to flee their homes to escape certain destruction. Or Steven had somehow convinced the sheriff to evacuate the town so he and Jim could take down the specimen without another incident. There was no change of plan from head command that Brooks was aware of.

With every rambling premonition that danced around in his brain, not one of them could soothe his queasy stomach.

As soon as Brooks cleared the shaded terrain of the road, the sun immediately saw fit to emerge from behind the clouds. Just a few feet ahead in the distance, he could spot a speck of wood that was hidden behind a cluster of withered weeds. He pulled the truck to the side and got out.

Brooks stepped around to clear away the rotting bush before studying the dusty, worn sign that read: **Welcome to Sull**. The rest of the writing had been scratched away as if it had been that way for decades.

Brooks was aware that it was an old town, so he gave it no more thought as he climbed back into the truck and proceeded to enter through.

He roared into the obscure little town. From left to right his eyes rapidly shifted as he tooled down the road. He glanced over at a barren creek that had a large hole directly in the middle. The surrounding grass was brown and yellow, while a discolored **No Trespassing** sign swayed back and forth in the breeze.

Brooks recalled in Steven's message to meet him at the sheriff's office, but after turning down road after road, just being able to find another human being, let alone the office itself, seemed fruitless.

One thoroughfare led to the wrecked ruins of a white chapel, while another path took him to a quaint little house that had its front door left wide open to the world.

Just about fifteen or so minutes down another lane sat a sprawling piece of decrepit property. A once tall barn was leaning to its side, while a shack with its entire roof caved in sat clear across the yard. Right in front of the shack sat both a rusted, blue pickup truck with all four of its tires missing and a station wagon that had weeds growing from the inside out.

Once he was done viewing the morbid remains of the property, Brooks carried on down more roads and paths that led to more of the same every time. The man made double sure to keep an attentive eye glued to the gas needle that was nearing the E spot. The very last thing he wanted was to be stuck right smack in the middle of a town that seemingly didn't even exist all of the sudden.

The more he traveled around the more it became apparent that perhaps the old men weren't as senile as he once thought.

The young man cut down a road the led to the town square. The town's only grocery store and all the other shops were abandoned. Some store fronts had their windows shattered into pieces, while others were suffocated in a healthy collage of cobwebs.

The very moment he cleared the square, right around the corner sat a crumbled structure which appeared to be at one time a diner with a twisted cable antenna that sat at the top of the rubble. The sheriff's station was only five minutes down the road.

Brooks stopped the truck in behind one of the two patrol vehicles and got out. His skittish behavior only increased a hundred fold the moment his feet hit the earth. He listened to hear something that was completely out of sync; there was no sound outside whatsoever. No birds chirping or bugs sounding off, just a warm and quiet summer breeze that calmly whistled through the muggy air.

Brooks carried on towards the station and pushed open the already unlocked entrance door. Inside were two cells and a front desk. Yet, there appeared to be one flaw, everything looked as if it was decades old. The cells were lined from top to bottom with cobwebs. The desk was lopsided thanks to its one missing leg.

Brooks' mouth was dried out. He kept on reassuring himself that even after only three beers the night before he was still in the proper frame of mind when he listened to Steven's voice recording over his cell phone.

He snatched his phone from out of his pocket and again tried to replay the message as he blindly passed by a calendar on his way over to the sheriff's private office. For some odd reason, the calendar's date was specifically circled in black marker, **Thursday, June 23, 1988.**

Instead of receiving the same message he had been hearing since the night before, the phone's automated female voice kept informing him that the number he had dialed was no longer in service.

"What the fuck," Brooks mumbled before looking at both the date and time of the message on the phone that read, **Friday, June 23rd, 2006. 9:07 pm.**

He kept his jittery eyes strangely glued to his phone's data as he twisted the knob on the office door, pushed it open and found a desk littered with papers. Brooks cut off his cell phone, stuffed it back into his pocket and walked over to the desk to pick up one of the dusty pages.

The paper he was reading was a log of daily reports on town activities. Brooks tossed the paper aside and started to rummage through the rest of the musty wreckage, trying to find anything that could make some kind of earthly sense.

Page after countless pages read only of cow tipping incidents, a little boy who was electrocuted the day after a storm and a moonshine bust down at a place called Ray's Hardware Store.

Thanks to regular updates from his colleagues, Brooks was kept apprised on all of the important happenings in the town ever since the specimen's escape, so it was even more mind boggling that not one report of a single murder that had taken place was anywhere to be found amongst all the clutter.

Brooks let the papers fall from his quivering hands and onto the floor, he then reached for his phone and again tried to contact Steven, only to listen to the operator translate the same communication.

Once his phone was slid back into his pocket, his right hand fearfully made its way over to the holster that was next to his left pocket, and the chrome plated forty-five that was tucked within it.

He whipped the gun out and eagerly turned and bolted out of the station and back to his truck. Brooks didn't waste a single second to cut on the ignition and tear down the road.

He wanted to see his newfound buddies Andy and Jack again. Mercifully, they didn't live in or anywhere near Sullinger.

Brooks placed his gun down onto the passenger's seat. His entire body was sweaty and shaking. It was inconceivable to him that an entire town had been vacant all those years and that no one outside would even have the slightest care to investigate what had possibly taken place. And then of course, there was the matter of his two colleagues and the ill-fated message on his phone that nagged at him. The more he glossed over it the harder he gritted his teeth.

"Dammit," he yelled, pressing down on the gas pedal. "Can't this fucker move any faster?"

The man needed something potent, for the time being, to soothe his frayed mental state while trying to backtrack out of the town. He cut on the radio, expecting to hear the same jazz station that he had been listening to ever since entering the Jackson city limits. But, rather than hearing a melodic jazz tune, the radio scratched and screeched to Paula Abdul's, *"Straight Up."*

It wasn't that Brooks didn't know or even liked the song, it was the station's D.J. that informed his audience after the closing of the tune that they had been listening the new song from newcomer Paula Abdul. It was at that very instant Brooks' hands shook so violently that he could hardly maintain a stable grip on the steering wheel. He closed his eyes for only four seconds, hoping that God would wake him up.

With every lane that Brooks tore down, the more he began to realize that he was going in circles; from the sheriff's station and back to a shabby apartment complex where a series of downed power lines layered the parking lot. He knew that he had passed by there at least three times before, and by the look of his gas gauge he would be fortunate to make it back to the edge of town in less than five minutes. By then, however, Brooks didn't care if the truck ran out of gas; all that mattered to him was getting himself out of Sullinger as fast as humanly possible.

He floored the pedal and flew past each and every landmark until they all were mere blurs. If one endless road led to another, then he would take the opposite. All the young man could think of while blasting through the town was his two small children whom he hadn't seen face to face in well over a month.

Roaring at speeds well over a hundred mph, Brooks screeched around a bend, nearly barreling into a collection of withered bushes. He right away spotted the dried up creek that he had passed earlier on. He recalled that it was the same hole that signified the beginning of the tortuous town. Once the wheels regained their bearings, Brooks straightened out and rocketed towards the creek.

Suddenly, a serene sensation massaged his every muscle. Brooks' heavy and erratic breathing ceased. Never before had such an ugly looking hole in the ground appeared so glorious.

Brooks let up on the gas and sat back in his seat while allowing the truck to cruise its way out of the seemingly uninhabited town. He began to ponder on just how he was going to explain everything to his superiors. The abrupt disappearance of nearly four hundred people, his two friends, and most of all, the specimen, couldn't just be chalked up to some freak accident. A plausible explanation would have to come sooner than later.

The more he contemplated on the subject that was all the more he just didn't care, just as long as he reached the town line. Nothing after that mattered.

Just a few more yards until the clearing up ahead. Brooks looked over at the barren creek bed. What seemed like yards relentlessly turned into miles as the man pressed on. He couldn't see the entrance or the back of the welcome sign, all he could spot in front of him was yellowish, dry weeds where he thought the entry was located.

Brooks stopped the truck and discovered an odd number of new weeds were all of the sudden covering the area.

"Fuck this shit!" He hollered before reaching for his gun and noticing an ominous stench emanating from the back of the truck.

He turned around to see just what was stinking behind him. His jumpy eyes couldn't stop themselves from moving so wildly as he held his gun in the air.

"*Don't scream,*" a soft voice whispered directly into his right ear.

Out of vicious fear, he shot his gun, shattering the windshield in front of him. Right after that, from behind, something cold and wet grabbed a hold of his arm. Brooks spun around to see the creature slowly materialize right before his very eyes.

Too stunned at that point to even move, Brooks sat stuck to his seat while his entire body shivered uncontrollably. The beast, with its one claw holding the man down, carried with it its customary, innocent expression. It was never an evil grimace, but rather one of childlike wonder. No matter, all Brooks could see was shining, sharp teeth that glared back at him.

The creature, with its claw still secured to Brooks' arm, calmly dragged the man out of the truck and onto dry land.

"Please…please, I have kids." Brooks gasped for air as he stood face to face with the specimen.

The creature released Brooks' arm before wrapping his own arms around the man's back and simply snapping his vertebrae like it were cracking a measly twig.

Brooks' eyes rolled to the back of his head before faint wheezes and pants cooed out of his mouth. At that, the man's body went completely limp inside of the beast's stringy arms.

Batting its eyes and flashing its teeth, the creature picked Brooks up and carried him down into the wide open hole where the creek's water once resided.

For nearly five unimaginably long and excruciating minutes, not a single, minuet sound was to be heard within the vicinity. That is until the rustling of a cluster of bushes to the side of the road erupted.

At the edge of the woods stood a fur-faced old man who had silently witnessed the entire tragedy.

A cold tingle slipped down his crooked spine the second the beast and its prey vanished into the chasm. The old man then unclenched himself while trying in vain to control his shaking jaws and hands from the Parkinson's disease that had overtaken them.

He was never a man for many words, but even he knew that the poor fellow that had been taken down to God knows where deserved a quiet and poignant prayer to send him off. The old man had run out of tears to cry at that point.

With his nearly blind eyes, the man gazed around the hushed wasteland of a valley without allowing another remembrance to enter his mind.

He then tipped his faded Union Workers ball cap, and with his wooden crutches, he turned and carried his one-legged self back into the darkness of the forest from which he regretfully emerged.

Printed in the United States
By Bookmasters